Something
LIKE LOVE

Something LIKE LOVE

International Bestselling Author

MONICA JAMES

Editing: Editing 4 Indies
Formatting: E.M. Tippetts Book Designs

Follow me on:
authormonicajames.com

Other Books By
MONICA JAMES

THE I SURRENDER SERIES
I Surrender
Surrender to Me
Surrendered
White

SOMETHING LIKE NORMAL SERIES
Something like Normal
Something like Redemption
Something like Love

A HARD LOVE ROMANCE
Dirty Dix
Wicked Dix
The Hunt

MEMORIES FROM YESTERDAY DUET
Forgetting You, Forgetting Me
Forgetting You, Remembering Me

SINS OF THE HEART DUET
Absinthe of the Heart
Defiance of the Heart

ALL THE PRETTY THINGS TRILOGY
Bad Saint
Fallen Saint
Forever My Saint

The Devil's Crown-Part One (Spin-Off)
The Devil's Crown-Part Two (Spin-Off)

THE MONSTERS WITHIN DUET
Bullseye
Blowback

DELIVER US FROM EVIL TRILOGY
Thy Kingdom Come
Into Temptation
Deliver Us From Evil

IN LOVE AND WAR
North of the Stars
Fall of the Stars

REVENGE IS SWEET SERIES
Crybaby

HEART MEMORY TRANSFER DUET
Heart Sick
Love Sick

STANDALONE
Mr. Write
Chase the Butterflies
Beyond the Roses
Someone Else's Shadow

"Love cannot save you from your own fate."
—Jim Morrison

I've never really understood the saying blood is thicker than water. I mean, of course it is.

Blood is essentially made up of platelets, plasma, and red and white blood cells. And water—well, water is made up of oxygen and two hydrogen atoms. So it makes sense that blood is indeed thicker than water.

But it was only recently that I realized that the saying itself does not refer to the literal meaning but more to the philosophical notion of family and the strong ties that bind them. And the reason for my epiphany is because I found my family. We may not have been related by blood, but we were a family nonetheless.

A family of misfits.

However, I left my family of misfits in hopes that when I located my blood kin, the grass would be greener and blah, blah, blah

But now that I've found my nearest and dearest, which I am related to by blood, I understand another saying—you can choose your friends, but not your family.

And the reason I can relate is because sometimes the family you're born into…just fucking sucks.

One

One could use so many words to describe their mother—caring, devoted, compassionate, loving, but most of all, a protector.

It's a mother's job to protect her child unconditionally, devoting her life to ensure her offspring grows up happy and feeling safe. But the lady before me fails on all accounts, as she was never devoted or a protector.

Maybe the words heartless, cold, callous, and selfish could best describe her. Yet I am utterly fascinated by her, as this is the woman who gave me life. She is also the woman who took it away.

"What are you doing here?" she gasps, and just like that, my earlier adjectives seem totally justified.

My face contorts at her clipped question because she may as well have slapped me with her formality.

"It's lovely to see you too."

"I'm s-sorry, I just…" She stutters nervously.

"It's fine," I reply, finally finding my voice. "I should never have come."

I quickly turn to leave this train wreck behind.

As far as family reunions go, this one can be labeled a total disaster.

"No, Mia, wait!" she says, seizing my arm.

I yank out of her grip and face her with red-hot fury in my eyes.

She wrings her hands, obviously distressed by my hostile reaction, but I can't contain my rage. Her touch feels like manacles imprisoning my heart, and I fear I'll be sick if she lays her hands on me once more.

"Sorry," she quickly apologizes, hands raised in surrender. "Come inside. It's cold out."

Is it? I'm totally numb and don't feel a thing.

"Please," she pleads when I don't move.

I move only when I feel a familiar pair of hands wrap around my middle.

"Come on, Red," Quinn says, his warm lips pressed against my ear.

Quinn Berkeley—he's the only person I trust.

I nod, thankful his hands steady me since I'm about to fall flat on my face.

Cynthia gently guides the scowling teenager inside, and I follow apprehensively. I still cannot believe I'm here.

Quinn's hands are like my security blanket, and by the gentle, reassuring squeeze, he knows it, too.

As soon as I step into the grand foyer, a pang of anger hits me straight in the guts. This house is huge.

From the polished floorboards to the white spiral staircase

leading up to God knows how many floors above us, I can't help but compare this home to the house I grew up in back in LA.

My house was barely standing by the time I left, not to mention that it contained my dying father, bleeding out on the basement floor.

Sadly for me and the rest of humanity, he didn't die. And that's the reason I'm here.

"Come into the sitting room," Cynthia says over her shoulder.

I follow blindly, as I have no idea what a sitting room is.

The house smells like cinnamon and fresh flowers, and I notice a bunch of roses sitting on top of a mahogany coffee table as we enter. The room has a small brown sofa and two matching recliners. The bright embers in the fireplace, which are softly crackling, give the pretty room a homey feel.

"Sit, please." Cynthia gestures to the brown sofa with a shaky hand.

I look at it, and like everything else in this house, it's fucking perfect.

Gaping down at my ratty clothes and muddy boots, I realize I don't belong here. I will never fit in with all the perfect white linens, floral wallpaper, and fucking fresh flowers. I never will.

"Please, Mia," Cynthia begs again when I stand defiantly, gazing around the room.

"Fine," I gripe, sitting rigidly on the sofa.

Quinn takes a seat near me, ensuring our knees remain touching. His simple gesture is done with intent, illustrating he's here with me every step of the way.

"Let me get you some tea," Cynthia says, fiddling with her gold charm bracelet as she stands awkwardly in the middle of the room.

The teenager has slumped into a recliner, eyeing me something wicked. From her looks, I'd say she's about sixteen, but it's hard to tell under her layers of makeup. Her sizable boobs make mine look laughable, and she's all womanly curves, while I'm slender and toned.

We couldn't look more different. Well, apart from our eyes.

"Who is she, Mom?" she asks, glaring at me.

My gaze never wavers from her, as this little *brat* in front of me surely cannot be who I think she is. If she were, that would mean my mother left me alone in the care of my father while she was pregnant, and I would surely remember having a sister.

It would also mean my mother made a choice to save her, but not me. She left me there to rot, and by the looks of her house and her appearance, Cynthia hasn't looked back on her decision with regret.

Cynthia looks uncomfortable as she adjusts the belt on her gold pantsuit. I can't wait to hear her explanation because I, too, need to know the answer.

"Mom?" the teenager presses, anger lacing her tone.

Cynthia looks over at me and sighs once before replying in a mere whisper, "She's your…sister."

The color drains from my face, as hearing what I knew to be true is almost impossible to digest.

"What the fuck?" we say in unison.

Well, looks like we really *are* sisters.

"Pollyanna!" Cynthia scolds. "Language!"

Pollyanna slumps low, crossing her arms over her chest while sticking out her plump bottom lip. "Well, how do you expect me to react? You tell me this"—she scowls at me—

"*freak* is my sister, and I'm just supposed to be happy about it. I mean…look at her."

I feel myself redden from anger but also embarrassment.

"Enough!" Cynthia snaps, turning to look at my sist— Pollyanna. "Go to your room!"

"No! I will not!" she shouts, standing and stomping her foot. "Not until you explain what the hell is going on!"

I feel like I'm going to be sick. This situation has just gone from bad to worse.

Quinn squeezes my knee, and again, the simple gesture grounds me. However, with the way things are going, I'll need his hands on me permanently.

"You will calm down, Polly, before anyone explains anything to you."

"Fine!" She harrumphs, dropping onto the sofa. "I'm calm."

Her comment is laughable because no one is calm. This whole room is bursting with tension at its pristine, wallpapered walls.

"I'll make tea," Cynthia suddenly says, making a mad dash for the door.

"Cynthia, I don't want tea," I snap, feeling my sanity slowly evaporating with each passing minute.

She flinches when I use her name, and as petty as this makes me, I did so deliberately.

"Very well," she replies, her eyes darting around the room.

Finally, she sits in the chair across from me. The air is filled with an uncomfortable silence.

I wipe my face when Cynthia keeps staring at me. I know I look like shit, still beaten and bruised, but I don't understand what she's looking at.

Sadly, my question is answered as she gasps to herself,

"You look just like him."

No guessing to whom she's referring. But funnily enough, my dad always said I looked like her. And that's why I believed he hated me so and had absolutely no qualms pimping me out.

So it looks like both my parents hate me since I resemble the person they despise.

Whatever possessed me to come here has been exorcized, and I've seen the light. I don't belong here, and I was stupid to think I ever did.

"This was a bad idea," I say, jumping up from my seat.

"Mia, please wait." The panic in her voice is clear. "This is just a shock. I'm sorry. Maybe it's best you leave. I just need...time. I don't know how to behave. Or what to say," she confesses, but it's pathetic how she expects that to be a plausible excuse.

She's the adult here, and she's also my mother. It's her job to tell me that everything will be all right. But I guess that ship set sail long ago.

"It's fine. I don't expect anything from you. I never have," I add, closing my eyes to stop the tears.

I instantly feel Quinn at my side, reaching for my hand and interlacing our fingers. He's my family—the only family I need.

"Sorry to have bothered you," I whisper, my throat about to close as I open my eyes.

I practically run for the front door, needing an escape.

"Mia." She sniffles, and I barely restrain myself from punching her in the face.

What right does she have to sniffle? *I* should be the one sniffling, not her. But I'm done with the tears. And I'll be damned if I shed one more tear over this disappointment of a person.

"What?" I reply, my hand braced on the doorknob.

"Where will you go?" she asks, her heels clicking on the tiled floor as she steps toward me.

"Oh, who cares where she goes! She's not welcome here," snaps Polly, who is undoubtedly overjoyed to see the back of me.

The fact Cynthia has not refuted Polly's statement makes me believe that she's right, that I really am not welcome in their home.

"Mia?" Cynthia presses.

"Anywhere but here," I reply, ignoring Polly's malice. The cool breeze slaps my cheeks as I yank open the door.

Quinn is silent throughout the whole exchange, but I can tell by the way he's chewing on his lip ring that he wants me to stay and talk to her because we came here for a reason.

As much as she doesn't deserve an explanation, I'll give her one because once I do, it's the last thing I ever intend to say to her. When I leave this house, they will both be dead to me, and I will no longer miss something I never had.

"Oh, by the way," I say over my shoulder, casually meeting her uneasy gaze. "I shot my father...but he didn't die." Her eyes widen as I continue. "So now he and his drug dealer friend, Phil, who used to be my boss, are after me, and they probably know I'm in Canada. I'm also on the run from the police."

As my mother gasps at my news, I can't help but spit, "I came here to warn you. So consider yourself warned."

Then I take off into a dead sprint.

"Red, wait!" Quinn yells, desperately trying to catch me. But I can't stop, and even if I wanted to, I'm unable to.

A sister? A fucking *sister*?

With that thought plaguing my brain, I continue running to I don't know where—it just feels good to be free. But now as my decision to run like the wind catches up to me, I realize I'm lost.

I slow down when I reach an open field of wildflowers because I have no idea where I am.

"Feel better?" Quinn puffs from behind me.

Pushing my sweaty hair off my brow, I bend low, placing my hands on my knees, attempting to catch my breath. My ribs protest in pain, as they are still tender and sore, courtesy of the life-threatening beating I received from Justin Miller— the megalomaniac psychopath. Just thinking about him and what he did to me has my breathing escalating into panicked gasps.

"No," I reply breathlessly. "I do not."

Quinn stands in front of me as I pant into my knees, trying to slow my heart rate to a semi-normal pace.

I know I'm being a spoiled brat, but I honestly can't handle the gentle look in his eyes. I don't want kindness. I want to fight. But I don't want to fight him, and that's what will happen if I face him.

I need to hurt something as my temper slowly overtakes my sanity. This is why I learned how to box. It was a perfect way to release all my rage and anger so I don't hurt another. But sadly, the only thing to box right now is Quinn's face.

"Leave me alone, Quinn," I say from between my knees.

The only response I receive is a laugh—great. He's not going anywhere, and I'm about to faint at this angle, so I rise to full height, meeting his stubborn green eyes.

"Hit me," I order, my gaze never wavering from his stunned expression.

"Excuse me?" Quinn asks, taking a step back.

"You heard me. Hit me." I'm angered that we're still talking because the thought of violence is better than having to deal with this sinking, hollow feeling in my gut.

"What the fuck?" he gasps, shaking his head. "No. I will not fucking hit you. Why would you even ask that of me?"

"Because then I won't feel so bad when I hit you," I reply, taking a step toward him.

"*What*? You want to fight me?" he incredulously asks, retreating.

That's the last thing I want, but I'm about five seconds away from losing it, and I refuse to allow *her* to be the reason why I finally snap.

But I nod. "It's the only way I know how to deal with"—I point angrily in the direction of the house—"that."

"How about you talk to me?"

"No," I growl, violently shaking my head.

I can't confess my rejection out loud. The words will make me weak, and they will shatter the last tether of humanity I have left.

"It'll hurt a lot less if you do," he says, taking a small step toward me, his hands raised in surrender.

"That's where you're wrong!" I cry. "If I confess what a pathetic loser I am for wanting at least one parent's approval, you'll look at me with pity in your eyes, and I couldn't bear it."

My confession feels just as I thought it would—like utter shit.

"It's okay to be vulnerable," Quinn says, his eyes softening.

Thankfully, he's stopped advancing because I need some space.

"No, it's not. I'm sick of being the victim. I don't know what I expected coming here," I whisper, closing my eyes in defeat. "I mean, I wasn't expecting to be welcomed with open arms. I know my life will never be like that. It'll never be normal."

I open my eyes, and the reality of my life comes to a boiling point. "Everything is so fucked up, Quinn."

Quinn doesn't move to console me; he just stands and listens. And now that I've started, I can't seem to stop. This is why I never wanted it to start.

"I hate this feeling in here!" I shout, grabbing at my sweater and pulling at my chest. "I don't want to feel anything for her, but I do, and I'm so fucking pathetic to feel something for someone who feels nothing for me. I want acceptance from someone who abandoned me when I needed her the most!"

I laugh, but it's a crazy, maniacal sound. "You know what that makes me?"

Quinn shakes his head, his messy hair veiling his eyes.

"That makes me a victim. A pathetic victim searching for anyone's love or approval. How fucking sad is that?" I take a deep breath because there it is—the ugly truth.

Birds have taken flight from their perches as my rant has scared away any living thing in a hundred-mile radius.

Well, *almost* every living thing.

"That's where you're wrong," Quinn says, stepping toward me. "You know what that makes you?" He takes yet another step forward. "It makes you strong. It makes you a survivor."

"A survivor?" I ask, shaking my head. "I highly doubt that."

As I rub a hand over my face, my beaten body just wants to collapse in a heap and stay that way for a week. But my purge has made me feel slightly better, and I shamefully meet Quinn's gaze.

"I'm sorry for being a little psycho," I confess, pulling on my lip. "Forgive me?"

Quinn takes a step closer so we're standing toe to toe. "You're forgiven."

I lower my eyes, ashamed of my outburst, as he was in no way deserving of my anger nor my threats of violence.

"Let's get out of here," he whispers, resting his thumb under my chin and coaxing me to meet his eyes.

As awful as it was, my purge has made me feel somewhat saner. But I know the main reason I'm not homicidal right now stands before me.

"Okay." I sigh, feeling utterly exhausted.

Quinn's devilish lips tip up into a lopsided smile. "So you're not going to hit me?"

"Not today," I reply, stepping into his welcomed arms.

"Good," he says, his lips resting atop my head. "Don't ever ask me to hurt you again, Red. I would rather kill myself before I laid a finger on you."

I nod, knowing he means every word, and I'm more than ashamed of my hysterical actions.

"Sorry...for everything," I mutter against his warm chest, inhaling his unique fragrance.

I attempt to pull away, but his arms are like shackles, gripping me tight, and he only lets me go when I begin to feel human again.

The bright department store lights hurt my eyes, but it's a sacrifice I'm willing to make as my cart is full of items I so desperately need.

Knowing we can stay in Canada without the police on our tails is a relief. We still have to be on the lookout for my dad and Phil. But I doubt they would be stupid enough to attack us in such a bright and public environment.

So I'm thoroughly enjoying piling more items into my overflowing cart.

"You've already got conditioner." Quinn mock sighs, looking down at the leave-in treatment.

"Really? We're having this conversation again?" I smile as I reach for a minty mouthwash and toss it onto the pile of essentials.

Since my breakdown, I've tried to keep our conversation light because Quinn doesn't need me to lose it again. But I honestly don't even know where to go from here. I mean, I'm not naive, so I wasn't expecting a happy reunion with no issues. But I *was* expecting some kind of explanation as to why she left me.

I guess the truth was staring me in the face this entire time. And no matter how ugly, it's best I just accept the fact that my mother didn't want me.

I can't even begin to digest the fact that I have a sibling. Growing up, I never craved a sister because I never wished another living soul to go through what I did. But after seeing Polly, a part of me, in a sick, twisted kind of way, wishes I had her life.

I wish *I* was the one living in a mansion with a mother who actually gave a shit about me. Instead, I feel like the problem child who was left to rot.

Lost in my head, I fail to notice something sticky sliding down my cheek until it hits the floor with a loud splat. My eyes focus on the blob of pink goo to my right, and I quickly raise my fingers to my gluey face.

When my fingers pull away with the same pink matter coagulating on the floor, I say, "What the hell?"

Upon closer inspection, I can see the unidentifiable gunk

is actually some kind of cream. Cream that Quinn is currently holding.

"What was that for?" I ask, wiping my cheek with the back of my sleeve.

Quinn shrugs while looking at the jar with close scrutiny. "To see if this cream can actually rejuvenate the skin in under a minute. I have my doubts," he adds, examining my face with a smirk.

And that's it. He offers no other explanation. But he doesn't need to explain his actions because I can read him without words. And obviously, he can read me just as well.

I'm the luckiest girl alive to have Quinn's affections. After my deplorable performance earlier, I wouldn't blame him if he hitchhiked his way back to the US. The fact that he's a fugitive, however, may have something to do with that—another reason why he should just dump my ass and go back to his normal life.

But the past few weeks have shown me that Quinn is not going anywhere, and *that's* what makes me the luckiest girl alive. I've tried in vain to push him away, but it's like moving a stubborn, infuriating brick wall.

I know Quinn has secrets, just like me, but before we met, he wasn't a fugitive and wanted for a murder he didn't commit. Nor was he wanted for aggravated assault and kidnapping, which is what he most likely will be facing if caught, thanks to the stunt he pulled in the department store.

"We're in so much trouble." I sigh, sidestepping the blob of cream and walking down the aisle.

"How's that any different from our situation a week ago?" Quinn asks, tossing a pack of razors into the cart.

"Well, a week ago," I say, lowering my voice when a shopper squeezes past us, "you weren't wanted for kidnapping, and you hadn't threatened to blow an innocent shopper's head off."

Quinn only shrugs, casually brushing off my claims. "Well, a week ago, we weren't a hair's breadth away from being caught. I did what I had to, and when the time comes, I'll deal."

I latch onto his arm to stop his retreat, as his laid-back attitude concerns me.

"*We* will deal," I correct, raising my eyebrow, ensuring he understands I meant every word I said in that alleyway.

I won't allow him to take the blame for this whole mess. Whatever happens, we stick together.

"Promise me you won't do anything stupid."

"Define stupid," he says with a smirk, but it is quickly wiped clean when my face falls in panic.

"I'm *kidding*. I promise," he confirms, raising his pointer finger to his chest. "Cross my heart, hope to…" But he thankfully stops because what he's about to say is making me sick.

His eyes soften as he strokes a knuckle along my cheek. "Hope to live. I hope to live, Red. With you. After this is over, I hope to live a boring life…with you."

His heartfelt confession is music to my ears, and a small smile tugs at my lips as I place both palms against his warm chest.

"A life with you could never be boring, Quinn Berkeley," I whisper, slowly lifting my eyes to meet his, and I mean every word.

This is our first time openly discussing life together after this crazy roller-coaster ride ends. And I hope it's not the last. The thought of my future with Quinn firmly rooted in it is a future I can't wait to experience.

With that future fantasy embedded in my mind, I wrap my hand around Quinn's nape and say, "Well, tomorrow, let's take our first step toward that new life."

Quinn arches a brow, and I clarify, "Tomorrow, we call Abi."

Two

I've had the most restless sleep, and after finally getting five minutes, I'm rudely awakened by a banging. I try to focus on my breathing, hoping it'll lull me back to sleep, but sadly, as the banging now incorporates some moaning, I know I have no hope of dozing off.

Throwing my arm over my eyes, I groan, "What time is it?"

Quinn barely sleeps, and I know now is no exception, as no one could sleep through the ruckus next door.

"A little after six."

"A.m.?" I bark in shock, and he laughs in response.

"Jesus Christ! People are trying to sleep!" I yell as I reach over my head and thump on the wall.

This of course goes unnoticed by the amorous couple, who are saying some choice words I hope to never hear ever again.

So far, I hate Canada. It's cold, they talk funny, and oh, my family lives here. But I have to suck it up and deal since it's my sanctuary.

"Oh c'mon, it could be worse," Quinn says, obviously reading my thoughts.

"How?" I ask as I turn to face him and melt when I see his mussed hair flick into his emerald eyes.

"Well, we could be dead for one," he explains while I groan.

"Is this little speech supposed to make me feel any better?"

He laughs, his tongue ring catching the early morning light. "Yesterday it sucked, I get it," he says, passing the conversation baton over to me.

But I only sigh, rubbing my brow, as yesterday's debacle still gives me a headache, and I really don't want to talk or think about it.

"Do you want to talk about it?"

Sometimes I really wish he couldn't read me so well.

"No. I do not."

When he remains quiet, I guess I should at least explain a portion of how I'm feeling because I have no intention of discussing my so-called "family" ever again.

"Quinn, they're both dead to me," I state with finality, proud that my voice didn't betray my pain.

"But you have a sister," he gently says, as if that's meant to sway my decision.

The fact that I *have* a sister is what makes my choice easier.

Cynthia left me with my father for reasons unknown, but now I know part of that reason is because of the girl who is nothing but a stranger to me.

"I don't have a sister. I have someone who shares the same

bloodline as me. In no way will she ever be my sister. If I wanted a bitch in my life, I'd get Lucky a girlfriend," I spit, and Lucky whines at the end of our bed.

"What you did? It took a lot of courage. And if you never want to see them again, at least you can say you tried."

He's right, as usual, and I yank on the collar of his shirt, pulling him close. "Aren't you sick of always being right?"

"Well, it does get old," he says with a mock sigh.

Regardless of how shitty my day is, knowing that I have Quinn by my side makes this all a little more bearable.

"Hank would have been proud, too," he whispers, brushing a stray strand of hair off my brow.

It's the first mention of Hank, and although it still and will always hurt to know that I'm responsible for his untimely death, I don't feel like I'm about to break down with no hope of ever resurfacing without tears.

I guess this is what acceptance feels like because I know what denial, revenge, and regret taste like. They were the emotions that animated me through my quest for retribution on my father and Phil.

But now, all I want to do is remember the good times with him and not associate those two assholes with Hank. I want his memory not to be that of his death but of his wonderful life. And everything he did for me.

"That's my girl."

I cock my eyebrow at him, and he shrugs with a smirk. "You're the one who said I'm always right."

I knew that comment would bite me in the ass.

Alberta is huge, but I still can't help watching over my shoulder, always on the lookout for my dad.

I feel human after my long shower, and now my rumbling stomach alerts me to the fact I'm famished. We decide to eat at a quiet diner because even though we're not being hunted by the local police, I still don't want to flaunt our presence.

As I decide what to order, I hear "Jingle Bells" humming over the speakers for the tenth time today.

"What's up with the Christmas carols being played so early this year?" I ask, placing my menu on the tabletop and pointing at the speakers in the ceiling.

Quinn smirks before taking a small sip of his steaming coffee. "Christmas is next week, Red."

It is?

Being on the run has jumbled my days, weeks, and months, and I can't stop my frown. Christmas is the time to celebrate with your loved ones, and sadly, my loved ones would rather I didn't exist.

Well, that is, except for Quinn.

I would be completely content to wake up on Christmas morning with him sitting under my tree. But I realize how selfish that is because, unlike me, Quinn has a sibling who likes him.

"Sorry you can't spend the holidays with Tristan."

"It's okay," Quinn replies, reaching forward and clasping his fingers through mine. "I have you instead."

As I try not to melt at his adorable confession, I ask, "What did you want to do for Christmas?"

Quinn shrugs, running his fingers over my knuckles.

"Nothing. And besides, every day is Christmas with you."

I playfully roll my eyes at his tongue-in-cheek response.

"I'm serious," I say after he's done chuckling. "I know I'm not a very good substitute for Tristan, but I can try."

Quinn smirks, and his dimple will forever make me swoon. "Are you serious? You're even better. At least I can kiss you under the mistletoe."

He dodges my flying straw wrapper.

I know he's trying to make light of our fucked-up situation, but I don't want him to sacrifice his Christmas because of me.

Suddenly, I'm struck with a brilliant idea, and Quinn arches an eyebrow, obviously clueing in on my plan.

"We could have our own Christmas? I mean, it wouldn't be much, seeing as we're stuck in a shithole motel, but we could make it ours."

I go quiet. As much as I hate to admit it, I really want this. This is the first Christmas I've ever wanted to celebrate.

Usually, Christmas was the busiest time for me as I was run off my feet, delivering gear to festive junkies who wanted to spend their bonuses on Phil's merchandise.

They say Christmas is the time for giving, and I sure as hell gave to the point of falling into an exhausted heap on Christmas Day. And it all started again a few days later as people got ready to bring in the new year with a bang and a bag of blow.

"Let's do it," Quinn says, interrupting my messed-up trip down memory lane.

"Yeah?" I ask, meeting his warm eyes.

"Fuck yeah," he replies, giving me a small nod. "I couldn't think of a better person to spend Christmas with."

My breath gets caught in my throat as I whisper, "Ditto."

Feeding quarter after quarter into the phone we found off some deserted strip has my guts churning with dread. I haven't spoken to Tabitha for days, and although I know Quinn has filled her in on the events when I was unconscious, I'm frightened she'll be no closer to finding a way out for us.

"Hello, Bobby Joe's. This is Tabitha. How may I help you?"

A longing hits me so hard that finding my voice takes a minute.

"Hello?" Tabitha asks while I remain mute.

"Hi, Abi," I finally manage to choke out.

A stunned gasp greets me, and then I hear muffled noises as if she's walking, and I know she's going somewhere private.

After a minute, she says, "Oh, Mia, I miss you. I'm so sorry. Quinn told me what happened."

I cut her off, not wanting any sympathy. "I miss you, too. How are you?"

Thankfully, she takes the hint.

"I'm okay. I'm just worried about you. And Quinn. He's in a lot of trouble for what he did," she adds, the concern clear in her voice.

"I know." I sigh, looking at him. "How bad is it?"

"Well, the fact he pulled a gun on you and took you hostage has shifted things a bit."

"What do you mean?" I ask, watching Quinn roll a rock under his boot, totally undisturbed by our conversation.

"Don't be mad," Tabitha says, and I instantly freeze.

"What are you talking about, Abi? Why would I be mad?"

"Well, with the stunt he pulled and being on the run while wanted for murder, my dad has pulled some strings, and well, he has pushed that you both get the death penalty if found guilty."

I pull the receiver away from my ear. Surely, I haven't

heard her correctly.

Quinn is beside me in an instant, his eyebrows raised in question. But I don't have the answers until I find out what the hell is going on.

"Death penalty?" I spit, my voice rising in concern. "Please explain why your dad thinks that's a good idea."

As I see Quinn's mouth pop open, I calm down—only just.

"In most circumstances, Canada will only allow extradition if the person won't receive the death penalty. My dad had to push for that sentence so you can stay in Canada. Even if the Canadian police capture you, you'll be safer in Canada than you would be here."

"How so?" I question.

"Well, seeing as you're dubbed Bonnie and Clyde by the press, they're out for blood."

I rub my temples, my head about ready to explode. "So I guess this is good news?"

"It's as good as it gets for the moment, I'm afraid. Dad has ensured me that you're safe in Canada, but make sure you keep a low profile."

I close my eyes and sigh, sick of all the hiding. "We're nearly there. Dad said it's only a matter of time. They're building a strong case against Phil, and my dad said they should close in on your dad in the next few weeks."

"Thank you so much, Abi. Hey, what does your dad do?" I ask, realizing I never once asked how he could pull all these strings.

"My dad, well…he's a senator. And a powerful one at that."

My mouth hangs open because I wasn't expecting that answer.

"He has a lot of connections, Mia. But he's trying to do

this underground so it won't affect his name. If this were to get out, you can imagine what it would do to his career. But if push comes to shove, he would do what's right, regardless of the scandal it would cause."

My brain can't process this without short-circuiting, and I get out the only coherent word I can manage to express. "Why?"

"Why? Why is he helping you?" she questions, unsure what I'm asking. "Because I asked him to. My father lives in Washington DC. He left me with my mother, thinking I would be better off staying in my hometown when they divorced. But I knew he really wanted to focus on his career, and I'm okay with that. I have never asked anything of him before, so when I asked him to help me, he knew it was important to me, and he said yes."

My eyes widen at her confession, and I really don't know what to say because a simple thank-you seems like an unsatisfactory response.

As corny as this makes me, I whisper, "I love you, Abi. You're my best friend, and I really don't know what I would have done if I'd never met you."

Abi sniffs at my honesty, and I'm glad I went with my gut.

"You can thank me in person when you come home."

"I'll hold you to that," I quickly reply, wiping away the unfallen tears from my eyes.

Abi chuckles but turns serious. "Have you seen your mom?"

A groan slips past my lips, and Quinn rubs my back in support.

"I take that as ayes, and that it went well," Abi says sarcastically.

"Yeah, something like that," I reply with a tired smile.

"We have a lot to catch up on when you come home." I'm thankful she's not pushing a conversation I can't bear to have over the phone. "I haven't told Tristan about Quinn and what he did."

I nod, looking at Quinn. "Good idea. The less he knows, the better."

"It's not that," Abi says, concern touching her tone. "It's… he's different. This is really getting to him, and I think if he found out about this, it would be the final thing to tip him over the edge, and no amount of reasoning would be able to keep him from finding you."

I bite my lip, feeling my heart break. "Please look out for him. I couldn't live with myself…" I stop, unable to finish.

Quinn wraps his arm around my middle, kissing my head softly.

"I promise I will. You just missed him, actually. He went to Night Cats."

As soon as she mentions the one place I could call home, my feet feel unsteady and weak. Bracing one hand against the glass for support, I lower my head in defeat. Will this always be my response to a place where my fondest memories are held?

"Sorry," Abi whispers when I remain silent.

One day, I know I'll be able to deal with these emotions without having a mental breakdown. But sadly, today is not that day.

"It's fine, Abi. Don't sweat it. I better go. I'll call you in a couple of days to check in. Say hi to Tristan from us."

"Take care."

"You too." I hang up with a sigh, not letting go of the receiver. "Did you know Abi's dad was a senator?"

Quinn shrugs. "I knew he was powerful and in politics,

but not a senator."

"Well, at least we got the good guys on our side. Here's hoping they can clear our names, as I'm not keen on being a fugitive my whole life."

Quinn surprises me by pulling me into his embrace by my belt loops. "How does it feel to be in the arms of a criminal?"

"Crime has never felt so good." I loop my hands around his neck, toying with the soft hair at his nape.

He smirks, and I'm reminded of how lucky I am to have met him. Without him, I have no doubt I would be dead. He's saved me more times than I care to admit—but not just literally. He's saved me from losing myself in the memories of my past, and for that, I will always love him.

Even though I've never expressed my feelings aloud, I hope Quinn knows how I feel. Because the love I feel isn't just butterflies in your stomach.

I love him as a lover.

As a brother.

As a protector.

As a fighter.

And as a friend.

But most of all, I love him for being him.

And one day, I'll gather the courage to tell him all the ways I love him. But for now, I'll settle for showing him as I smash my lips to his.

As we walk up the stairs to our room, I wonder where we'll spend our Christmas. I ignore the stabbing sensation in my chest that my mother and Pollyanna will most likely be partying in style, eating and drinking the most expensive foods and wine, while Quinn and I eat frozen burritos and Pop-Tarts.

But who says that's what we have to do?

This Christmas, just like Thanksgiving, is the first I'm celebrating. Living with a drug addict whose Christmases all came at once every time he got high kind of took the fun out of celebrating.

I was always so busy dealing during the holidays that when the actual holiday rolled around, I wanted nothing to do with it. But this year will be different. And this year, I have someone I want to buy a gift for.

But what do I buy him? Whatever I decide upon, I know it has to be special.

"Whatcha thinking?" Quinn asks, slipping the rusty key into the lock.

As it wheezes open, I reply, "Christmas."

"What about it?"

"Just about your present," I tease, flopping onto the bed.

"Oh yeah? I'm listening," he replies with a smirk as he kicks off his boots and lies beside me.

"I'm not good at gift giving," I admit, using my hands as a pillow as I roll on my side to face him.

Quinn is the hottest man I have ever laid my eyes on. And when he nibbles on his lip ring, just like he's doing now, he takes that sex appeal to a whole new level. Suddenly, my cheeks flush as I'm struck with an idea of what I can give him for Christmas.

"You're enough of a gift," he replies with a smile as if reading my thoughts.

"I'm hardly a good substitute for chocolate, eggnog, and gingerbread," I say nervously, rattling off a list of Christmas goodies, hoping Quinn doesn't become aware of my blushing cheeks.

"Red," Quinn states seriously, his eyes scanning down my body. "If I were going to overdose on something sweet, I would much rather eat *you*."

My already flushed cheeks smolder at his admission, and I will my breathing to a normal pace before I embarrass myself.

But no matter how hard I try, his comment awakened my body. And that just makes my gift choice all the more perfect.

"Come here," Quinn whispers, and I instantly shuffle closer. "For as long as I can remember, Christmas was just another crappy holiday when I would purposely sleep the day away."

"Why?" I softly question.

"I know I haven't told you much about my past. And there's a reason for that. I don't want you to judge me for actions that I'll never be able to change. Or ever be able to redeem myself for."

"I would never—" I frantically reply, but he silences me by placing a finger over my lips.

"You say you wouldn't, but I judge myself every day for it, and although I'll never forgive myself for what I've done, you make it a little easier to forget the sins of my past. So trust me when I say you're more than enough of a gift."

Only then does he remove his finger.

"Quinn," I stumble over my words, at a loss for the right thing to say.

But how does one reply to something so sweet and also something so heartbreaking? I simply can't because there are no words to vocalize my feelings at this moment. Actions are the only thing I can employ to express my love for him.

We breathe in one another's exhalations, transfixed on the other. But a war rages inside me, threatening to break free at any second. And I don't have the strength to fight it at the moment.

I launch at Quinn, fisting my fingers into the collar of his T-shirt, desperate to draw him closer. He complies, allowing me to drag him onto my starving body, anxious to feel his touch. As soon as my lips meet his, I can't get close enough, quick enough. But too many clothes are in the way, and I'm desperate to be skin to skin.

"Lose the shirt," I say around his mouth, my hands frantically helping his as he reaches for the hem of his T-shirt.

As soon as he's bare, a shiver rocks me when he lowers his hard chest onto mine. His nipple ring digs into me, and I whimper, loving how the cool metal caresses my skin. His tongue drives forward, licking my lower lip, requesting permission into my mouth, and I open up wide, wanting to devour him whole.

His hand takes a leisurely tour of my body, stopping at my right breast along the way. I moan in pleasure, arching into his touch, but it's still not enough. I clutch at my T-shirt, and Quinn pulls away for the briefest of seconds to allow me to sit up and tear it off over my head. Before it even hits the floor, I'm pawing at Quinn to resume his position on top of me.

He bites my neck, and I bend backward, exposing the entire length for him to consume. His stubble scratches me in the most delicious way, and as I feel the stud of his tongue ring tickling a path down my neck to my collarbone, I know I'm about ready to detonate.

"Pants. Off," I manage to choke out, and Quinn chuckles in response, but thankfully, I hear a zipper being unfastened.

"No, yours, not mine," I reply breathlessly when I feel him slipping his fingers into my pants.

"Later," he replies huskily, biting my jaw.

I'm too highly strung to argue, and as his wicked fingers crawl into the waistband of my underwear, all rational thought goes flying out the window.

"Oh fuck," he hisses as he brushes over my aching center but never seeking haven inside.

Quinn teases me, sliding two fingers up and down my slick entrance, and I just wish he would…

Oh God.

He inserts a finger, and I moan at the feeling. It's exactly what I need. My body begins undulating beneath him, and by his labored breathing, I know he's just as turned on as I am.

His finger torments me as it skirts around where I want it to be, and I know he's doing this on purpose. But I'm really not in the mood for teasing, so I reach down and palm the huge bulge in the front of his pants, and he sucks in a breath of air at my forwardness.

"More," I beg, barely able to speak.

But to my horror, Quinn withdraws his finger.

My eyes flick to his, wordlessly demanding an answer.

The answer I get has my burning body engulfing into flames.

He runs the finger that was inside me seconds ago along his lower lip, spreading my arousal with his touch. If that's not hot enough, his pink tongue emerges, slowly licking my taste from his wicked mouth.

My eyes are glued to his, and as he places his finger into his mouth, sucking away my taste while reaching for the button on his jeans, I almost come from the sight alone. As he unfastens his zipper, my eyes drop to his pants, and the unmissable erection poking out of his jeans has my body demanding more.

Sadly, all thoughts of getting anywhere near him are

interrupted by a loud knock on the door. Both our movements cease, and I think I almost stop breathing when another knock, louder this time, thumps on the door.

I have no idea who it is, and as the knocking continues, quite impatiently, I know they're not going away.

"Who is it?" I whisper to Quinn, who quickly buttons up his jeans.

As he leans over and opens up the bedside dresser and produces a gun, I know he won't take any chances when he finds out. My eyes fall to the piece, and I jump up, frantically searching for my top on the floor.

"Go into the bathroom and lock the door," he demands as he slowly creeps toward the banging.

My response is a laugh as I reach into my backpack for my Colt. "I don't think so."

Before he can object, I follow him silently, ensuring my steps are masked by the soft green carpet.

"Of course not," Quinn replies with a sigh.

My heart beats at a deafening octave, and as the knocking gets louder and more insistent, I think I'm about to throw up in terror.

"Do you think they found us?" I whisper, not needing to clarify who *they* are.

Quinn shrugs as he replies, "I doubt they would knock, but I don't know. I really wish you would just go wait in the bathroom."

"How about *you* go wait in the bathroom?" I spit back, insulted.

Quinn blows out a breath, exasperated by my stubbornness. Too bad. Besides, he should be used to my pigheadedness by now. I mean, I have a very good teacher.

As he silently approaches the small window of our room,

he takes a shallow breath and uses the barrel of his pistol to inch the curtain open a fraction. I can't see a thing as his huge back blocks my view, so I stand on tippy-toes but still can't see jackshit.

As the knocking turns into a loud banging, I'm tempted to jump onto his shoulders so I can see who the hell it is.

"Who is it?" I demand, attempting to look over Quinn's shoulder as he turns to face me.

By his plagued expression, I'm not sure if I want him to answer my question. But of course, curiosity gets the better of me.

"Is it them?" I ask, holding my breath.

"Worse," Quinn replies, tucking the gun into the waistband of his jeans as he reaches for the doorknob.

"Worse?" I gasp, watching in awe as he stows away his piece. "Then why are you putting your gun away?"

But all my questions are answered as Quinn yanks open the door, revealing someone I never, ever expected to see.

Three

When I see Pollyanna's scowling face, I'm tempted to rub my eyes because there must be some mistake. But as she rudely shoulders past Quinn and me, I know I'm not mistaken.

I'm rooted to the spot as I vaguely hear Quinn shutting the door behind me, foiling my escape.

Pollyanna scrunches up her nose in disgust while gazing around our tiny lime-green room. As she runs her finger over the dusty breakfast table, she mumbles, "What a shithole," and wipes her hand on my jacket, which is draped on the back of a chair.

Quinn stands by my side, and we watch Polly sag into the brown armchair, making herself right at home as she kicks her boots onto the stained coffee table in front of her.

I lean toward Quinn, my eyes never leaving her as I

whisper in a catatonic tone, "Why did you put your gun away?"

Quinn chuckles as he kisses the top of my head, and the sound draws Polly's attention our way. I don't fail to notice her gaze fall to Quinn's chest, and the feeling I had yesterday of clawing her eyes out returns.

"What are you doing here?" I bark, thankful it came out coherent and not consisting of a string of profanities.

Polly's icy blue eyes flick to mine, and she crosses her arms over her chest. "Oh, trust me, I do not want to be here."

"Well, you know where the door is, seeing as you so rudely decided to break it down," I bite back, mimicking her actions. "So don't let it hit your spoiled ass on the way out."

Polly's jaw drops and Quinn sighs, obviously unimpressed by my bad manners.

"Pollyanna, hi, I'm Quinn." He walks toward her and extends his hand when I make no attempt to move.

She shuffles to the edge of the chair, graciously accepting his hand while batting her fake eyelashes. "Hi," she purrs, leaning forward, revealing an eyeful of boob in her low-cut top. "And it's Polly."

I clear my throat when she makes it more than obvious she's checking out my very half-naked man.

"Okay, enough with the introductions. What the hell do you want, Polly?" I ask, reaching for Quinn's discarded shirt and throwing it at him.

I have never been so thankful to see Quinn dress. The thought of this little troublemaker looking at him with that look in her eyes has me itching to reach for the gun in the waistband of my jeans.

"It's Pollyanna." She scowls, standing. "Only my friends get to call me Polly," she adds, waving at Quinn. "Hi, friend."

I take a menacing step toward her, about ready to break her jaw, but Quinn wraps an arm around my waist, holding me back.

"Polly, is there a reason why you're here?" he asks, and I suppress the urge to stomp on his foot.

Why is he being so nice to her?

Was he not present when she was a right royal asshole to me?

His kindness toward the Antichrist angers me, and I attempt to push away from him, but his arm sits securely around my waist, and I give up trying to break free.

"I'm only here because my mom is a mess," she replies, her bracelets jingling when she brushes a stray piece of straightened hair off her brow.

My ears prick up, and I narrow my eyes to slits.

"Why is that our problem?" I snarl, finally escaping Quinn's hold as I storm toward her.

"Because," she spits, not retreating from my warpath but advancing. "*You're* the reason she's a zombie! Since you left, she won't eat or speak. She's like the living dead!"

Being this close to her, there is no doubt she's my sister, as the look of rage contorting her features is one I live with every day.

"Not my problem," I say casually, shaking my head.

"Are you serious?" she wails. "You're the one who just turned up on our doorstep as a fugitive, ruining our lives!"

"Excuse me?" I gasp, incredulous of her accusations. "You need to leave. Now."

I take a step away from her before I smack her smug face.

Ruining *their* lives? She has no idea what a ruined life feels like. She has no fucking idea.

"I will not leave until you explain to me how in God's

name you are my sister. Daddy is on some business trip in Europe, and I can't reach him. Mom is a fucking nutcase, so I can't get a straight answer from her. As you can see, you're the only person who can explain what the hell is going on!" Polly screams, but I barely hear a word she says. The only word I can hear on repeat is…*Daddy.*

Who the *fuck* is her daddy? Because I know for a fact Thomas Lee is not traveling the streets of Europe on some business trip.

My brain can scarcely catch up, but when it does, I cover my mouth as nausea begins creeping up my throat.

"Polly, will you give us a minute?" Quinn asks, gently reaching for my arm.

I shrug out of his hold because as the events of the past few minutes become crystal clear, I know I'm going to be sick.

Running into the bathroom, I barely make it in time to lift the lid before I throw up the entire contents of my stomach. But it's still not enough, and I force my body to expel anything that might be left.

"This can't be happening. This cannot be happening," I mumble, thumping my fist onto the tiled wall.

"Red," Quinn whispers from the doorway. "Are you all right?"

I try not to scoff at his question because I doubt I'll ever be all right ever again.

Slamming the lid shut as I flush the toilet, I stand and a surge of anger overwhelms me because Polly isn't the only one needing answers. Shoving past Quinn, I storm over to Polly, who stands by the door, adjusting the brown strap of her leather handbag.

"Who is your father?"

"What?" she asks, and I don't fail to notice her voice

quivering when she can clearly see how pissed off I am.

But I don't care, continuing with my rampage.

"Who the fuck is your father?" I repeat, shoving into her chest. The action causes her to bump into the wall.

"Hey! Don't push me!" she shrieks, pushing off the wall and getting into my face, ready to slap me.

But it'll be a cold day in hell when I allow this brat to lay a finger on me. So I do something, and in hindsight, it's probably not the best idea I've ever had.

Reaching for my gun, I pull it out and aim it at her face. As soon as she sees my piece, she gasps and quickly raises her hands, freezing on the spot. Tears instantly spring to her eyes, but I don't care because I want answers.

"Red!" Quinn yells from behind me, his voice rising in distress when he sees what I have done.

I ignore him. There is no way I'm dropping this gun until she starts talking.

"Answer the question!" I yell, waving the pistol when she remains mute, her eyes transfixed on the gun.

This only has her breaking out into a loud sob, her chest heaving with each intake of winded breath.

I feel a pinch of guilt for pulling a gun on her when she begins howling and squeezes her eyes shut, afraid to look at me. But if she answered the damn question, then I wouldn't have pulled the gun.

"Red, you're scaring her," Quinn says softly, but he wisely stays put, leaving me to make a decision on what to do next.

Closing my eyes, I realize that no matter how mad I am, I'm no better than Phil for pulling a gun on an innocent person. I have no right to scare her, and I instantly feel sick for losing my temper in the worst possible way.

Quinn's calmness has the desired effect, and I slowly

lower my arm, placing the gun on the table. With my hands raised in surrender, I take a step toward a terrified Polly.

"Polly, I'm unarmed," I say, hoping my voice conveys some composure.

Her sniffles are loud and amplified, but I continue to press, softer this time...and without a gun pointed at her.

"Who is your father?" I ask, watching her tremble when she opens her red-rimmed eyes.

"Chandler Ashfield," she finally replies, shakily wiping away her fallen tears.

I take a step back at her confession, bumping into the sofa.

Who the *fuck* is Chandler Ashfield?

I shake my head, unable to process this information right now because it makes no sense. None of this makes any sense.

"Polly, I think it's best you leave," Quinn says, walking toward her as I stand catatonic. "Do you need money for a cab?"

Polly shakes her head, her long black hair sticking to her tears. "I...I...d-drove," she stutters, her eyes still glued on me.

"Will you be okay to drive home?"

She nods as her lower lip quivers, and another stowaway tear slips down her cheek.

I would have apologized to her for my deplorable behavior if I could speak right now. But when she steps toward me, my intended apology gets kicked in the teeth.

"I wish I'd never met you! Stay away from me and my family. Mom deserted you for a reason, and although I don't know why, I'm so glad she did. You're obviously a huge, disgusting mistake. Neither she nor I want you here, so stay away!"

And she turns on her Prada heels, slamming the door shut behind her.

There is no way that what happened, just happened. There is no fucking way that my mother had an affair and had another child with someone named Chandler Ashfield.

But the guttural pain I feel in my chest tells me that it's very, *very* true.

My mother got pregnant, and then she left. She chose her other family, leaving me behind like yesterday's trash. How could she do that to me? I was three. I was three fucking years old! But she didn't care.

She doesn't care.

Maybe Polly was right. Maybe I *am* a huge mistake, one she wishes she never made.

I'm going to be sick—again.

Running to the toilet, I flip the lid, but no matter how hard I try, nothing comes out. I'm dry heaving, but my body has nothing left to give. It won't allow me to purge my memories, the one thing I so desperately want to push out of my body forever.

How can this be happening?

I thought coming here would answer all the questions of my past. But it has done the opposite. I am now plagued with so many questions, ones I'm afraid may never be answered.

I feel dirty and unclean. I feel used and lied to. I just wish I didn't feel because the pain is choking me alive.

A pair of hands wraps around my middle, pulling my back to his warm front, and I sag in exhaustion.

"How can this be happening?" I whisper to Quinn, closing my eyes in defeat.

"I wish I had the answers, Red," he replies, resting his chin on my shoulder and kissing my cheek.

I know who does, and as much as it kills me, I have to find out why. I won't be able to move on until I face my past head-on.

"How do you feel?"

"Dirty," I reply honestly. "I fucking pulled a gun on an innocent girl. What the hell is wrong with me?"

I squeeze my eyes shut, as I won't allow myself to cry.

"Nothing is wrong with you," Quinn says, and his kindness has a single tear rolling down my cheek.

"I want to take a shower."

Quinn slowly rises and walks over to the shower before turning it on. As the steam from the hot water fills the room, my aching body gathers what little strength I have left to stand, and I reach for the hem of my T-shirt.

Without a second thought, I pull it over my head and toss it into the corner of the room. As I work on unzipping my jeans, I realize Quinn remains in the room. But biting my lip, I continue to shimmy them down my legs until I'm standing in nothing but my black bra and underwear. Unsure if this will freak him out, I reach around and unhook my bra, holding the front when it snaps free.

Quinn turns to look at me, and as he takes in my near-naked appearance, he gives me a small smile.

Standing bare in front of a boy a year ago would have scared the shit out of me, but now, it really doesn't.

I have grown and overcome the fear of connecting with a stranger. And I know I have to do the same with my mother. I don't expect miracles, but I have to at least try. Even if I *was* a mistake, I need to know why.

No matter how hard it'll be, I'm no quitter. I've come this far, and I refuse to give in.

Quinn reaches forward, and when his fingertips lightly brush over my fallen bra straps, goose bumps break out over my entire body. His gentle touch gives me the strength to slowly peel my hands away from my chest and let my bra drop to the ground.

I raise my eyes to meet his, and he's the perfect gentleman as his gaze never wavers from my face.

Taking a small step forward with his eyes still focused on mine, he gently reaches for my waist and draws me toward him, his fingers flexing on my skin. He then hooks his thumbs into the waistband of my lace underwear and slowly drags them down my legs. Once they pool around my feet, I step out of them, standing completely naked.

I shiver, but I'm not cold.

I shiver in yearning, as I have never felt as desirable as I do right now.

Quinn's hands glide up my flesh and then down my arms as he interlaces our fingers, leading me to the shower. I step into the bathtub, and as soon as the warm spray hits my skin, I let out a small moan of pleasure. It feels better than I could have ever imagined, and I close my eyes, stepping farther under the mist of water.

As my body instantly warms to the scalding temperature, I sag in relief, and the heat does wonders for kneading out the knots in my back. Reaching blindly for the shower gel, I suddenly feel it being placed into my outstretched palm. I give Quinn a small smile as I open my eyes, not able to really see him too well through the dense mist, but I see enough.

Unlike him, I am not chivalrous, and I can't stop myself as my eyes drop to the huge arousal in his pants. The sight has my mouth running dry, and I reach for the faucet to decrease the temperature before I combust.

Quinn smirks when he sees my actions, and with a faux sigh, he says, "My eyes are up here."

A small smile tugs at my mouth, as this conversation is

one we had all those months ago. However, now I've been caught staring.

I decide to reply with the same response as he gave me. "I know where your eyes are," I whisper, and Quinn shakes his head with a dimpled grin.

We remain silent, no doubt lost in the past and recollecting how far we've come since our first encounter.

Only when Quinn removes the shower gel from my hand and lathers it up into his palm does reality kick in. I gasp when he reaches forward with strong fingers and begins rubbing the vanilla-scented body wash all over me.

He starts at my neck and slowly works his way down, not missing a single inch of skin. As he rubs over my breasts, my nipples immediately pebble with his touch, and I whimper. But he continues to be the perfect gentleman, ensuring my needy body does not deter him from his task at hand.

However, when he arrives at the junction between my thighs, we both softly groan at the sensation.

His deft fingers stroke over my core, and I bite my lip to keep from screaming out in pleasure, as I know this isn't sexual. This is him showing me how much he cares.

Once my front is cleaned, Quinn turns me so I face the white shower wall, and he begins the same treatment as he did on my front. His skillful fingers lull me into a sleepy bubble, and I lightly shudder when he massages my ass.

But again, he's only there to take care of me, something no one has ever done for me in my entire life.

By the time he's done washing my hair, I'm about to fall asleep standing up. I'm pretty sure I'm halfway there because I don't remember getting out of the shower, drying off, or climbing into bed.

It's only when I feel Quinn's naked flesh press up against

mine that I barely register where I am.

"Sleep, Red."

I do as he says because sleeping beside the man I love sounds like a perfect thing to do.

Four

The following morning, I wake before Quinn, which is unusual. So I steal this moment to examine the man beside me.

Quinn's epic looks are beyond being simply amazing—they are *fucking* amazing.

His hair has grown so much longer since we first met, and I reach forward, brushing his dirty blond hair off his brow. My finger traces his thick but well-groomed eyebrows, and continues to glide down the slope of his nose.

When I reach the seam of his top lip, my heartbeat begins kicking against my rib cage. His mouth has kissed me in ways I never thought possible. I lightly rub over the silver hoop that hugs his plump lower lip, and as a tiny moan escapes him, I catch a glimpse of his tongue ring.

But regardless of his looks, I know I would still feel the

same about him. Quinn Berkeley is beautiful, inside and out. He's shown me how to live, and through his strength, I have never felt so alive.

As he shifts, the sheet slinks lower, exposing his entire chest for my viewing pleasure. But there is one thing I am interested in—his tattoo.

Believe it or not, I actually have never been close enough to read the intricate script writing, which is buried in swirls of red and orange. But now that the opportunity has arisen, I can't stop myself as I slowly glide the sheet a little lower so I can read it in its entirety.

I turn my head to the side as his tattoo originates just under his armpit and flows across his ribs, leading into the waistband of his black boxer briefs. It's a beautiful side piece, and as I look closer, I can see that the bursts of red and orange are actually flames.

However, these flames are drawn with such fieriness that I'm almost afraid to reach out and touch them just in case I get burned. These flames, I imagine, are what the flames of hell would look like.

I lean closer and lower his briefs to read it all, as the last word is inked down his hip. I gasp when I softly read aloud what the tattoo says.

Love cannot save you from your own fate.

I don't know what to do because I suddenly feel like I'm intruding on a private moment. I know that's ridiculous, seeing as it's tattooed on his body forever. But like my ink, I never got it to show others. I got it for me. It reminded me of who I am and what I did until that point in my life to mark my body forever.

And I have a feeling Quinn did exactly the same.

It really is a beautiful tattoo, but I slowly pull up his briefs and glide the sheet back over his body, not wanting him to know I've seen it.

Although he doesn't hide it, I still feel like this is a private memory he'll share with me when he's ready.

I slip out of bed, not wanting to wake Quinn, and make some coffee.

As I cradle the coffee cup, I think about my decision. Even though every bone in my body tells me not to go, I've decided to see my mother. As selfish as this makes me, though, it has nothing to do with her being a "zombie," as Polly phrased it.

It has to do with me.

I've done my part and warned her about my father and the danger she may be in. So now it's her turn to start talking.

I also want to apologize to Polly for pulling a gun on her.

My temper got the better of me, and even though that's no excuse, I still have to try and make amends. I have no doubt she'll tell me to shove it because I know that's what I would do if I were her, but I'm not her.

So I have to at least try.

This whole situation has my already nauseated stomach doing somersaults.

"Morning," says a croaky-voiced Quinn as he lays a kiss on my forehead before pouring himself a cup of coffee.

We sip our coffee in silence, but the inevitable lingers.

"What are we going to do now?"

"I thought I would keep up the crazy and go see Cynthia."

"You're right, that *is* crazy," he says, tongue in cheek.

"I never claimed to be sane," I reply with a playful shrug. "This is your last chance to run screaming for the Canadian hills."

"I think you mean the Rocky Mountains," he corrects with a smirk, kissing the tip of my nose.

I love that Quinn and I can always be dorks together regardless of our situation.

"Your hair is getting so long," I say, unable to take my eyes off his bed head.

"Don't you like it?" He chews on his lip ring, which is totally distracting.

"Like what?" I ask, enthralled by his actions.

No matter how many times I see him tug at that hoop, I can never get enough.

"My hair." He chuckles, reading my dirty thoughts.

"Oh right," I reply, my eyes shyly meeting his. "There's nothing I won't like about you, Quinn Berkeley."

And I mean every word of it.

My comment has me thinking about his tattoo and his confession about his past sins. What has he done that's so bad he could never forgive himself?

Looking into his gentle eyes, I know that whatever it is, it'll never change how I feel about him.

We all have skeletons in our closets. I should know. But no matter what he's done, we all deserve a second chance, right?

With that thought, the decision to go see my mother feels all the more fitting because even *she* deserves a second chance.

However, what if that second chance isn't enough?

Looking at the mansion through the windshield of our stolen truck, I sigh, totally unprepared for round two.

The closer we get to Cynthia's home, the more I regret my decision. But now that I'm here, there's no turning back. I've dealt with worse before, so I tell myself to slip on my big girl panties because I'm not leaving this place until I get some answers.

Patting Lucky on the head for luck, I exit the truck and interlace my fingers through Quinn's warm ones.

I scoff when I see a dancing Santa and his entourage of reindeer and elves displayed on the front lawn. I never noticed this ridiculous Christmas exhibit when I was here last, and that's a good thing because I would have taken an axe to it.

Quinn sees me eyeballing the reindeer and chuckles. "What did Rudolph ever do to you?" he asks as we walk the long gravel driveway to the front steps.

"His carol sucks. Out of all the Christmas carols, it's fucking 'Rudolph, the Red-Nosed Reindeer' that gets stuck in my head for days. Rudolph needs to go into retirement or stop having such a damn shiny nose," I add as we climb the marbled stairs.

Quinn laughs at my outburst. "Okay then, how about I just call you the Grinch from now on?"

"One nickname is more than enough, thank you very much," I reply, leaning forward and ringing the doorbell without hesitation or second thoughts.

As the heavy sound resonates inside, I panic, realizing that I have alerted the occupants of my presence due to my anti-Rudolph rant.

I need time to prepare and maybe do breathing exercises to calm down. But there's no time for that as the white door opens, revealing a sooky-faced Polly.

As soon as she sees me, she attempts to slam the door shut, but I wedge my boot into the frame to stop it from closing.

"Polly, hear me out," I say, inching closer and using my arm to hold the door open. "Please."

She narrows her eyes at me, and her red-painted lips pull into a tight scowl. "Why? So you can shoot me? I don't think so. Fuck off," she snarls, still attempting to shut the door.

I use my body weight to stop it from moving an inch.

"Look, you have every right to be mad, and I get that. I'm sorry for pulling a gun on you. That wasn't cool."

"You think? I should have you arrested. You're a fucking psycho!" she cries, but thankfully, her hold on the door slackens.

"Look, I said I'm sorry," I grit out through clenched teeth. Her attitude is pissing me off.

"So what? Sorry isn't good enough. Now leave," she says, feebly attempting to shut the door.

"Mia?" a weak voice asks. "Mia, is that you?"

Both Polly and I freeze when we hear the voice of our mother, and I can't deny she sounds like shit.

"Polly, is that your sister?" Cynthia questions, her heels clicking on the tiles as she quickly approaches the front door.

Polly doesn't turn to face her. "Yes, Mother, it's Mia. The gun-wielding lunatic," she adds under her breath as she finally opens the door.

I return the stink eye she gives me, but my mouth parts in shock when she has the audacity to flip me off.

Quinn bites his lip in amusement, but all hilarity disappears when Cynthia stands in the open doorway beside Polly.

I actually recoil backward when I see her because she looks like death.

Her long black hair sits in a messy bun. The defiant tufts sticking out at odd angles make her look like she stuck something shiny into an electrical socket. Her clothes are the same ones I saw her in when I was last here, but she's wearing mismatched heels. One is black, and the other is purple. She has a serious case of raccoon eyes, and her grimy stench is masked under the perfume of cigarettes.

I should take pleasure in seeing her look so damaged, but I don't.

"Oh, Mia," she sobs, running toward me and throwing her arms around my neck.

I don't have time to move, but there's no way in hell I'm about to return her embrace, so I stand rigid, watching Polly glaring at me over Cynthia's shoulder.

Once she's done with the PDA, she lets me go, reaching into her pocket and pulling out a handkerchief.

"I'm so glad you're here." She sniffs, dabbing at her eyes.

I grunt in response. I have no idea what to say, seeing as she was the one who asked me to leave when I was here last.

"Come inside, Mom," Polly says after a few moments of uncomfortable silence. "You'll catch a cold."

She steps back, opening the door wider for her to enter.

Cynthia nods, her eyes brightening slightly when she says, "Mia, please come inside. And your friend too." She seems surprised to see Quinn, like she only just realized he was here.

"I'm Quinn," he says, extending his hand, which Cynthia lightly shakes.

"Nice to meet you. Are you Mia's boyfriend?"

On that note, I pull Quinn by the hand and push past Polly. I am so not ready to have that daughterly talk with my mother just yet.

Now that rage isn't clouding my vision, I can see this home is pretty. All sorts of artwork adorn the walls, and I can't help the sick feeling gurgling in my stomach as I wonder if my mother still paints.

It's one of the only memories I have of her.

I remember how excited she was to have her artwork chosen and displayed in a gallery downtown. It was her dream come true. But sadly, that dream wasn't enough to make her stay. And that thought has me grinding my teeth as I enter some glamorous living area off to the right.

This room is bigger than the other room I was in last time, and again, it's beautiful and tasteful. And I hate it.

I hate that I think it's pretty.

I hate that I'm not slashing at the walls and breaking all the crystal figurines in rage.

"Sit, please," Cynthia says, pointing at a black leather sofa.

I don't resist and quickly sit, and Quinn sits beside me.

Polly and Cynthia also sit down, and the awkwardness begins.

How do you start off a conversation such as this? No matter how I intend to phrase it, or how many questions I ask, there only seems to be one word that sums it all up.

Why?

No matter what I ask or how she replies, the result will always be why.

"Mia, I'm so sorry for my behavior the other day," Cynthia says, breaking the silence.

Crossing my boot over my knee, I slouch backward because I feel like I'm about to collapse.

I really think she needs to apologize for a lot more than just the other day. But I give her a small nod, indicating I'm listening.

"I don't even know where to begin." Cynthia sniffs, wringing the handkerchief into a knot.

"How about you start by telling me why you left?" I suggest louder than expected. Cynthia jolts, startled by my hostility.

Quinn places a warm hand on my bare knee through a hole in my jeans. He squeezes it lightly, and I know he's asking me to calm down. If I don't, I'll never get the answers I desperately seek.

With that in mind, I sigh, slightly annoyed that I have to be the rational one. "Look, I know this isn't easy for anyone…" I ignore Polly's disgruntled "humph" in the background as I continue. "But you owe me the truth. No matter how painful, I want to hear it."

Cynthia nods, her hair shrouding her face as it slips free from her loose bun. "You're right. I do owe you the truth. From start to finish, you deserve to know it all."

My heart races because I've been waiting for this moment my entire life. How will I handle the truth? Will it shatter me? Or will it empower me to start anew once I know everything?

There's only one way to find out.

I look at Cynthia, waiting for her to speak, but she doesn't. She just buries herself further under her veil of hair, sobbing quietly.

I know she needs a moment. I have no doubt these memories are painful for her to relive—but too bad, as I'm not leaving this house without answers.

I look at Quinn, hoping he'll give me some magical solution to get her to talk, but he only shrugs and toys with his hoop.

Polly is the first to speak. "Mom, are you all right?" Her concern for her mother is evident in her soft tone.

Cynthia looks over at Polly with a slight smile on her face. "I'm fine, sweetheart. This is just very hard for me to talk about. I buried these memories long ago, and I need a minute before opening the door on a past I wish I could forget."

Well, fuck her.

That past she so wishes she could forget involves me.

Chewing the inside of my cheek to stop my string of

profanities, I patiently wait, hoping her minute is nearly up.

When she meets my eyes, I tell myself, *This is it. No matter what happens, you stay till the bitter end.*

"Mia, is what you said true?" She sniffs, wiping away her tears.

"Which part?" I ask, annoyed she's asking me questions and not vice versa.

"That you...worked for Phil?"

I have no idea how that's important, as shooting the man she once loved takes precedence over some lame-ass drug dealer.

But I humor her as I nod in response.

She muffles her cries with a trembling hand and begins weeping once again.

Why does she care about Phil? Shouldn't she be questioning why I shot that pathetic excuse of a man who used to be her husband?

"I'm sorry, I can't do this." She jumps up from her seat like it's on fire.

But no way am I about to let her leave.

Latching onto her arm as she storms past me, I demand, "What the hell is going on?"

She recoils from my touch as I know I'm gripping her hard, but I won't let go without knowing what the fuck is going on.

"Mia, I..." She pauses, tears sliding down her cheeks. "I can't do this."

"No, you don't get to do that!" I cry, shaking her harder. "You owe me answers! After all these years, you owe me the goddamn truth!

"I know I'm a disappointment to you, but please," I beg. "Please, just please, please tell me the truth."

52

A betrayal tear slithers down my cheek, but I wipe it away with the back of my hand because I will not allow her to see my grief. But more only follow in its place.

Before I have a chance to wipe them away, Cynthia does something that catches me off guard. With trembling, apprehensive fingers, she slowly reaches forward and brushes away my tears.

I recoil from her touch, but the gentle, unexpected sentiment has more tears falling. "You were never a disappointment to me, Mia."

"Then why did you leave me? Why did you leave me with *him*? Why did you leave me with a monster?"

Cynthia bites her lip, swallowing her tears as she sobs. "I had no other choice."

"What does that mean?"

But she only shakes her head, indicating this conversation is over.

I feel like I'm about to be sick because I'm left with more questions than answers every time she opens her mouth.

Pollyanna decides now is a good time to intervene.

"Enough," she spits, yanking on her mother's arm, pulling her away from me. "You need to leave!"

As I look at the trembling woman before me, who looks about ready to have a mental breakdown, I agree with her for once because no one will surrender today.

But tomorrow, tomorrow I will get what I want.

Five

What the *fuck* was that back there?

If possible, I'm now even more baffled about my past than I was before. And the one person who has all the answers decides to clam up.

Leaving Cynthia a blubbering mess in her daughter's arms has me realizing I may never get the answers I so desperately seek. If these memories are buried so deeply within, what happens if asking Cynthia to unearth them breaks her? Or worse yet, what happens if she refuses to tell me?

I never took that factor into consideration.

Cynthia owes me nothing. I'm just a ghost of her past, one she no doubt wishes had remained dead and buried. The honorable and decent thing to do would be to tell me the truth. But after today's performance, I think getting the truth will be a lot harder than I originally anticipated—which is just my luck.

When the truck's tires crunch over gravel, I register we've stopped driving. "Where are we?" I ask Quinn, and after hours of silence, my throat sounds raspy and hoarse.

"Pride Rock," he replies, and I cock an eyebrow.

"Like out of *The Lion King*?"

Quinn chuckles as he kills the engine. "Something like that."

I have no idea where we are, so I follow Quinn as he jumps out of the truck. He reaches into the back and pulls out his black sweater. Does he want us to go for a hike? In the dark?

I'm too tired to argue as he wraps his zip-up hoodie around me like a cape. I'm thankful for the extra warmth and snuggle into the fleecy material, sniffing his unique fragrance on the cotton.

"Where are we going?" I ask as Quinn reaches for my hand. He silently leads me into a forest of tall green pine trees.

My boots trudge over mushy dirt, and I latch harder onto Quinn's hand as I nearly trip over a rock. But this reminds me so very much of the first trek we took back home when Quinn showed me the twinkling lights of South Boston.

So I remain silent and follow.

We walk in silence, but the farther we hike, the harder it is to see, and when I hear a gentle rustling in the bushes, I launch onto Quinn's back.

"What was that? A Canadian bug?" I ask, my eyes darting from left to right.

Quinn chuckles as he pries my fingers from around his neck. "I think you should be more afraid of bears than bugs," he replies, reaching for my hand and pulling me alongside him.

Bears?

"This better be good, Berkeley." I yelp when I hear a loud hooting overhead.

"Trust me," he replies, and the sliver of moonlight reflects off his beautiful features, illuminating his mischievous smile.

We trek for a few minutes, and when the terrain gets impossibly steep, I lag behind, attempting to gain my footing. But I refuse to stop because I have a feeling that what I'm about to see will be life-changing. And besides, when I slow down, the bitter wind has my teeth chattering.

Thankfully, the landscape becomes a little easier to maneuver, and before I know it, we're standing at the edge of a cliff looking over an enormous lake. The sight leaves me breathless as I have never seen anything so calm or untouched.

I attempt to take everything in, but the view extends farther than my eye can see. In the distance, however, I can see snow-capped mountains, and with the moon settling low, the sight is pure tranquility.

The overwhelming feelings of today suddenly submerge, and I can finally breathe for the first time in forever.

I now understand why Quinn brought me here.

In the grand scheme of things, my problems seem so small, so trivial when looking out into the vastness of absolute nothingness. I could get lost in this place, so that's why I'm here. This is my private oasis.

My personal slice of heaven.

"Thank you," I say, my eyes never leaving the landscape before me.

In response, Quinn wraps his arms around me from behind, resting my back against his warm front. His exhalations tickle my neck, and I sag into him, the tension slowly seeping out from every pore in my beaten body.

"So this is our Pride Rock, hey?"

"It can be whatever you want it to be," he explains, softly kissing my temple as my eyes slip shut.

And he's right.

Life is what you make it, and today, my life sucked. But the fact I'm standing here, in the arms of someone who gives me a reason to smile, gives me the strength to soldier on.

Our mingled breaths are the only noise for a long time, and I think Quinn needs this stillness as much as I do.

His soft voice breaks the silence. "I'm sorry about today. I know you didn't get the answers you wanted."

"There's no need for you to apologize. If it weren't for your support, I would hate to think where I would be now. You're the only thing getting me through this, and if anything, I should be the one apologizing to you."

"Hey, stop that," Quinn says, spinning me around to face him. "You know I'm here because I want to be."

I nod, but I still feel like shit that he feels that way. He should be out on a date with some normal college girl or having a beer with his friends. Instead, he's here with me, emotionally supporting a girl who is slowly forgetting why she's here and who she is.

Suddenly, the stillness and the peacefulness break down my walls. They come crashing down with a loud bang, and word vomit is about to overtake my sanity.

"Everything is so fucked up. I came here thinking that I could get some kind of closure. But I don't even know who I am anymore. I started this journey just wanting to escape a life I so desperately wanted out of. And for a while, it was nice to pretend I was normal. But who am I kidding?

"I'll never be normal, and I was naive to think I ever could be."

There it is—the ugly truth. The truth I've been trying so

hard to squash down.

But I don't have the strength to suppress it any longer, as it eats away at my already fragile mind.

At that precise moment, a shooting star blazes across the night sky, and its beauty is gone before I can appreciate it. But the small glimpse was enough.

"Make a wish," Quinn says, also looking up into the atmosphere. "That was the universe's way of telling you it's listening."

Raising a confused eyebrow, I look at Quinn, waiting for him to elaborate because I'm not sure what he means.

"Tell the universe how you feel. Shout it out. Shout out that you want a fucking break. It's only you and me. Let go, Red. Let it out," he declares, hands spread out wide.

"I think the universe stopped listening a long time ago," I say with a small smile. "And besides, I think I've purged enough. All I feel like I've been doing is crying or complaining. I'm sure you've had enough, and it's getting old pretty quick.

"I mean, even I'm getting sick of—"

But before I can finish my sentence, I watch Quinn bite down on his lip before he brushes past me and stands at the edge of the cliff.

I don't make a sound, as I have no idea what he's doing, but I watch with close scrutiny, curious to see what comes next.

He remains utterly still for a few moments before unexpectedly tilting his face to the sky and yelling, "I wish I could take it back! All of it."

I remain motionless, unsure of what to say or do.

But as I watch Quinn, standing with his eyes shut tight, completely at the mercy of the heavens and baring a piece of his guarded soul, I know there is only one thing I can do.

Slowly walking over to stand beside him, I take a deep breath before mimicking his position, throwing my head back, and screaming into the starless sky, "I wish I could be normal! I just want to belong!"

The scream that tears from my throat scorches my esophagus, but the burn feels so good.

"I wish I never made her leave!" Quinn suddenly screams, his arms spread out wide.

My heart breaks at his confession, but I don't make a fuss, as this, in a weird way, is somewhat like our confessional box. And now that I've started, I can't seem to stop.

"I wish I'd killed him! I wish he'd fucking died!"

As awful as that sounds, it's the God's honest truth.

And the truth has never felt so good.

Quinn sighs, his hair trailing in the wind as he softly confesses, "I wish I hadn't come home early from school that day. I wish I never saw it."

Piece by piece, Quinn shows me a sliver of his soul, and what I see is simply beautiful.

"I wish my mother wasn't such a disappointment. I wish she cared," I profess, and my voice, just like Quinn's, is a lot softer and reflective.

However, to my surprise, Quinn takes a deep breath before he whispers, "I wish my mother wasn't such a disappointment. I wish she cared."

My hands itch, needing to reach out and console him. But I stop myself because this purge is cathartic for both of us.

As a lightning bolt cracks across the night sky, it lights up the universe for a split second, and everything at that moment is so much clearer.

"I wish I'd fucking said no!" I scream, punching my fist into the sky, and at that precise moment, the heavens open up, dumping rain on both of us.

But we don't move a muscle.

We stand motionless with our faces raised to the sky, our drenched clothes sticking to our bodies.

"I wish I fucking said yes," Quinn says softly, but he may as well have screamed it because I heard him loud and clear.

Peeling back the layers of Quinn Berkeley is beautiful. It washes away all the bullshit insecurities I've ever had.

And at this moment of clarity, I know that no matter what he did, I will love him for all the days of my life. And although I'm afraid he won't feel the same, I want him to know.

Turning slowly to face him, I can see that his eyes are still closed, but his mouth is tipped up into a smile that radiates freedom.

I've never seen him look so carefree. He looks like the punishing rain is washing away his past sins.

I know it's not that simple, but we have bonded and gained strength through pain and loss. And that strength suddenly animates me to tell Quinn how I feel.

"Quinn!" I scream to be heard over the harsh rain.

My eyes are mere slits since the rain is so heavy, but the moment Quinn opens his, I see that he has changed. Something inside Quinn has shifted, and it's beautiful.

"Quinn, I…" I repeat, my teeth chattering from the cold but also from what I'm about to confess.

"You what, Red?" he questions, running a hand through his wet hair.

Another thunderbolt slices through the sky, animating me. But I'm still afraid.

So I place my hands over his ears.

I want to tell him how I feel, but I'm scared.

Droplets of rain cascade down his cheeks, but he doesn't

stir to brush them away, and I know I have his undivided attention as his gaze never wavers from my face.

This is not how I wanted to do this, but I know this will have to do for now.

"Quinn…I…I love you," I whisper, my hands still sitting firmly over his ears.

Once I say those three little words, the tightening in my chest lessens, and a small smile tugs at my lips because nothing has ever felt so right.

His eyes widen, and I know he read my lips, but I don't care. Whether he feels the same or not, I'm just happy I said it. Maybe next time, I'll gather the courage to tell him without any barriers.

He parts his wet lips, but I don't want him to feel obligated to return my declaration, so I quickly remove my hands, place a trembling finger over his mouth, and slowly shake my head.

Quinn's eyes are deep black pools of desire, and as another lightning bolt strikes above us, the yearning is highlighted with a sliver of silver.

Nodding, he carefully places a cold hand over mine, removing it from his lips and slowly resting it over his beating heart.

The sentiment has tears stinging my eyes, but before they have a chance to fall, Quinn reaches forward, brushing them away.

I don't know how long we stand this way. All I know is the feeling of Quinn's heart beating under my palm is one I never want to end.

But sadly, all good things must come to an end. "Hey! You can't be out here!" a voice yells over the rain, surprising us.

Turning to the right, we see a park ranger with a flashlight pointed our way.

As I see Quinn's mouth slowly tip up into a lopsided smile, I know we're on the same page. I reach for his hand at the exact moment he lunges for mine. We gently lock our fingers and take off at a dead run.

"Hey, come back here!" the ranger shouts. Quinn and I quicken our pace, never looking back as we flick up mud in our hurried getaway.

The rain blinds me, so I'm thankful that Quinn leads the way. I happily follow, trusting him completely because I have no idea where to go. The adrenaline of the chase has my heart beating wildly, and I've never felt so free.

"Jump!" he says, and I obey, jumping over a fallen branch.

"Stop! You stop right there!" the ranger, following in hot pursuit, yells through his red megaphone.

I can't help the laughter that bubbles from my throat as I turn to see the young pursuer lagging behind as he attempts to catch his breath.

Before long, it's not only the rain that clouds my vision but also my big, fat tears. Because I'm laughing so hard at this ridiculous situation, I'm giving myself a stitch and gasping for breath, slowing us down. The intense rain isn't helping either, and I'm slipping and sliding since the tread on my shoes has been obliterated after years of constant wear.

My ribs protest with every step I take. Quinn must sense my pain because he suddenly stops and picks me up, draping me over his broad shoulders effortlessly in a fireman's carry, then continues pounding the soaked ground like a damn athlete.

I twist my neck and look behind me at the poor-winded ranger, who has no hope in hell of catching up to us.

However, his last attempt to stop us has me laughing so violently that Quinn has to secure his hand around my thighs so I don't fall flat on my face.

"Stop!" the ranger yelps, blowing a whistle loudly.

But the whistle dies abruptly as he face-plants into the dirt with a loud splat.

"Holy shit!" I cry, tears rolling freely down my cheeks as the ranger slowly raises his mud-caked face with the whistle still firmly planted between his lips.

As he blows out an exasperated breath, it rattles through the mud-clogged whistle, and the sound resembles a dying hyena.

Quinn continues running like the wind, ignoring my fits of laughter until we reach our pickup. By the time I'm sitting in the truck, I'm laughing so hard that I can't breathe. However, when I turn to look at Quinn, who's sitting behind the wheel and speeding away from yet another crime scene, I almost choke.

The fact I never noticed his wet white T-shirt sticking to his gloriously muscled body is a mystery to me. But now that I've seen it, I can't look away.

Chewing on his lip ring, Quinn concentrates on the road because the rain makes it difficult to see. But I can see perfectly fine, and I like what I see.

As I admire the way his soaked T-shirt highlights his nipple ring and the synchronized manner in which the little droplets of water trickle down his neck from his slicked-back hair, my mouth begins to water, and my cold body begins to sizzle.

Just as my eyes are about to wander lower, Quinn chuckles. "I'm trying to drive, Red."

I bite my lip and can't help but think some wishes really do come true.

Six

My hair feels like a matted bird's nest, and my clothes are still damp, but I have no energy to move. Nor would I want to since I'm wrapped up in Quinn Berkeley's arms.

After our law-breaking trek, we returned to our motel and crashed, absolutely beat from the events of an exhausting day.

I didn't realize how far Quinn had driven, as it took us over two hours to get back to Alberta.

I dozed in and out of sleep throughout our drive back to the motel, but I somehow managed to walk to our room without breaking a leg. However, as soon as I stepped inside, I collapsed face-first onto our tiny bed, falling fast asleep, fully clothed.

And it's here I have remained with no intention of rising. Well, that is until I hear hushed voices just outside our door.

Raising my weary head, I brush my tangled hair off my face as I turn my ear toward the doorway. The sunlight slipping through the lacy curtains indicates it's daytime, but I have no idea what time it is.

Quinn is still sound asleep, breathing lightly, and I don't want to wake him for fear that my jumpy nerves are just playing tricks on me, and the voices outside our door will soon disappear.

Unfortunately, they don't.

And when I hear the unmistakable static over a walkie-talkie, I know it's the cops.

I don't fail to see the pattern when I wake before Quinn and make a mental note to never let him sleep in.

I also make a mental note to train my dog to be more alert because he's still sound asleep.

"Quinn," I whisper, lightly poking him in the chest as I'm wrapped in his arms in a vise-like grip.

But my whisper falls on deaf ears.

Quinn tightens his arms around me, drawing me closer against his warm chest. This has my arms being caught between us, and as Quinn begins snoring softly, and with my arms literally tied, I know I'll have to utilize other methods to wake him.

His head is slanted upward, so I can't subtly wake him up with a kiss.

But as the voices outside our door begin getting louder, I resort to desperate measures and bite him on his stubbled chin—hard.

"What the fu—!"

But I widen my eyes to imply something is wrong.

He thankfully reads my facial expression and nods, indicating he's listening.

I gesture with my head toward the doorway. At that instant, the crackling over the radio sounds, and Quinn curses under his breath.

We arise in a synchronized manner, both reaching for our guns, which have taken up permanent residency on our bedside tables.

We start a slow crawl toward the voices, and Quinn nudges his head toward the bathroom, indicating for me to wait in there.

My response to his offensive suggestion is a light snicker, and I follow him as we silently tiptoe toward the window.

Quinn scoffs, shaking his head, obviously annoyed by my stubbornness.

I don't know how much longer I can keep doing this. Every day seems to be a vicious circle, and the thought of turning myself in crosses my mind briefly.

But as I hear the familiar voice of someone who shouldn't be here, my thoughts of surrender are put on hold.

I need to know what the hell she's doing here.

"Good morning, Mike," says my mother's chirpy voice.

As soon as Quinn hears her, he turns to me, eyes wide, mouthing, "What the fuck?"

I only shrug in response because I'm just as stumped as he. We both freeze, listening intently.

"Mornin', Cynthia. Whatcha doing out so early?" the man, who I'm presuming is Mike, asks.

"Oh, I just had to take care of some business for Chandler," she replies flippantly. The mere mention of his name has my teeth grinding in annoyance.

"Is he back for the holidays?" asks another male voice.

"I'm not too sure yet, Dean," Cynthia replies.

Her voice sounds like it's just outside our door.

I have no idea why she's here, playing nice with the police officers about to arrest us.

I attempt to move to look out the window, but Quinn squeezes my hand, so I stay put.

"What are you boys doing here?" Cynthia asks, but surely, she knows—they're here for me.

"Well, this pickup has been reported stolen. We're just about to go inside and talk to the manager to see who checked in with the vehicle."

"Oh, stolen? That's just awful. What's happening around here? Just this morning, I was talking to Mr. Bourke, and he told me someone broke into his home and stole some money and documents out of his safe," my mother concludes with a sigh.

"Mr. Bourke?" questions an officer I think is Mike. "You mean Mr. Bourke, who lives on Cherry Lane?"

"Yes, that's right. Do you know him?"

From the choice curse words Mike uses, I dare say he does.

"Isn't that Amanda's grandpa?" asks Dean.

"Amanda…she's your girlfriend?" Cynthia innocently asks.

"Shit," mutters Mike.

There's a long pause, and I look at Quinn, hoping he can shed some light on what the hell is going on, but he looks just as puzzled.

"If you'll excuse me, Cynthia. I better go check that out," Mike says, and I can hear his footsteps retreating.

"Yeah, Mike. You're in the doghouse as it is with her, and you've only had two dates. Maybe checking on her pops will win you some brownie points." Dean chuckles loudly.

"It certainly would help," replies Mike, and suddenly,

Cynthia's plan becomes clear.

"What about the pickup?" she asks.

I can see her silhouette just outside the window.

"Oh, it's probably just a bunch of kids," Mike replies in the distance. "We'll come back later to check it out. Have a good day, Cynthia."

A car's engine revs to life and pulls out of the parking lot with a loud squeal.

It's only when I hear silence do I let out the breath I was barely holding on to.

Although I think I know what's happening here, I have to find out for certain because Cynthia lying to save us from getting caught makes no sense.

"You can open up. They're gone," she says through the door, jiggling the locked handle.

Quinn looks at me, ensuring I'm okay with allowing her inside.

I nod, sitting shakily on the sofa as he opens the door.

When she quickly enters, I try not to recoil. The memories from yesterday come flooding back, but I suck it up and meet her flighty eyes because I want answers.

"What are you doing here?" I bluntly ask, crossing my arms over my chest.

I don't fail to see the hurt flicker across her face at my direct question, but I don't care. I'm done trying to play nice and leaving with nothing in return.

"Hi, Mia," she says, taking a small step toward me. She at least seems a lot more coherent and groomed today.

"Hi," I reply curtly, my arms still crossed.

I make it clear I'm not talking until she starts giving me some answers.

"Polly told me where you were staying, and I saw the

officers sniffing around your car, so I had to come up with some excuse to get them off your trail," she explains, nervously fidgeting with the neckline of her pink sweater.

"So that was all bullshit? No one got robbed?" I ask, raising my eyebrow at her.

"No," she replies softly as she attempts to sit near me.

I almost fall over my feet as I jump off the sofa quickly, not wanting to be anywhere near her.

She bites her lower lip but settles on the stained cushions, ignoring my insolence.

"What happens when they find out you were lying?" Quinn asks from behind me.

"Oh, Mr. Bourke did get robbed, but that was in 1984. It's a story he loves to retell over and over as he still thinks it's 1984," she explains, her eyes flicking to Quinn's.

My mother preyed on the senile, old mind of poor Mr. Bourke, and as much as I hate to admit it, that was ingenious thinking on such short notice. But I would rather cut out my own tongue than admit that to her.

"Thanks. But that doesn't answer my question."

"You have every right to be angry with me, Mia. I have been awful to you. But I'm here to ask for your forgiveness," she says nervously, lowering her eyes when I scoff at her suggestion.

"Forgiveness? Forgive you for what, exactly? Because from where I stand, that's a shitload of forgiveness you're asking for."

Every time I open my mouth, I tell myself to shut up because she's making an effort, something she hasn't done before. But the anger and rage overtake my sanity, and insulting her is the only way for me to deal right now.

"You're right. You're absolutely right." She stands up and

reaches out to me.

Again, I back away and bump straight into Quinn. I calm down because I want to know why she's here.

"I'm sorry for everything, and you're right. You do deserve answers."

I try not to prematurely celebrate until I've heard the last of her speech.

"But you must understand, this is hard for me, too. I have repressed these memories for a very long time, and I can't just speak about them right away. I also need time to digest it all."

Rubbing my forehead in frustration, I realize I may be eighty by the time she's ready to talk. Of course, I understand what she means, but that doesn't make it any easier to process.

"So I propose you stay with me and Polly, and let's get to know one another. I promise to answer all your questions in time. And I promise to listen to everything you have to say."

"How long?" I press through clenched teeth. The thought of living under the same roof as Pollyanna sounds like a bad, *bad* idea.

Cynthia straightens out her pressed slacks as she replies, "I don't know. I mean, there isn't really a timeframe on something like this."

"No," I spit, stepping away from the comforting sanctuary of Quinn's body. "No way am I playing happy families. I can't stay with you, pretending nothing has happened."

"That's not what I'm asking, Mia. My home is big enough for you and Quinn to come and go as you please without fear of being on the run from the police and your fa—" She doesn't finish her sentence as she clutches the gold locket around her neck.

The events of the past few days have totally shifted my priorities, and my father has been low on the list of things to worry about, which has been careless. She does have a point, but I won't submit just because she thinks it's a good idea.

As I'm about to object, Quinn speaks softly. "Red, she has a point. I mean, today was close. At least we wouldn't have to keep looking over our shoulders. And we can also figure out what to do next without fear of your dad and the cops on our asses."

He's right, but my stubbornness yells at me not to surrender.

"Red?" my mother questions with a small smile, looking over my shoulder at Quinn.

"Yeah." Quinn quietly chuckles. "Her temper earns her that well-deserved nickname."

My mother smiles, brushing a piece of hair behind her ear, and nods at his comment.

I turn to glare at Quinn for consorting with the enemy, but he looks at me, faking innocence.

"It's true," he says with a slight shrug.

"It's a lovely nickname," Cynthia has the gall to say.

Well, fuck them both.

I clear my throat. "I'm glad you approve."

"Mia," Cynthia says with a small frown, but I cut her off, ignoring the miserable look on her face.

"The answer is no. Thank you for the offer, but I'd rather be caught by the police or my father"—Cynthia flinches as I mention him—"than live under the same roof as you."

I turn on my heel and slam the bathroom door behind me, needing to get the hell away from her.

Bracing my head into my hands as I slump onto the toilet lid, I scold myself for being so stubborn because Quinn is right. It *is* a good idea, and I should suck it up and agree.

I should meet Cynthia halfway because this is what I

want, isn't it?

I just wanted her to open up and tell me the truth. But now that the opportunity has come knocking, I'm slamming bathroom doors in its face instead of embracing it.

A knock on the door interrupts my pity party for one, and I raise my head as Quinn enters the bathroom.

"She's gone," he says when I look over his shoulder to ensure she isn't loitering behind him.

I'm suddenly embarrassed that I'm behaving like a two-year-old, but I can't help it. The thought of trying to mend bridges with my mother scares me. What if she's still a disappointment after everything is said and done?

Or worse yet, what if *I'm* a disappointment?

Returning to my pity party, I groan and clasp my head with my palms, unable to face Quinn.

He gives me a minute to sulk before he kneels on both knees before me, lightly placing his hands on my thighs.

"Whatever you want to do, I'll support you. You know that," he says softly, and I know he means every word by the concern in his voice. "I'm on your side. Always."

"I know. I'm sorry for acting like a spoiled brat. She just brings out this awful, childish, rebellious side to me." I remove my hands, ashamed of my outburst.

"It's okay," he replies, thumbing my pouty bottom lip.

"So…" I sigh, feeling every bit as miserable as I probably look when the realization of what is about to happen hits home. "We're doing this?"

Quinn nods with a smirk. "I've grabbed a few of your things."

"That was a little presumptuous, don't you think?"

"No, presumptuous would be telling your mother we'd see her in an hour." He quickly stands to avoid my playful slap.

"You're lucky I lo—" I stop myself before I drop the L-bomb.

Looking at Quinn's rigid stance, I'm glad I stopped myself before embarrassing us both.

But as Quinn takes a step toward the door, he suddenly stops and slowly turns over his shoulder and whispers, "Every moment spent with you has me realizing how lucky I really am."

"This is a bad idea," I grumble as I dawdle up Cynthia's driveway.

Just to rebel, we're late, and I did this deliberately. My mother expected us an hour ago, but she can wait.

"C'mon, stop dragging your feet," Quinn says, grabbing my hand as he hauls me through the inches of snow.

The door opens as we ascend the first step, and Cynthia greets us with a beaming smile. "I'm so glad you're here," she says, opening the door wider for us to enter. "Hello, little guy."

She bends forward and pats Lucky on the head. He happily accepts her pats as he seems to like her. *Traitor.*

Quinn stands behind me and practically shoves me through the door. He must be afraid that I'm going to turn away and run screaming bloody murder.

Once inside, every muscle within my body seizes up, and I feel claustrophobic as the walls begin to close in on me. This house is to be my prison for the next God knows how many days or weeks, and I suddenly question my decision to come here.

"Your room is upstairs," Cynthia says.

She nervously fiddles with her locket before leading the

way up the glorious staircase.

Quinn slides my backpack off my shoulder as I remain firmly rooted to the floor, gazing up at the endless steps that no doubt lead to my impending doom.

He lugs my bag onto his shoulder and reaches for my hand, pulling me toward the stairs.

But my hand snags in his because I have no intention of moving.

Turning to see what my problem is, he cocks a brow.

But I animatedly shake my head.

"I can't go…up there," I say, raising my eyes toward the stairs.

"So you want to stay down here all night?" he asks with a smile.

I nod because that option is far better than entering a room that will never be mine.

"Well, all right then, but with all the Christmas cheer going on down here," he says, looking at the front window where I can see the ridiculous Christmas display, "I just may feel the need to break out into song. And I know just the one."

He takes an exaggerated breath, which puffs out his chest, and he bellows, "Rudolph—"

Before he can continue, I slap my hand over his mouth and smile. "You sing. You die."

I know what he's doing, and it's worked.

Cautiously removing my hand in hopes he doesn't feel like belting out another carol, I lean forward and kiss him on the cheek.

"Thank you, Quinn."

"Anytime," he replies, slowly reaching for my hand, and we take our first step toward what, I don't know.

I don't want to be here, but a small part of me does. This

is my chance to find out who I am.

The staircase leads up to the second floor, which is just as lavish as downstairs. I almost trip up the last step when I see how many rooms this floor has. Beautiful paintings decorate the white walls, and as I look down the long hallway, I can see they extend all the way down the corridor.

"This way," Cynthia says, leading us down the beige-carpeted walkway as Quinn and I silently follow.

My shoes squish on the plush carpet, and I look behind to ensure I'm not leaving a mud trail.

We stop at a white door, and inside, I can hear the recognizable voice of Kurt Cobain over the radio.

"Polly?" Cynthia says, knocking softly. "Your sister is here."

It looks like she'll be waiting a while as the only response she gets is the volume being turned up all the way and Kurt yelling at us to stay away.

With a sigh, Cynthia rubs her brow as she faces us with a strained smile. "She mustn't have heard me."

No one addresses it. This situation is awkward enough without adding Polly to the mix.

We arrive at a door a few down from Polly, and Cynthia stands aside. "Well, this is your room. Just let me know if you don't like it or want another."

"It'll be fine," I reply, which are my first words to her since my arrival.

"Please make yourself at home. My room is at the end of the hall," she says, looking back the way we came.

"Peachy," I reply, reaching for the knob.

I stop when Cynthia says, "It's really lovely to have you here, Mia. I hope you treat this home as your own."

I nod in response, but I hate that when I look at her, I

actually feel sorry for her. I know she's trying, but I'm not ready to play nice just yet. I need time to process everything before I think of anything that's hers as mine.

"Thanks," I mutter quickly, turning the doorknob and running into the safety of the room.

As soon as I enter, I stand staring, dumbfounded. This place is huge. The king-size canopy bed is draped in a black silk, jeweled duvet. The jewels throughout the design twinkle as they catch the light rays from the white lamps on the mahogany bedside tables.

A dresser with a huge mirror sits against the wall, and as I walk toward it, I can see a familiar-looking porcelain jewelry box on the smooth surface. Stepping closer, I run my finger over the ceramic and gently lift the lid, revealing an aged onyx hair comb. The brightness of the stone catches the light, and again, this item looks familiar, just as the jewelry box does.

Quinn switching the light on in the walk-in closet jars me out of my daze, and I turn to see him looking above his head at all the shelf space, whistling in awe.

"I don't know if I'll be able to fit all my clothes in here," he says, dumping our bags onto the floor.

I shake my head at his sarcasm but focus back on the comb because I don't understand why I'm drawn to it.

"You like that?" Quinn asks from behind me as he rests his chin on my shoulder.

"Yeah, I've seen it before," I reply, fingering the teeth of the comb.

"Yeah? It looks really old."

"It does," I reply after a few moments of silence.

Taking one final look at it and realizing that this mystery is one I won't solve tonight, I gently close the lid and tell myself to forget I ever saw it.

"So," I ask, turning to face him, "what do we do now?"

Quinn smirks. "Well, I don't know about you, but I really want to check out that tub," he says, looking over his shoulder into the huge bathroom.

I chuckle. "Go for it. I might take a look around."

"You don't want to join me?" He winks while toeing off his boots.

As appealing as that sounds, I need to be on my own. Everything has happened so quickly, and I just need time to digest it all.

"Maybe later." I consider changing my mind as Quinn slips off his T-shirt, revealing a sight of pure perfection.

"I'll be here when you get back," he replies with a smirk as he witnesses me gawking at his snail trail.

As he reaches for the button on his jeans, I make a quick exit before I follow him into that tub, forgetting all about my plans of exploration.

Once out into the hallway, I take a deep breath and start my journey of this foreign land that Cynthia and Polly call home.

It's safe to say Cynthia still loves her art. Abstract statues sit inside hidden alcoves along the wall, making the passageway seem like it's inside a trendy museum. But it's not pretentious or tasteless.

It actually gives off a calming, cultured vibe.

As I tiptoe past Polly's room, I hear Fiona Apple humming softly, and I wonder if she's calmed.

I know this must be hard for her, but it's hard for me too. I don't know if we'll ever see eye to eye, but maybe one day we'll get to the stage where we can stand to be in the same room together.

There are ten doors on this floor, and I've opened all but

three.

The first was Polly's since I'm sure that wouldn't go down too well, and the second is Cynthia's, for obvious reasons. However, the third door, which is the room next to Cynthia's, is the room I desperately want to enter.

All the doors, except this one, are white.

This door is a pale purple, and unlike all the other doors, this door is locked.

I can see by the keyhole that the key that opens this door is a big, old-school brass key, which seems out of place with the modernized home.

Just as I am about to jiggle the handle again, a voice scares the shit out of me, and I yelp, jumping back guiltily.

"It's locked."

"I can see that. Why?" I ask, turning to look at Polly.

"I don't know. It always is," she replies simply as she glares at me.

"And you've never wondered what's inside?"

"No." Polly is obviously bored by our conversation as she examines her peach-colored nails. "Besides, whatever is inside can't be good because every time Mom goes in there, all she does is cry. Then when she emerges, hours later, she looks like shit."

"Oh?"

"So whatever is in there can stay in there," she says after ensuring her nails are symmetrical.

I only just suppress the urge to kick down the door as I realize Polly and I are actually having a semi-normal conversation, which is a first.

"So...I hope you don't mind me staying here?" I say, hoping we can continue to be partially civil to one another.

Polly narrows her icy blue eyes as she kicks off the wall.

She walks over to me, stopping a few feet away, and subtly looks from left to right before she leans forward into my personal space. "Mind? I more than fucking mind."

Taking a step back, I'm stunned by her hostility, but I allow her to finish.

"I don't really have a choice now, do I? Mark my words, I'll do *everything* in my power to make sure you don't stick around. Welcome to the family," she mocks inches from my face before turning on her heel and leaving me with a mouth full of nothing.

After my ever-so-pleasant conversation with Polly, I explored the rest of the house and gardens, and I would be lying if I didn't confess I was considerably impressed with what I saw. However, the bitter cold and snow have me cutting my outdoor explorations short, and I enter through the back door leading into the kitchen.

The instant I'm inside, my stomach growls at the mouthwatering smell of freshly baked sweets. Only then do I realize I haven't eaten all day. But my appetite is shot when I see Cynthia pulling out a tray of muffins from the oven, looking all motherly in her strawberry-print apron.

"Sorry," I utter, not really sure why I'm apologizing.

I attempt to duck past her without stopping to talk, but I'm not that lucky as she quickly places the muffins onto a cooling rack and slips off her mittens. "Mia, would you like one?"

As I stand rigid, unsure of what to say, she quickly reinforces, "They're chocolate chip."

I can see the hope behind her affectionate blue eyes.

Deciding to try this mother-daughter thing, I nod half-heartedly and pull up a stool at the marbled kitchen island as I watch her hunt in the cupboard above her head for a plate.

"Would you like coffee?" she asks, placing a muffin on a small floral dish.

"Only if you've already made some. Don't go out of your way for me."

Cynthia cringes at my unintentional, snippy remark. "It's no trouble, really," she says, passing me the muffin.

I accept, and she turns on the machine and begins brewing us some coffee.

She seems to be deep in thought, silently watching the coffee percolate, so I remove the top of my muffin and bring it to my lips, eager to take a bite.

But Cynthia's unexpected confession stops me from moving or breathing. "I did love your father."

I'm so glad I wasn't chewing, as I would have choked on my food.

Placing my muffin onto the plate, I silently wait for her to continue.

"We were high school sweethearts, and I always knew we'd get married," she says in a faraway voice, her back still turned. "He was such a good man, always doting on me, and during our senior year, he surprised me by proposing right before prom. Of course, I said yes. We got married right after graduation."

She pauses before continuing with a sigh. "I was so happy back then."

Hopeful I don't disturb her reminiscing, I ask, "What happened?"

She remains still, her soft sigh the only thing alerting me to the fact she's listening.

"When I got pregnant with you, Mia, I was the same age as you are now. The day I found out I was pregnant was the happiest day of my life. I always wanted a family because it was only me, my brother, and my mother growing up."

"I have an uncle?" I question. I never really considered the prospect of having uncles, aunts, and cousins.

"Yes," Cynthia replies, but the sharp tone of her voice has me thinking my uncle is someone she wishes to forget.

"When you were born, I counted each of your perfect little fingers and toes, and at that moment, I knew my purpose in life had become clear. I was put on this earth to look after my baby girl." A small sob escapes her.

As touching as this story is, a lash of anger overtakes me because a mother abandoning her three-year-old child doesn't really classify as looking after her "baby girl."

"Yeah, well, you failed on all accounts," I bite back, unable to control my annoyance.

"I know," she whispers, and I see her wipe at her eyes. "If I could take it all back, I would. But I thought it was the right thing to do."

"What was?"

With her head bowed, she replies, "Leaving you."

Rage boils to the surface because deep down, I hoped that maybe she was suffering from some kind of amnesia, or maybe she suffered a mental breakdown or was abducted by aliens, and that was the reason she left me.

But to hear her admit she intentionally left me with my father fucking hurts. I mean, what kind of mother does that? What kind of mother admits abandoning her child was the right thing to do?

"I was three," I say between clenched teeth, barely containing my fury.

"I know, Mia," she says, spinning around to face me, her mascara tears running down her porcelain cheeks. "But I—"

"You what?" I demand, kicking back my stool as I stand.

"I thought it was for the best," she whimpers, her lower lip trembling when she meets my enraged eyes.

"How?" I yell, slamming my palms onto the marbled counter, frustrated with her heartless excuses. "Please explain to me how you thought leaving a three-year-old with her unstable father was for the best? Because from where I stand, that's just a fucking weak and selfish thing to do."

When my mother begins sobbing, choking on her tears, I storm over to her, tempted to shake the answers from her.

But instead, I decide to share how her decision to leave was in fact not for the best. She needs to know how her decision ruined my hope of ever living a normal life.

"Do you want to know all the things he made me do?" I cry, ignoring all personal boundaries. "Do you want to know all the things he *wanted* me to do?"

"Stop, Mia," she wails, raising a quivering hand to her mouth. "I don't want to talk about this anymore. Please, just stop."

"No, I won't stop just because my fucked-up childhood makes you uncomfortable. Try living it! Try living with memories that will never disappear, no matter how hard you try! Try being an eight-year-old little girl, scared out of your mind because your father has left you with a disgusting drug dealer who has no qualms about ruining your innocence.

"Try being an eight-year-old little girl who has no friends because you're too busy dealing drugs to every lowlife scumbag in LA.

"And try being a confused eight-year-old little girl attempting to wake up your father, who has passed out in his own vomit and shit after being on a three-day bender. Go on, *Mother*," I sneer, "walk a day in my shoes, and then have the nerve to tell me it was for the best."

I am mere inches from Cynthia's terrified face as she sobs uncontrollably, sliding onto the kitchen floor.

I think I've broken her.

She slumps against the cupboard, sobbing hysterically, and I look down at her with nothing but disgust.

"You have no right to cry. An innocent man is dead because of you!"

The mere mention of Hank has tears springing to my eyes. But I angrily wipe them away because my sorrow can wait.

Cynthia slowly raises her head, her face stained with tears. "I'm sorry, Mia. I'm so sorry."

"Yeah, so am I. I'm sorry that I ever thought you were worthy enough to be my mother."

I turn my back to her. Today's therapy session is over.

Storming from the kitchen while Cynthia is an inconsolable mess may seem cruel, but it's either that or I continue to divulge my past. And judging from today's performance, it's safe to say she's had enough.

Charging up the stairs two at a time, I speed down the hall to my room before I totally lose my shit and go back for round two.

However, when I push open the door, my anger boils to the point of no return, and whatever reasoning I had explodes.

"What the fuck are you doing in here?" I demand. Polly sits on the edge of my bed, chatting with my boyfriend while patting my dog.

"What crawled up your ass and died?" she retorts, and her snide comment has me seeing red.

"Get out!" I storm over to her, seconds away from pulling

out her long hair.

Polly must realize she has three seconds to move before I throw her out because she launches off the bed and hides behind Quinn, who has quickly moved to act as a barrier between us.

"What's going on?" he questions, nothing but concern lining his face.

"I could ask you the same thing," I spit, glaring at Polly, who cowers behind Quinn's shoulder.

Quinn opens his mouth, no doubt about to give me a reasonable explanation, but I cut him off. I'm in no mood to listen to any more excuses.

"What is she doing in here?" I demand, pointing at her as I stalk forward, but Quinn's huge frame stops me from moving any farther.

"She came in here to talk to you, that's all," Quinn says, bracing his hands out, attempting to stop my rampage.

"So why is she still in here?" I ask. "She could obviously see I wasn't here, so what, you thought you'd entertain her while I was gone?"

Quinn looks beyond mortified at my accusation, and so am I, as I don't mean a word of it. But I can't stop the venom bubbling from my throat because everything inside me feels tainted and confused.

I feel like I'm losing it with every breath I take.

"You need to calm down," Quinn says with a touch of hostility. He's in no way impressed with my allegation.

"Don't tell me what I need to do."

"I'll go, Quinn. Sorry for getting you into trouble," Polly says in a soft voice from behind him, and I begin to shake in anger when I see her lips curve into a small, sinister smile.

"Don't sweat it, Polly," he replies, his eyes watching my

every move.

"Okay, well, I'll talk to you later."

As I glare at her, her lips turn up into a full-blown snicker, and I now know that her plan to make me leave has everything to do with the one thing making me stay.

"You little—" I scream, lunging forward to tear out her eyeballs, but Quinn launches for me, wrapping an arm around my waist to prevent me from charging at her.

"Polly. Leave," he spits while I fight him like a wild cat, clawing at him with all my might.

I watch as she quickly exits the room, but not before she blows me a kiss with her middle finger, then slams the door shut.

"Come back here!" I bellow, my feet skidding on the floor as Quinn's arms restrain me. "Get off me, Quinn!"

"Not until you calm down," he breathlessly replies, holding my back to his heaving chest.

"I'm calm!" I yell, trying to pry his fingers off me as he lifts me off the ground.

"Oh yeah, I can see that."

The fact I'm trapped infuriates me more than I already am, so I do something stupid. I throw my head back and connect with Quinn's nose. Stunned, he loosens his grip, and I scramble out of his hold, running toward the door to kill that little bitch.

However, I take about two steps before I'm tossed onto the bed, bouncing with the momentum.

I try and scramble off, but Quinn is on top of me before I have a chance to move.

"Get. Off."

My cheek is pressed into the mattress because Quinn is lying on my back. He doesn't budge an inch.

Attempting to use my arms as leverage, I push off the mattress, hoping to throw him off balance. But the move has Quinn reaching for my arms, and he extends them above my head while securing my wrists in his palm. He then pins my flailing legs with his thighs, and any hope of escape dwindles to none.

My last endeavor to buck him off proves futile as he's too damn heavy, and I realize I've lost this war.

Sagging in defeat, I stop fighting him as my exhausted body surrenders.

"Would you care to explain to me what the fuck is going on?" Quinn breathlessly asks, inches from my ear.

"Nothing," I stubbornly reply, blowing my tangled hair off my face.

"Nothing? I don't call two minutes ago nothing, Red. I mean, I was waiting for your head to rotate and you to puke up some wicked green vomit."

I roll my eyes at his lame *The Exorcist* reference because I wasn't that bad—was I?

Thinking back to my tirade, which commenced downstairs, and how I ended up here under Quinn's warm body, I realize his analogy isn't too far from the truth. But I'm done talking because whenever I open my mouth, it always ends with a screaming match and me losing my cool.

What's happening to me?

Closing my eyes, I hold back my tears. If I allow them to fall, they'll never stop.

I hate this toxic feeling inside me. And as each day passes, it only seems to be getting worse.

I'm lashing out more than ever, and I hate it. I hate this irrational, unstable brat I've become, but I don't know how to stop. Years of mental and emotional abuse have come crashing down around me, and I have a feeling it doesn't even skim the surface of the shit that lies buried within.

"Please let me go," I whisper, my eyes still shut tight.

Quinn must be able to sense my mood shift because he slowly releases my palms and slides off me.

However, I remain lying on my front with my head turned away from him, not able to meet his eyes.

"What's happening to me? I don't even know who I am anymore. Maybe coming here was a mistake," I confess, sniffing away my tears.

"You're you, Red," Quinn replies gently.

I can't help but let out a sarcastic chuckle as I counter, "Yeah, well, I don't want to be this person who lashes out at everybody. I don't like who I've become. But I don't know how to stop being so angry."

We remain quiet, and I realize I owe Quinn yet another apology.

"Sorry for before. I never meant all those things I said about Polly. I was just angry because I had my first proper talk with Cynthia, which was just peachy," I scoff, letting out a frustrated breath.

"This is normal. I mean, you've got years of fucked-up shit you need to get out. You deserve to have a tantrum or two."

Opening my eyes, I turn to face him.

I frown when I see how beat he is. This whole saga, *my* saga, has aged us both, and I can't help but wonder what'll happen when it's finally over.

I'm at a significant crossroads in my life, and whichever path I decide to take, I hope Quinn will hold my hand and take it with me because all this seems worthless without him.

"You okay?" he asks, brushing my hair off my face.

"Ask me tomorrow," I whisper, leaning into his touch. I hope that when tomorrow comes, my answer will be yes.

Seven

My heavy eyes flicker open, and I don't feel tired for the first time in forever.

Looking over at the clock, I see the reason could be because of the marathon sleep I've just had.

Over twelve hours ago, I fell asleep in Quinn's arms, and I woke up the same way.

By his heavy breathing, I know Quinn is still asleep, and I realize this is the first night we've had in so long when we're not sleeping with one eye open, awaiting the police or my father to kick down our door.

This is one big pro of staying here, and I realize I should be a little more grateful.

So I decide here and now that my New Year's resolution will be just that. I'll try my absolute hardest to stop losing my shit and also to be a little more patient with Cynthia and Polly.

That thought has me wondering when New Year's or Christmas actually is, as all my days seem to blur into one lately.

"Why are you up so early?" a croaky voice asks, disturbing my thoughts.

My lips tip up into a small smile as I love the way his husky voice sounds first thing in the morning.

"It's not early; it's after nine. We've slept for about fourteen hours," I joke, pulling away from his chest to see his early morning beauty.

When I see him, I barely suppress my sigh as he looks epic. His tousled hair falls over his brow, partially veiling his bright eyes, which are vividly clear when he first arises. This man doesn't look like he's just woken up after a lengthy slumber.

I, however, probably look as if a family of ravens has taken up permanent residency in my hair.

"What did you want to do today?" he asks, and I suddenly appreciate the fact we don't have to pack up and go, leaving behind yet another town that provided us sanctuary for the night.

We don't have to keep driving until Quinn falls asleep at the wheel, forcing us to check into some shithole motel, only to wake up and repeat the same thing the next day and then the next day after that.

Here, we can be normal. Well, something like normal.

"I'm not sure," I reply with a yawn. "What day is it?"

Quinn smirks, and the sight has my heart doing a tiny somersault. "It's Thursday, the twenty-third of December."

I widen my eyes because there is no way that's right. "Holy shit! Tomorrow is Christmas Eve?"

He nods.

"Damn, how did that go by so quickly?"

"The fact we've been running since Thanksgiving might have something to do with it."

He's right.

We have been on the run for roughly four weeks. Four weeks is a long time.

It's exactly twenty-eight days. It's six hundred and seventy-two hours. It's forty thousand, three hundred, and twenty minutes. And it's also way too many seconds to count.

I can't believe how different things are. How my life has changed from the moment I decided to start anew. Each day is definitely a challenge, and although I've come close, I haven't broken down—yet.

And I know the reason for that stares straight at me with those damn inquisitive eyes.

But he doesn't push. He only leans forward and kisses me lightly on the forehead. "Want to get something to eat?"

I nod, but my stomach turns when I realize I'll have to face the music with Cynthia and Polly sooner or later. I really wish it were later since my behavior yesterday was deplorable.

Slipping on Quinn's sweater, I take a deep breath.

"You'll be okay," he says as if reading my thoughts.

"I just want today to be uneventful and boring," I say, drawing out the G when we reach the staircase.

As we peer over the railing, my wishes for an uninteresting and ordinary day get shot down in flames of glittery greens, glitzy golds, and radiating reds.

"Um, what the hell?" I mumble, taking in the scene of pure Christmas bedlam below.

Quinn remains quiet, no doubt his eyes glued to the sight of about fifty workmen decking out the downstairs with every imaginable Christmas ornament known to humankind. And in the center of all that craziness is Pollyanna, clutching a bright pink clipboard to her chest while giving orders to a poor minion on where to hang the mistletoe.

"Good morning, you two," my mother says from behind us, startling me.

"Hi," I reply, slowly turning to face her, and I'm thankful she looks better than when I saw her last.

Feelings of guilt overwhelm me, and I avert my eyes back to the activity downstairs, ashamed that I left her the way I did.

"What's going on down there?" I ask, looking at the transformed Christmas wonderland, hoping to make small talk that doesn't involve profanity.

"We throw a Christmas Eve party every year. It's been a tradition for as long as…" She leaves the sentence unfinished, no doubt not wanting to tell me all about the lavish Christmas parties she's thrown while I've been slumming it on the streets.

I tell myself to breathe and not freak out. "Cool."

"Honestly, Edward, are you deaf? I've told you twice. The ice sculpture goes in the front room. I'll just do it myself," Polly says, snatching the cart away from a poor, humiliated Edward.

"We were going to cancel this year because of current circumstances," Cynthia says with a hitch in her voice. "But as you can see, this is Pollyanna's thing. This is also Chandler's first Christmas away, so I didn't want to take it away from her."

The mere mention of Chandler's name has my semi-calm composure slipping.

Cynthia must read my discomfort because she quickly backtracks.

"Oh, Chandler is Polly's…" But once again, she leaves the sentence incomplete, and I'm thankful because I don't want to start another fight with her.

"I know who Chandler is," I say, turning to meet her uncomfortable gaze.

"You do?"

"Yes." I leave it at that. "Looks like Polly is in her element, bossing everyone around. I'm glad you decided to go ahead and have the party."

Cynthia smiles and looks relieved I've made a joke. "Yeah, she sure is. She loves this time of year. She loves these social gatherings. Any excuse to dress up."

I nod but can't help but think how different we really are.

I would much rather hide in a dark room, watching a horror movie, than liaise with strangers who are only there for the free food.

The thought of a dark room reminds me of my idea for Quinn's Christmas gift. I don't know if I'll actually be able to follow through, but I'll try my best.

"You're both invited to join us. If you want to attend, that is. Of course, there's no pressure," she adds when I scrunch up my face, thinking I would much rather hibernate upstairs than socialize with guests.

But that stupid promise I made to myself has me opening my mouth before my brain can protest. "Sure. Thanks. We would love to come."

Quinn places a hand around my waist and gives it a gentle squeeze.

I'm proud of myself...that wasn't as hard as I thought.

"Is there a theme?" I ask, looking at the ostrich feather centerpieces, diamanté jeweled fans, and elegant laced candles that look out of place alongside Santa.

"Oh, it's a masquerade ball. The theme is black and white," Cynthia replies, looking over the railing at the mayhem below.

"Edward! Seriously, are you deaf *and* blind?" Polly says, taking hold of a fondue fountain and slamming it onto the mahogany table.

Looking down at Little Miss Bossy Boots, I'm struck with an idea that is probably one of the worst I've had in a very long time.

"This is the worst idea ever!" Polly groans from the back seat of Cynthia's red Mercedes.

My ingenious plan was to attempt to bond with Polly, and I figured what better way to do that than while shopping.

Obviously, I thought wrong.

"I have a million and one things to do today, but thanks to my mother's bright ideas, I'm stuck babysitting you." Polly huffs, slamming back into the leather interior.

After twenty minutes of circling the local mall, we finally find a parking spot, and Quinn zips into the space with ease.

"Ooh, there's something so hot about a man who can handle a high-powered vehicle," Polly purrs, running her fingertips through Quinn's hair as she leans over from the back seat.

Before I have time to break her fingers, she quickly exits the car and slams the door shut behind her.

Quinn places a hand over mine, stilling my fingers from clawing at the upholstery. "She's doing it to get under your skin," he says with a chuckle as he turns off the car.

"Yeah, well, it's working," I scowl, hating that I get so jealous when Quinn is involved.

"Don't let it."

But that's a little hard when I watch Polly through the

driver's window, intentionally leaning over to tie her laces up with her butt pointed directly at Quinn's face.

"Do not look out that window," I order, grinding down on my jaw as she turns over her shoulder and winks.

"That shade of green suits you." Quinn laughs, chewing on his lip ring.

"I'm not jealous." I pathetically scoff because I am *so* jealous.

"Oh, okay then," he says, slowly turning toward the window to look at Polly.

"Don't you dare," I say, snagging his jaw and turning his face my way. "You're a jerk."

"You know what would really get to her?" He grins, inching closer to my lips.

"What?"

"This." He closes the distance between us, painstakingly slow, before finally placing his warm lips on mine.

The kiss is meant to be innocent, but my hungry mouth has other ideas.

The moment our tongues intertwine, we both moan at the contact, and Quinn takes control, wrapping a hand around the back of my neck and drawing me impossibly close to his devilish mouth. As his barbell seeks out every corner of my mouth, a loud knocking on the window breaks us apart.

It seems we've both forgotten we're out in public.

Looking over Quinn's shoulder, I see an unimpressed Polly glaring at me.

"I hate to interrupt," she spits. "But can your gross make-out session wait until *after* shopping? I have better things to do than watch you dry hump one another."

She turns on her heel, her long ponytail thrashing like a whip as she storms off.

I bite my lip, feeling a touch guilty because, as usual, I lose all sense of space and time when kissing Quinn.

"Oops." I smirk, so not sorry for my PDA.

Quinn grins, giving me a light kiss before he sighs. "Let's get this over with."

After much debate, Quinn left me alone with the spawn of Satan, as he too needs an outfit for this masquerade ball.

However, I'm currently hiding in the changing room, avoiding going outside and confronting a scowling Polly, who has hated every outfit I've tried on.

This barely-there garment, which scarcely passes for a dress, is Polly's pick, and I have a feeling she chose this to make me squirm.

The only thing I like about it is that it's black. Other than that, the indecent plunging neckline and short hemline make me afraid to move the wrong way because I'm certain if I sneezed, this thing would turn into a scarf.

The shoes are also ridiculous, and I feel like an utter fraud pretending to feel comfortable walking in glittery stripper heels.

But I'm here to try and bond with Polly. So I suck it up and slowly open the changing room door.

Polly sits outside on a round plush sofa, checking her phone, totally uninterested.

As I clear my throat, she lifts her head and stares at me for a moment before saying, "Wow, who would have thought you could actually kinda look like a girl."

I don't know if that's a compliment, but it didn't involve profanity, so I'll take it as a positive.

"It's really, um…short," I say, tugging at the creeping hemline.

Polly stands in her red-heeled boots, tapping her chin.

Moments like these, when we're not yelling at each other, I can see our similarities.

We both stand at the same height and have similar facial expressions when we're unhappy or pissed off. Her hair is longer than mine, and I can see Polly has a natural kink in hers too, but she straightens it daily so the stubborn curls stay away. Her body is curvier, but we both have an athletic build.

We do also have many differences; our varied dress sense is obviously one of them. But our smart mouths are definitely something we share.

"Just make sure you don't eat or breathe, and you'll be fine." She laughs, pointing at the midsection of my sucked-in torso.

I sarcastically laugh, holding my sides in fake amusement, and trip over my skyscraper heels in the process.

Polly rolls her eyes while I clutch onto a mannequin for support.

"You're really not good at this whole 'being a girl' thing, are you?"

With my patience wearing thin, I retort, "Well, the fact I spent my entire teenage years as a drug dealer might have something to do with that."

Polly's eyes widen, and I'm taken aback when I see a flicker of pain cross her features. But it's gone before I can question it.

"I guess you would look ridiculous dealing in those shoes," she says after a pregnant pause, pointing at my feet.

I'm speechless. Surely, she didn't just make a joke, did she?

We stand staring at one another, and I can't believe how this person can be my kin. I can't help but wonder if things had been different and Cynthia never left, would we have been friends? Would I be standing here, feeling comfortable with this lifestyle?

I guess that's something I'll never know because we can't go back, but we can move forward, and that's what I'll try to do.

"Okay, I'll buy it if you think it looks okay," I say, cringing when I look down at the glittery disco ball I'm currently wearing.

Polly must be able to read my apprehension as she sighs. "Wait here."

She quickly walks away before I have a chance to question where she's going.

Just as I'm about to sit down, Polly returns with a white dress and matching shoes. "Here, try this on," she states, shoving the items into my chest.

As I look down, I'm nearly blinded by its brightness because it's so…white.

"It's, um…white," I stupidly say, stating the obvious.

"Congrats for knowing your colors. Now hurry up." She pushes me in the direction of the changing rooms, huffing in annoyance.

I decide to humor her, as there's no way I'm wearing a white dress, but at least it's longer than the one I'm currently wearing.

The shoes make a loud thud as they smash against the wall when I impatiently kick them off, and the balls of my feet sing in celebration as soon as they are bare.

I let out a relieved breath as I remove the skintight garment from my body, and my lungs thank me because I can finally breathe again. I throw it into the corner, about to rejoice, but then my eyes fall onto the hanger behind the door.

Sighing, I rip it down, and as I'm shimmying into the ridiculously shiny white dress, I can't help but think this is an awful idea. I'm not the type of girl who can wear white without getting it dirty. I'm the type of girl who just looks at a white garment and marks it up with invisible dirt.

But as I turn to look into the mirror, I almost trip, not recognizing the reflection staring back at me.

"Do the shoes fit?" Polly asks from outside the door.

The moment I slip them on, my feet thank me for not subjecting them to those other heels. Even though these shoes are high, they're platforms, making it much easier to stay balanced.

Still gaping at the reflection staring back at me, I can't believe the mirror image is mine.

My legs look lengthy and toned, thanks to the five-inch white diamanté platforms, and the dress, which is still short but modest, sits mid-thigh, giving my legs a longer, suppler look.

The sweetheart neckline is held up by crystal-beaded spaghetti straps, which match the dazzling crystal beads on the corset-style bodice. The white skirt balloons out like a tutu, but it's softer and flows naturally, as the hem of the three-layer skirt is rimmed with white silk.

"Hello? Are you alive in there?" Polly impatiently knocks on the door.

Taking a deep breath, I open the door with poise and step out, but I feel extremely self-conscious when Polly and the sales clerk both gasp when they see me.

I pull at the plunging neckline, and Polly slaps my hand away. "Do not cover them up because they look awesome. We'll take it," Polly says to the smiling shop assistant, pointing at my attire.

"Good choice, Polly. Your friend looks amazing," she innocently says, not realizing that Polly and I aren't exactly friends.

But I nearly fall flat on my face when Polly replies, "Yeah, she kinda does."

I give her a small smile, and she returns it for the briefest of moments before she produces a plastic card and hands it to the store clerk.

"Oh no, I can pay for it," I quickly object, waving my hands to stop the assistant.

"Don't worry about it," Polly replies dismissively, nodding at the poor girl looking back and forth between us, confused. "It's on Mother."

"I still don't feel right about it." But it's too late as the beaming sales clerk has taken off for the registers with the credit card in hand.

"Honestly, it's fine," Polly reaffirms when she sees me chewing my lip.

"Okay. Well, thanks." I nod before ducking into the changing room to get undressed, seeing as Polly won't take no for an answer.

As I drape the dress onto the hanger, I have to do a double take to ensure I've seen the correct eight-hundred-dollar figure on the price tag.

I've never spent that amount on anything before and feel guilty for allowing Cynthia to pay for a dress I'll only wear once.

"Polly, this dress is eight hundred dollars," I whisper as I exit the changing room, waving the hanger in the air.

"And?" she replies, looking up from her phone as if I've gone mad.

"That's a lot of money for a dress."

"Daddy can afford it," she says, reaching for my shoes and dress as we make our way to the register.

Her comment has me thinking. I don't actually know what Chandler does. And come to think of it, I know nothing about him.

"What does he do?" I ask, hoping I don't get my head bitten off.

"He's a lawyer but deals with international law. At the moment, he's dealing with some Geneva Convention or something," she says with a brush of her hand, not too interested that her dad has dealings in some serious shit.

"Oh, right. That explains why he's in Europe."

"Yeah, I guess so. Also explains why he's such a shitty dad," she adds, and I don't miss the hint of resentment behind her tone.

Her comment has us waiting in silence while my items are bagged up, and as the total of the shoes and dress come close to fifteen hundred dollars, I nearly choke.

But as a nonchalant Polly signs the receipt, I know she's done this a million times before, and I can't help but think money really can't buy happiness because it seems we have a lot more in common than just our mother.

The house is still in a state of chaos when we get back.

Cynthia stands in the foyer, looking up at the wall, obviously debating whether the decorations are appropriate enough.

"Oh, hi, girls," she says when she sees us. "Quinn, do you think this is too much?" Her eyes are focused on a gory, morbid painting of flying limbs and heads.

I have no idea what I'm looking at, so I remain mute because to my untrained eyes, it looks kind of gruesome and has me wondering if we're celebrating a public execution instead of Christmas.

"It's a great replica of Guernica," Quinn says beside me.

"Oh, you're a fan of Picasso?" Cynthia asks, looking at Quinn, obviously impressed.

"Yeah, he's brilliant. This piece is actually one of my favorites," Quinn says, mesmerized by the picture.

Cynthia nods animatedly, clearly excited to be in the company of a fellow Picasso lover. "You must go visit the National Gallery. There is an original piece on display. Just breathtaking," she says, hand over her heart.

"Haven't you had some pieces on display there too, Mom?" Polly casually asks.

Cynthia shyly nods, brushing a piece of midnight hair behind her ear. "Yes."

"Did you paint this?" he asks, pointing at the painting whose name I cannot pronounce.

"Yes, I did. It's a very poor duplication, but I had limited time to get organized." Cynthia sighs when looking back at her artwork, clearly disappointed.

"No way, it's fucking cool," Quinn says passionately, and I watch my mother swoon over Quinn's comment.

But any female would because witnessing Quinn Berkeley grow passionate about something is a sight that would have any human drooling with desire.

I should know.

"Thank you, Quinn. That is really lovely of you to say."

As we stand staring at the painting, I can't help but think that she's made a name for herself here too, just like she did when in LA.

I sadly remember the last picture I drew for her and how my father discarded it like it was nothing.

Feeling my eyes well with tears, I clear my throat because I will not cry. "Well, I better call Abi," I say, and Quinn turns to look at me, giving me a small nod.

"Who's Abi?"

"My friend back home," I reply without thought.

"In LA?"

"No, South Boston, Virginia," I correct, and am amazed I think of Virginia as my home.

"Oh? That's where you're from?" she asks Quinn, who nods in confirmation.

There's so much she doesn't know about me, about what I've done, and I wonder when she'll finally open up and ask. But we remain quiet because now is not that time.

Cynthia clears her throat. "Well, feel free to use the phone in the den."

I look at Quinn, chewing my lip.

What if the diner's phone is tapped, and we lead the police straight to our whereabouts?

I know it's stupid, seeing as we haven't been masking our phone conversations in the past, but we've always called on the run and not from a direct location. Calling from here makes me nervous, and as paranoid as this makes me, I have to refuse.

"Um, thanks for the offer, but I'll just use a pay phone."

Polly scoffs as she joins us. "You do realize this is the twenty-first century, right? I don't even think they exist anymore."

Cynthia sees me squirm uncomfortably and gasps with understanding. "Of course," she says before she flutters off down the hallway.

Polly cocks an eyebrow in confusion, so I decide to be honest, as there's no point in lying to her. I also think we made progress today, so hopefully, by being honest, we will continue that progression.

"If I call from here, I'm afraid the police may track me."

"Oh, well, that sucks," she flippantly replies.

"Welcome to our world."

Quinn wraps a hand around my waist, drawing me into his side.

Polly watches the exchange, and I don't fail to notice her eyes lower, saddened by our actions. It makes me wonder if she has someone like Quinn in her life.

"Here, you can use this," Cynthia says, handing me a black iPhone.

"Um," I say, stumped, as cell phones are still traceable.

"It's untraceable. It's Chandler's," she clarifies as if that's supposed to explain anything.

"I'll return it as soon as I make the call."

"No need. Keep it. Tell your friend to text you on that too if there's any news."

I don't know what to say, as having an untraceable phone is invaluable. "Thank you. I really appreciate this."

She smiles. Who would have thought we'd have a civil conversation about something illegal?

A cake the height of Quinn gets pushed into the room, and Polly gasps. "I said white, not off-white!" She dashes off, following the poor pastry chef in hot pursuit.

"I better go save Philippe." Cynthia chuckles, and for a split second, she looks as if she wants to reach out and touch me, but she changes her mind at the last minute and gives me a small nod instead.

I let out the small breath I was holding when she races off, and Quinn kisses the top of my head. "Untraceable phone? That's some high-tech Batman shit right there," he whispers, and I chuckle, thinking the same thing.

We make our way outside, away from prying ears, as I dial. But the person who answers has tears stinging my eyes.

"Hello, Bobby Joe's."

"Tristan?" I say on a gasp, pressing the iPhone against my ear, afraid I imagined the voice on the other end.

Quinn appears just as surprised as me.

"Mia?" Tristan asks when I remain silent.

"Yes—yes, it's me," I stammer after clearing my throat.

"Oh fuck, it's so good to hear your voice," he says on a rushed breath.

"Yours too."

"How are you? Where are you?"

"Canada," I plainly reply, not giving away my exact location.

"Everything okay?"

"As good as it can be, considering. How are you?" I quickly ask, changing the subject.

"I'm fine. Abi needs to stop telling you stories about me. She's ruining my image."

I chuckle because I've missed his humor.

"How's the pain in the ass?"

"He's still a pain."

Quinn smirks, but it doesn't quite reach his eyes.

"He's right here. Hang on, I'll put him on." I pass the phone to Quinn, who happily accepts.

"Hey, brat."

I can't hear too much, but from what I can see, this is the first time in a very long time a genuine smile has spread across Quinn's face. Undoubtedly, he loves his brother, and not seeing him is taking a toll on them both.

I feel like I'm intruding on a private moment only meant for Quinn and Tristan, so I decide to look at the rose garden a few feet away.

I can only imagine the pain both siblings feel at being apart because I know Quinn would do anything for his brother.

We need this to be over with soon. I'm not sure how much longer we can deal with this fucked-up situation before one of us snaps or does something rash. I came close, but I think I'm making progress.

Well, I'm trying my best.

"Tris, just stay there, all right?"

Quinn's sudden raised voice catches my attention, and I can't help but listen.

His back is turned, so he hasn't noticed my return as he openly says, "She doesn't need you to protect her."

I sigh, hating that the only thing Quinn and Tristan seem to argue over is me.

"Here, tell her yourself." Quinn turns and holds the phone out to me.

This won't end well.

"What do you need to tell me?" I ask Tristan, prepared for almost anything.

Almost.

"I'm coming to Canada."

"No, you're not," I counter firmly.

"Why not? What good am I here? At least I can help protect you over there," he says, and I can feel his frustration over the phone.

"I don't need you to, Tristan. You'll protect me by staying safe where you are."

He huffs, and I feel awful for being so harsh. "Look, we're

in the home stretch now. Abi said her dad is working hard, so it's only a matter of time. Please, just stay put. Okay?" I reinforce when he remains silent.

"Yeah, okay. Fine," he stubbornly replies.

"Thank you. It's bad enough I have one brother facing the death penalty."

The moment the words are out of my mouth, I regret them. But I can't take them back.

"Death penalty? What are you talking about?"

"Nothing. Don't worry about it," I say, trying to brush it off.

I look at Quinn and mouth, "Sorry."

"Hey," I quickly say, hoping to change the subject. "You got a pen?"

"Yeah," Tristan suspiciously replies.

"Write this down." I rattle off the cell number. "You guys can contact me anytime on this number. The phone is untraceable."

"That's some high-tech Batman shit right there," Tristan says, parroting his brother's earlier comment. I'm thankful I hear him scribble down the digits.

"We'll talk more tomorrow, okay? Oh, can you pass the number on to Abi also?" I ask, realizing Tabitha mustn't be working today.

"No problem. Hey, Mia..."

"Yeah?"

"I miss you," he says sincerely.

"I miss you, too."

Quinn lowers his head, and I feel like I've done something wrong, but I shouldn't. I tell Abi I miss her all the time, so why is this any different?

I know the answer.

"Say goodbye to Quinn for me," Tristan says, filling the silence.

"Will do." I nod, looking at Quinn, who's toying with his lip ring.

"Bye, Mia. I'll see you real soon." He hangs up before I get a chance to say goodbye.

I leave the phone pressed to my ear, realizing that real soon is not soon enough. I just want this shit to be over with.

I remain still, waiting for Quinn to break the uncomfortable silence.

But he doesn't.

I can't help but notice how uneasy he gets when I talk to Tristan, which is ridiculous since we're just friends. But being on the run and focusing on not dying has really made me blind to the fact that before we ran, Quinn stayed away from me because of Tristan.

Tristan had a crush or something on me, but it was purely innocent on both our parts. Tristan never tried anything. I think he knew I would have freaked out.

But his last comment back in South Boston rings in my ears, and I know he knew something was going on between Quinn and me the entire time.

He said, "Take care of our girl."

In his eyes, I was his girl as much as Quinn's.

It's fair to say he didn't know the extent of Quinn's and my relationship, but that didn't matter to him because he still took a knife for me that could have ended his life. I owe him so much. I owe them all so much, and I intend to pay up as soon as I can.

Quinn is still quiet.

I hate this distance between us, so I step into his arms and wrap my arms around his neck. "You okay?"

"Yes," he blankly replies as he settles his hands low on my waist.

"What's wrong?" I ask, as his reply surely doesn't imply that.

"Nothing, I'm fine. It's all fine."

But it's far from fine.

"Have I done something to upset you?" I ask when he won't meet my eyes.

He shakes his head.

But I'm not fooled because I've come to read Quinn just as well as he can read me.

"You're not a very good liar." I nestle into the side of his neck, kissing it softly.

"I guess not."

"So what's wrong?"

Quinn sighs, the deep sound echoing throughout me as he meets my worried gaze. "I just know my brother, and I have a feeling he won't do what he's told. I think he's going to come to Canada."

My eyes widen in horror. "He said he wouldn't. But then again, he is your brother."

Quinn chuckles, but by the hard set of his jaw, I know he's serious.

Shit.

Does Quinn really think Tristan will come here? But he doesn't know where here is.

"He wouldn't, would he?"

The thought of Tristan getting hurt again because of me has my stomach roiling.

Quinn only shrugs. "When it comes to—"

But he doesn't continue.

He only chews on his hoop, looking away.

"When it comes to what?" I press, shifting my head to meet his gaze.

"Nothing," Quinn says after a long pause, leaning forward and kissing the tip of my nose to distract me.

"Quinn," I retort, but I'm silenced as he swoops forward and kisses me.

Taken off guard, I latch onto his biceps for support as his skillful tongue begs for permission to enter my mouth. However, begging is not required as my body instantly responds before my brain can catch up, and before long, we are making out like our lives depend on it.

Since being here, we haven't been as intimate as we once were, and I miss it. I miss the closeness of being with him in a way I've never been with another.

Kissing Quinn is like eating chocolate. One bite is never enough. But Quinn is like nothing I've ever tasted before, and his flavor is one I could happily eat again and again. And that's exactly what I plan on doing.

I suck his hoop into my mouth and draw on it with a long, wet pull. Quinn moans, and his response spurs me on. I reach between us and softly rub over the firm arousal pressing against me.

Quinn groans once again.

That simple sound is all the motivation I need as I unsnap the button on his jeans and slide my hand into his pants. He's not wearing any boxers as usual.

"Red—" he pants from around my mouth since we are out in public for everyone to see. But that's what makes this all the more fun and exciting.

I pay no attention to his warning, and the moment I wrap my hand around his shaft, we both moan. I slowly stroke up and down, loving how Quinn surrenders and lets down his guard.

His mouth slackens, and he exhales hot, needy breaths, his hips thrusting forward, moving in time with my quickening strokes.

"Oh fuck."

I like that I can elicit this response from him, and I think Quinn needs this physical reassurance because showing him that I want him and no one else is what he needs to chase those insecurities away.

We all have insecurities, and the fact this man is afraid I would want anyone other than him is just absurd.

"You feel amazing," I whisper against his lips. "Does it feel okay?"

"Okay? Oh fuck." Quinn hisses, driving his hips onward.

"Is a...oh fuck me," he moans, his sentence structure intermittent as I stroke harder. "Understatement. I'm about five seconds away from coming in your hand."

I avert my eyes, still embarrassed by his honesty.

"Let me...oh fuck...let me finish you off first." He hisses, reaching for the button of my jeans, but I nudge out of his grip.

"No way. I like...being in control."

The confession stuns us both.

Quinn nods, closing his eyes, and arches his head back. The sight is fucking breathtaking. When he lets down his walls this way, what I see is simply beautiful.

His zipper is in the way, so I try to push it down without breaking contact with his arousal. However, when I hear Cynthia calling out for us, I realize this will have to wait.

We quickly disengage while Quinn attempts to act normal when Cynthia appears. "I hope I'm not interrupting."

I bite my lip because this situation is a little funny. "Not at all."

Quinn mutes a pained groan.

"I was wondering if I could borrow Quinn for a second. I just wanted to see if he could hang an ornament on the porch. I can't climb a ladder because of my vertigo, and Polly is busy, and the workers have gone for the day, and oh dear—sorry to be a bother," she concludes, taking a breath.

It's safe to assume she has an inkling about what she interrupted.

"It's no bother. I'm happy to help."

"Er, thank you, Quinn," she says, unable to meet his eyes.

We're so busted, and this is actually kind of comical as I've never experienced being caught out by a parent. I try to bite back my smile at this feeling of normalcy because maybe, just maybe, there is hope for Cynthia and me.

"Right, well," Cynthia says and waves goodbye to me before practically running away.

I burst out laughing while Quinn playfully narrows his eyes at me before trailing her.

I can't help but think a situation that should have been awkward and uncomfortable really wasn't. It felt normal. Today is the first day I've felt like me. And I hope today is the first of many more to come.

Eight

"**H**ow many more of these do I have to fold?" Polly groans, throwing a white napkin onto the mound in the center of the table.

"Until that pile is finished," Cynthia replies with a smile. "You're the one who wanted the cocktail napkins shaped like swans."

"I know." She huffs, reaching for another napkin, and begrudgingly begins folding some origami-style swan.

For the past three hours, we've been folding these napkins into ridiculous birds, and after a few sad-looking birds, I've finally got the hang of it.

"This is slave labor." She pouts, folding the corners over.

"Hardly." Cynthia scoffs. "Besides, a day's work isn't going to kill you. Consider yourself lucky you've never had to work a day in your life. Many sixteen-year-olds would have earned a small fortune by now."

"Yeah, well, many sixteen-year-olds don't have a slave driver for a mother," she replies with a smirk. "And besides, I'll be seventeen soon."

I totally ignore her flirting with Quinn. I'm more focused on the fact that my insides are screaming that my theory of Cynthia being pregnant when she left me was correct. There has to be some reasonable explanation as to why she would leave when pregnant.

Obviously, the fact my father isn't Polly's dad gave her reason to run, but why did she not take me with her? Did my father know she was pregnant with another man's baby? Or did she leave me behind because her new beau, Chandler, didn't want a child he didn't father?

I have so many damn questions. So here's hoping after yesterday's breakthrough, the next time I ask Cynthia about my past, it won't end in a screaming match.

"Everything okay?" Quinn whispers into my ear, picking up on my thoughts.

"Yeah, all good," I reply with a smile, bumping into him playfully with my shoulder.

"Ugh, you two are nauseating." Polly crinkles her nose in disgust.

I can't help but laugh as I guess we kind of are, but holy shit, look at him. How can I not want to touch him any chance I get?

His long bangs sweep over an eye as his head is bowed, expertly folding some fancy-looking bird, which in no way resembles my limp-looking handiwork. The way his deft fingers work with precision has me thinking of the way he touches me and how he also applies as much care to my body as he does to these stupid birds.

He must feel me visually undressing him because he flicks me a quick wink over his shoulder before continuing with his creation.

My cheeks heat as I start to think about what my Christmas gift entails and how I intend to give it to him. It'll have to be after the party because I don't want to rush this. And besides, I don't want him opening his present early.

"Do you want me to do something with your hair?" Polly asks, and when I raise my head, I see she's addressing me.

"What's wrong with my hair?" I ask, slightly insulted.

"Nothing is exactly wrong with it," she says, gesturing with a tiny bird at my head. "But nothing is exactly right, either. I'd be happy to work my magic on you. You won't recognize yourself."

She shrugs, not at all concerned she's just insulted me in a roundabout way.

"Gee, thanks," I reply sarcastically. "I'm at your mercy. But don't turn me into a Barbie doll."

"Red, I honestly don't think Polly can work that kind of magic."

I open and close my mouth, unsure what to say before I burst into laughter.

Polly and Quinn soon join in my laughter. They're both laughing at my expense, but I don't mind because as I turn to look at Cynthia, I see her discreetly dab at her eyes. This very weird, very stupid conversation actually feels normal.

There is no way I can go down there.

I've been hiding up here for the past hour, avoiding setting foot downstairs to face the music—literally, as Frank Sinatra is singing some cheesy Christmas carol.

But I can't hide up here any longer because I know Quinn waits for me downstairs.

We both got ready in separate rooms since tonight is a masquerade ball and all about mystery. I eye the mask, which Polly insists I must wear. I can't deny it really is stunning. It goes well with the beautiful jewels on my dress, which catch the light when I turn to examine myself in the bathroom mirror.

Polly wanted to pull my hair into some twist thing, but after much debate, she begrudgingly agreed to leave it down, but only if she could style it. So we came to a compromise. I asked if she could style it using the onyx comb I found in the jewelry box.

I don't know what it is about this piece of jewelry, but I know I've seen it before. I just can't remember where.

As I look at the clip, holding up tufts of my thick hair so it sweeps across my shoulder, I can't believe this is me. Polly curled the ends so my hair falls elegantly over my left shoulder, draping over my breast which is pushed up to the heavens, thanks to my push-up bra.

My makeup is simple, and I've replaced Polly's bright red lipstick with a sheer pink, which I feel more comfortable with. My eyes are painted a smoky black, and Polly added some subtle glitter to my upper lids, which reflect the light when I turn the right way. My cheeks are naturally tinted pink as I feel beyond embarrassed to go downstairs and face a room of complete strangers looking like someone other than me.

I finger the small diamond earrings Polly lent me and smile. They match the diamond piercing in my nose, which was not done intentionally. I was going to wear my hoop, but Polly made it very clear that the second set of earrings and nose ring had to go. Again, we came to a compromise, and I ditched the hooped nose ring and the second set of studs but left my tragus and replaced the hoop with a small diamond stud.

Polly seemed satisfied with our negotiation and said I looked like a punk version of Cinderella, but I don't see the resemblance unless she means my shoes. The heels were an issue since I would break my neck wearing those things, so I'm wearing my Doc Martens instead.

Reaching for my white mask, I carefully place it over my head, positioning it so it sits snugly and comfortably on my face, hiding the white ribbon ties under my hair. The eye holes are like cat eyes, and the ends flick into high peaks, accentuated with glittery edges and diamonds.

Polly said this mask is made of some kind of metal called filigree, which is meant to resemble lace, as the mask is not solid but has tiny sections cut out, revealing my flushed skin underneath. I like it as it still provides some mystery because just enough of my face is covered.

Ensuring my comb is securely fastened, I take a deep breath and tell myself to stop stalling.

Smoothing out my skirt, I like how my black nails contrast with the white. I open the door and can't help but think that Polly may be right. I am kind of like Cinderella. I'm the perfect rags-to-riches story and even have the evil stepsister to prove it.

But that's not entirely true.

As Polly transformed me, she did so with care, and I sat, mostly silent, trying not to overthink how someone I passionately loathed is slowly becoming a little more likable. It's fair to say we've got a long road ahead, but the past couple of days of not fighting with her or Cynthia have been nice.

Even in these ridiculous clothes, I feel more like me for the first time in a very long time.

Maybe things are looking up.

I open my door and make my way down the stairs. As I descend the final step, my pounding heart feels like it's about to splatter all over the polished floorboards.

I subtly look around the room for Quinn. Surely, he'll be easy to spot, but as I look around the crowded house, I realize every male is wearing a suit. I really should have thought this through before trekking into a room filled with complete strangers who all look a little kooky.

Ladies have opted for long, elegant gowns, which complement their elaborate masks, and even though the color theme is kind of cool, it's also a little creepy. We all look like chess pieces.

A masked server waltzes past, offering me a glass of something bubbly off a silver tray. I gratefully accept because I need something in my gurgling stomach. I down the drink in one mouthful, cringing when the acidic burn hits my throat. But the burn calms my raging nerves, so I look around for a server because I need another glass.

However, the moment my eyes lock with *his* across the room, my frantic heartbeat kicks into an unhealthy staccato. At this moment, everything fades, and the only thing that exists…is him.

Quinn casually leans against a wall, watching me closely behind his plain black mask. I almost choke when his sensual mouth tips up into a dimpled smile, his silver hoop catching the light from the crystal chandelier above him. He's wearing a simple tuxedo, but nothing about Quinn could ever be simple.

The crisp white shirt draws out the bright green of his

eyes, and the pressed black suit fits him perfectly, highlighting his muscular, broad frame. The lapels on the jacket are black silk, and as my eyes drop to his pants, the snug material falls just the right way. I can't help but smile as I see a pair of black Chucks adorning his feet, completing his sexy, rebellious look.

He gives me a small wave, and I'm barely able to register a response as I watch his bright eyes do a slow, deliberate appraisal of my body. I suddenly feel naked under his probing gaze. As he tugs on his lip ring suggestively, I almost buckle at the knees.

But it's not his piercing eyes that have me almost leaping over the guests to kiss the hell out of him; it's his hair. It's been cut and styled like a freaking supermodel. His bangs are still long, but they're fashioned into a messy peak, and the shorter sides are gelled stylishly, giving him the ultimate bed-head look.

"Oh, Mia, you look beautiful," someone gasps, standing directly in front of me.

Taking a minute to compose myself, I see Cynthia smiling before me, looking rather stunning herself.

Her long black hair is twisted into a messy side chignon and clasped together with a small topaz clip, very similar to the one I'm currently wearing. Her strapless black silk dress sweeps the floor behind her, hugging her petite frame. Her mask is akin to mine, but is black instead of white.

"Thank you. So do you," I reply, realizing I'm staring at her without a word.

A pink hue brushes her skin, and I see where I get my scarlet cheeks from. "Thank you. Have you seen Quinn?"

I give her a small nod.

"Polly cut his hair. I hope you don't mind."

I don't mind in the slightest. Quinn actually looks

hotter—something I believed wasn't humanly possible. "Not at all. It suits him."

"She said it's called a faux-hawk or something. I have no idea what that is." Cynthia chuckles, reaching for two glasses filled with orange juice.

"You don't drink?" I ask, accepting the flute glass.

"No, not really, it messes with my medication," she confesses, looking happily around the room, obviously pleased with the sight before her.

Medication? This is news to me. I wonder what she's on. But this isn't really the time nor the place to ask.

I suddenly see someone who no doubt has to be Polly. She's wearing an extremely tight ball gown, resembling Belle's *Beauty and the Beast* gown. However, while Belle's dress is yellow, Polly's is a deep, fiery red.

She looks beautiful.

Her hair is styled into a messy twist, but long curls drop down from the elegant weave, shaping her face and long neck. The dress has about four hoops underneath it and is so wide she has a permanent barrier of about four feet around her. But with her frame, it makes her look majestic. The bodice has silver jewels encrusted across the neckline and scattered sporadically throughout the skirt.

A young suitor reaches for her gloved fingers, kissing her lightly on the back of the hand. Polly flutters her long eyelashes underneath her red mask, loving the attention.

"Cynthia," an older gentleman with a curly mustache says, reaching for her hand. "You look ravishing."

That's my cue to excuse myself because I need to find Quinn and make out with him like yesterday.

I search the wall he stood against but am greeted by an older couple eating canapés.

Disappointed, I do a quick sweep but come up empty.

Deciding to take a walk and look for him, I enter a few rooms, but he's nowhere to be seen. I start to panic. Has Polly locked him away in her bedroom? Just as I begin to envision every possible kidnapping scenario, a familiar pair of warm hands lace around my middle, drawing my back to a very taut, divinely scented body.

I instantly sag when I press against him. My body tingles in all the right places.

"You look so beautiful," Quinn whispers against my ear, his lips tickling my lobe.

I need to turn around and face him, but his grip implies I'm not going anywhere. He drags me to a darkened alcove.

"Th-thank you," I stutter, my eyes slipping shut when his lips trail delicate kisses along my arched neck.

My skin instantly heats from the delicious contact, and my body demands I smash my lips to his and never let go. I turn, and thankfully Quinn loosens his hold as we both dive for the other, pawing the shit out of our fancy clothes, which are an unwanted barrier.

Quinn reaches for my mask, ripping it away, as the stupid thing is making it hard to keep up with his frenzied kisses. I run my fingers through his hair and am happy to feel there is still a little length for me to grab onto and pull.

He moans into my mouth, and holy shit, the sound hits me just the right way.

I want him like I've never wanted him before, and as his hand creeps under my skirt, caressing my bare ass cheek, I dare say he feels the same way.

I'm breathless as we recklessly kiss, but I need to pull away before I pass out from lack of oxygen.

"I want you," I whisper, unashamed by my blatant

confession as I stare into his eyes.

Quinn's hand slips out from under my dress, and he takes a calming breath, slipping off his mask. "Do you know how hard it is to keep my hands to myself? You're driving me crazy, and then you go and say something like that."

"It's the truth."

"I know it is, and that's what makes me the luckiest son of a bitch in the world."

I smile at his openness, as I love that we can talk freely like this and not be embarrassed or ashamed.

Back home, Quinn and I weren't like this. Quinn had some notion he had to stay away from me because of Tristan. He thought it best at the time, but now I can't imagine not being this way with him. To have to hide my feelings for him feels almost unnatural and wrong.

I'm so happy we've come this far, and I can't wait to move forward.

Resting my hand on his stubbled cheek, I state, "No, that would be me."

He unexpectedly turns serious, reaching for my cheek and drawing our foreheads together. "You're my poison," he whispers, and I gasp at the passion behind his words. "You're my one weakness…but I've never felt so alive."

He lowers his lips to mine.

This kiss isn't filled with lust. It's filled with love, and it's my favorite kiss of all.

We make out until my lips are bruised and swollen, and I'm about ready to ditch the whole party and drag Quinn upstairs.

But he pulls away with a small smile.

"Later," he says, thumbing my pouty bottom lip.

I raise an eyebrow in confusion, but he makes himself

very clear.

"Later on tonight, I plan on stripping you naked and possessing every…single…inch of you."

I can only nod because I know nothing remotely coherent will pass through my mute lips for the next few minutes.

"But for the moment, I'll get us something to drink. I won't be long," he says with a smirk as he lays a final kiss on my eager lips before slipping on his mask and walking away.

Is tonight the night?

It makes sense that sex would be the next step in our relationship, and I'm not scared or having second thoughts. I just know that when we do, Quinn is right. He will possess every inch of me.

I know it's not something I will ever regret because I want nothing more. This thing with Quinn is real, and no matter how far I run, I know he'll run with me.

"What are you doing hiding out here?" Polly asks, snapping me out of my thoughts.

"Just waiting for Quinn," I reply, hoping my scarlet cheeks don't give away what we were doing out here.

"You're welcome," Polly says, straightening her gown.

"Pardon?" I reply, totally confused about what I'm thanking her for.

"Tell me you weren't drooling all over yourself when you saw Quinn," Polly confidently replies, aware of how good he looks.

"Oh, right." I chuckle, thinking she's right, and I do owe her a big thank-you for making the hottest man alive even hotter.

"You both scrub up okay," she says, which surprises me.

"Thanks, so do you. Love your dress. Although, red?" I query with a smile, looking at her satin gown.

Her glossy lips tip up into a calculated smirk as she replies, "Well, now you're not the only one with the nickname Red. Anyway, I better get back out there. There's one guy, holy shit. I don't know who he is, but I'm going to find out."

"Good luck," I reply, feeling sorry for whoever's caught Polly's eye.

"I don't need luck. There's just something about metal in a guy's face that drives me wild," she adds over her shoulder before skipping off.

I don't like her comment, as it makes me feel uneasy knowing she's probably drooling over Quinn's piercings. She has made it more than obvious she enjoys flirting with him, and she did threaten to do everything in her power to make me leave. What if this is all just a bullshit charade?

She's putting on a little show, and when I've let my guard down, she pounces and punishes me for believing that she actually has a genuine bone in her body.

With that thought plaguing my mind, I realize I really could use a drink, and I wonder where Quinn is. I pull on my mask and decide to look for him.

Nat King Cole plays over the speakers as I walk into the vast living room where the party is in full swing. Looking around the lavish room filled with happy guests chatting while picking at the endless selection of finger foods, I know finding Quinn will be impossible.

I decide to walk around. The living area opens to a den, which leads into an alfresco area, then wraps around into an adjoining balcony. He could be anywhere.

The decorations look classy, and Polly has transformed this house into a black-and-white Christmas wonderland. I sigh when I see her dragging some poor chump over to the hanging mistletoe, puckering her ruby lips.

Thankfully, the chump isn't Quinn, but suddenly, I begin to worry. It's not like he would bump into anyone he would know to stop and chat. My anxious eyes do a quick, last sweep, but I don't see him anywhere.

"Shit," I mumble to myself.

Politely pushing past the mingling guests, I make my way into the den, which is a little smaller but still nothing. Dammit, where is he?

The cold air brushes my cheeks as I step out into the alfresco area, where patrons enjoy a cigar and liquor. They stand, casually chatting around the in-wall fireplace, none the wiser that I'm about five seconds away from losing it.

Stepping out onto the balcony when Quinn is nowhere to be seen inside has my teeth chattering because it's about zero degrees. Thankfully, it's not snowing.

Doing a quick look around, I don't see him anywhere, so I take a look over the railing, just in case he took Lucky out to do his business. Pushing into the banister, I look out into the open vastness. All I see are tiny candles lining the driveway and manicured lawns. But no Quinn.

Where is he?

My eyes once again fruitlessly search the area below, hoping he'll magically appear, but deep down, I know something is wrong. I have to find him because wherever he is, I know he's in trouble.

With my heart in my throat, I quickly turn but am stopped mid-spin when a set of warm hands wrap around my middle. I instantly sag in relief, but as I lean back, I realize the body is not Quinn's.

But it's also not a stranger.

"Don't be mad," the husky voice whispers by my ear as he loosens the grip around my waist.

Spinning around so quickly, I stumble in utter shock. His hand shoots out to steady me, and I let him because I'm seconds away from collapsing.

The moment I see those familiar blue eyes hidden behind a black mask, my pounding heart threatens to rip through my rib cage, unable to accept the reality of who stands before me.

And that's because there's no fucking way I am staring into the eyes of…Tristan Berkeley.

"Tristan?" I choke out, holding the wooden banister for support as my eyes widen, not believing the sight before them.

"Hi, Mia," he gingerly replies, confirming he's real and standing before me.

"Wh…what are you doing here?" I stutter, apprehensively reaching out to touch his arm to ensure he's actually here.

"I had to come. I couldn't stay away. Abi told me everything. She told me what Quinn did. You should have told me." He sighs, taking off his mask.

"I…I…" I can't construct a coherent sentence because I still can't believe he's here.

"I'm sorry for lying to you."

But I remain immobile; the only things moving are my eyes as they appraise the man in front of me.

I've forgotten how much he resembles Quinn, but while Quinn is sharp planes and rugged angles, Tristan is softer and easier to read. However, now that Quinn's hair is shorter, they do bear more of a likeness to one another than they did before. But the differences between them are what make them unique in their own personal way.

"Mia?" Tristan asks softly as I remain frozen.

"You're really here?" I stupidly ask just above a whisper.

"I'm really here," he affirms with a nod, his blond hair catching in the breeze.

"Oh God, you're really here," I reiterate, my hand falling to the center of his chest over his beating heart.

The memory from when I saw him last plagues my mind, and my eyes fill with tears.

I slowly trace my fingers down his side, stopping where his stab wound gushed out bright red blood. I squeeze lightly, staring at the spot and remembering the pain I felt when I saw his life source rapidly draining out of him.

"I'm okay, Mia," Tristan coos, placing a warm hand over mine, interlacing our fingers, and with the other, he gently removes my mask.

My eyes focus on our union, and tears spill down my cheeks because his hands took part in saving my life, in saving me. These hands belong to a selfless man who has already risked so much for me, yet here he is, consoling me and telling me everything is okay.

A sob tears from my throat, and I unexpectedly throw myself into his arms. Thankfully, he catches me, crushing me to his chest.

Pressing my nose into his neck, I inhale his unique fragrance and weep because the memories of who I was when I first met him and who I am now haunt me. I know I'm free from who I was, thanks to him.

"Thank you," I whisper, my arms encircling his neck, never wanting to let him go.

"It's okay. Everything will be okay," he replies softly, rubbing my back. "I've missed you so much."

"I've missed you, too," I confess, sobbing into his shoulder. "I can't believe you're really here."

"Me either...I can't stay away from you." He quickly corrects himself. "I mean, I couldn't stay away from you, knowing what's happening."

I don't have the energy to read too much into his admission because I'm so damn happy he's here.

After a minute or two of being in his arms, I no longer feel cold—I feel warm, and I also feel complete. My family is slowly coming together, and I wouldn't trade the feeling for anything.

"Sorry for the PDA." I sniff, unwrapping myself from his body and wiping my eyes with the back of my hand.

He chuckles with a shrug, rewarding me with his trademark dimpled smile. "Don't mention it."

It doesn't feel weird that I threw myself at Tristan because this is how we were back home. But now, now because of Quinn and me, I should maybe hold back on my enthusiasm.

Scanning our surroundings, oblivious to my inner thoughts, Tristan asks, "Where's Quinn?"

I bite my lip, ashamed that I allowed myself to forget about him for a split second, and reply, "I don't know. I was actually out here looking for him."

"He's not around?" he asks, furrowing his brow.

"No," I reply, shaking my head. "I've looked everywhere, but I can't find him."

"I'm sure he's here somewhere. Have you looked upstairs?"

"No, I didn't get a chance."

"Let me go look. You do another sweep down here, and we'll meet back in ten minutes, okay?" Tristan says, giving me a small smile. "He's fine, Mia."

I nod because he's right. I know I'm just overreacting, but I won't calm down until I know where the hell he is.

"Okay, see you soon," Tristan says, putting his mask back on and giving me a dimpled smile over his shoulder before pushing through the crowd.

I watch him disappear into the sea of people and let out a

shaky breath. I need a minute to compose myself before I go back out there. I still have a sinking feeling that something sinister has happened to Quinn.

Turning to look over the railing, deep in thought, I still can't believe Tristan is here. I know that's selfish, but having him here brings back all the memories of our good times together and also of Hank. Tristan brings back memories that sometimes I too easily forget.

Wiping the stolen tear that falls from my heavy eyes, I take one final look at the twinkling lights, feeling collected enough to go out there and not break down. I push off the railing, but suddenly, the hair on the back of my neck stands on end. I feel as if I've swallowed a bucket of acid, and it's quickly eating away at my soul.

Instinct kicks in, and I instantly reach for my knife. Of course, it's tucked away upstairs because I carelessly let my guard down for one fucking night.

A hand painfully seizes my arm to stop me from turning around and taking a swing. I know without a doubt that I'm trapped when that hand ensnares my waist, thrusting me backward and holding me prisoner.

Everything at this moment is heightened.

Every sound is amplified.

Every single disgusting memory of my past overloads my senses, and I almost black out, unable to take the pain.

But three simple words, three harmless words, have me wishing I was anywhere but here because those words open up a wound I wish would close over and let me be.

"Merry Christmas...princess."

Nine

"**N**ot so fast," my father warns as I strike my head back, praying I make contact with his nose.

But he's too quick and dodges my attack with a menacing chuckle.

"Too slow," he chides. "Some things never change."

"Obviously not. You're still a fucking asshole," I spit, attempting to twist out of his painful grip, hoping to break free. But he has a strong hold on me, and I'm futilely expending the energy I need to survive.

"I'll scream," I threaten. Looking around me, I wish someone would look my way.

But everyone is in party mode, too intoxicated on expensive spirits and Christmas cheer to notice my dilemma.

"Go ahead," he mocks, and I experience the unmistakable feeling of a gun being pressed into the small of my back.

Most people would be afraid, but I'm not most people.

I respond to my father's threats of violence by letting out a sarcastic laugh. Is he really that pathetic that he thinks I care about my survival right now?

All I can think of is what happens when Tristan returns.

My father will have no qualms in taking us both prisoner, and that's the only thing that has me afraid.

"Just in case you missed it, I'm holding a revolver against your spine. One wrong move, and you can say goodbye to your legs."

I cringe at his marijuana-scented breath as he inches his lips to my ear.

"I know. I just don't see how that's supposed to scare me. If you're going to kill me, just do it already, and stop boring me with your melodramatics," I say, hoping he buys into my detachment.

Now it's his turn to laugh as he replies, "Kill you? If I wanted to kill you, I would have done so weeks ago."

I realize he's right.

He's had ample time to do it, so now I know for certain that he has another plan for my fate.

"So what, you're going to bore me to death?" I laugh, roughly attempting to pull out of his clutches.

"Always the smart-ass," he growls, pressing the barrel into my back.

"I've learned from the best," I reply, holding the railing as he digs the gun deeper into my spine.

He takes a deep breath.

The fact I'm no longer afraid of him obviously pisses him off. "We're going to move, and you're not going to cause a scene."

I know this is my chance to save Tristan from walking in

on me and trying to save the day.

"Fine, but lose the gun. It doesn't really imply I'm going anywhere willingly with you." I hope he believes me because the moment he sheathes that gun…I'm going to kill him.

I don't know how, but there's no way I'm going anywhere with him because if I do, I'm as good as dead.

"You will come willingly, Mia."

I've never hated my name more than I do right now.

"What makes you so sure?" I ask, attempting again to break free as I buck against his hold.

But his reply has me ceasing all movement because there's no way there is any truth to what he just said.

"Because Phil has your little boyfriend upstairs, and if we don't move now, he'll put a bullet in his head—just like he did to that stupid old man."

"Don't you *dare* talk about him that way."

I roughly pull out of my father's grip and turn around to face him.

I don't care if he shoots me because there's no way I'll allow him to speak about Hank as if he were nothing. It's bad enough that they have Quinn, but to speak so callously about Hank has my rage bubbling.

"You killed an innocent man, and for that, you will pay, and you'll pay in the most painful way possible." I calmly inch toward him, my eyes narrowing as anger clouds my vision.

But he places the gun flush against my stomach, stopping my advance. "One more step and he's dead," he warns, referring to Quinn.

"He'll kill Phil before Phil has a chance to pull that trigger," I growl, fury lacing my words.

Deep down, I knew Quinn was missing because something sinister had occurred. I just never imagined this would be the cause.

Looking at my father in disgust, I realize this is the first time I've seen him since the night he killed Hank. My feelings of hate and loathing are amplified tenfold, and I decide this asshole doesn't deserve the title of being my father.

"Thomas," I sneer, and I don't fail to see him flinch at my formality. "If you're holding my boyfriend as collateral, then good luck with that. He's a bigger pain in the ass than I am."

I chuckle with indifference, hoping I'm doing the right thing. I don't want him to see how affected I am that they're holding Quinn prisoner.

If he knows how much he means to me, he'll be the one leverage they have over me, and I won't risk his life that way.

The shock is clear across Thomas's hollow face, and it's only now I realize he's also dressed for the ball in a cheap suit, his mask pushed back off his face.

"Maybe I'll just kill you in front of him, then. Or even better, kill him in front of you."

The thought of Quinn's life being in danger kills me, but I must remain composed and make sure my poker face doesn't slip.

"Fine, let's go," I spit, shoving past him.

"Slow," he hisses between clenched teeth, replacing his mask just as I do mine. "You make a scene, and I shoot the first person I see. Here's hoping that person is your whore of a mother or her bastard child."

I freeze when he mentions them, as there's no denying the sheer vehemence in his tone. I have no doubt he'll shoot them because they are of no value to him. But I am. Why? What does he want with me? I'm almost too afraid to find out.

"You make one wrong move, and I'll make sure you regret it," Thomas says, roughly grabbing my bicep and leading me through the sea of clueless people as he conceals the gun in the waistband of his pants.

The black-and-white effect, which I once thought clever, is now utterly disturbing, and the masks, blinding people to what is happening before their eyes, now seem ironic. But would anyone help me if they realized? I knew this day would come sooner or later, and I refuse to bring another soul down with me.

Considering my circumstances, I walk as casually as possible, trying to avoid eye contact with anyone and blend in with the crowd. As we walk through the den, I pray we don't bump into Polly or Cynthia, afraid for their safety if we do.

Once we pass, invisible to the happy partygoers, we only have the living room left—the hardest room to pass through undetected. I wedge through a swarm of strangers who are thankfully too intoxicated to notice my startled appearance and heavy breathing.

We're steps away from the foyer when Polly calls out to me. I curse myself for celebrating prematurely.

She runs over, holding her gown in her hands so she won't trip.

I attempt to lunge forward, but Thomas squeezes my arm. "One more step and I'll kill her."

A breath hitches in my throat at his threat because I know it's not empty.

"Mia, my mystery man has gone missing. Have you seen him?" she asks, oblivious to the man grinding his jaw behind me.

"No, I haven't. Now move," I abruptly say, attempting to push past her.

The hurt that passes over her face crushes me, and I know I've just undone whatever headway we've made.

"Well, excuse me." She narrows her eyes, still ignoring my brooding shadow. "What the fuck is wrong with you?"

I have three seconds to get rid of her, as I know Thomas will blow her head right off in five.

"Go bother someone else, you fucking brat!" As her eyes widen at my harsh words, I mouth the word, "Run."

For a nanosecond, I see confusion flutter across her features, but as her eyes flick to Thomas, she gets it.

Giving nothing away, she retorts, "Fuck you!" and shoves past us, storming away.

I let out the breath I was holding and quickly continue walking until we reach the quiet foyer, awaiting further instruction.

"Upstairs," Thomas hisses, pulling me toward the staircase.

As I ascend each step, I know that whatever I'm walking into will change me forever, but I continue walking. With Thomas breathing down my neck with his rank-smelling breath, I'm actually thankful when we arrive at the study so I can get the hell away from him.

"You ready to face your future?" Thomas chuckles, reaching over my shoulder to open the door.

"Fuck you," I respond, which is met with a gun barrel being whipped across my temple.

I barely register the pain because as he opens the door, my eyes fall to the slumped, unconscious man tied to a chair, his hair covering his face. Behind him stands Phil, wearing a shit-eating grin when he sees me.

The person tied to the chair isn't Quinn. It's someone I keep dragging into my mess.

However, I don't have time to react because Phil addresses me, making my skin crawl.

"Mia, it's so lovely to see you. It's been so long." He smiles, his arms outstretched for a hug.

"Not long enough," I bark, blood staining my white dress from my bleeding wound.

"Oh, still the little smart-ass, I see." He chuckles like this is all a big joke. "How I've missed you and your tenacity."

"Go fuck yourself, you lowlife asshole," I snarl, proud of myself for not submitting to either him or Thomas.

"Well, look who's all grown up," Phil sneers, the smile disappearing off his face.

This is the Phil I know. The evil, sadistic psychopath I've known my entire life.

"Maybe you'll show some respect if I start carving up your boyfriend here." He yanks the hair of the tied man backward, exposing his beaten, bloodied face.

I gasp, covering my mouth with a trembling hand because the face I see may not be Quinn's, but it's Tristan's. They must have been watching us when we were on the balcony and grabbed him as soon as he left to search for Quinn.

So that leaves one question—where the fuck is Quinn?

Tristan is out cold, and his face has been beaten with enough force that his right eye is incredibly swollen and looks almost closed over.

"She does have feelings, it seems." Phil snickers while Thomas stands on the other side of Tristan, pointing the barrel at his temple.

"No!" I scream, lunging forward. "No, I'll do whatever you want. Just leave him alone."

He's hurt once again because of me, and I can't stand for him to pay penance for my crimes a second longer.

"Oh, I like when you beg." Phil snickers, letting Tristan go and running a hand over his gleaming bald head.

"Whatever you want, I'll do it. Just let him go," I plead,

refusing to cry as I meet his beady eyes.

"That's your problem, Mia. You care. You could be something in our world, a queen."

I flinch because we are worlds apart.

"But you decide to lead with your emotions, a sure downfall because you leave people like your little boyfriend here an open target for people like me to use for my gain. Pathetic." He scoffs, curling his lip at me in disgust.

Tristan groans, and I bite my lip, scared of what'll happen next. Scared of what happens when he becomes a witness to all this fucked-up shit.

I know Phil, and he doesn't like witnesses who could potentially bring down his empire. He'll dispose of Tristan as easily as he did Hank, and I can't allow that to happen—not again.

"What the fuck do you want from me?" I yell, angrily wiping the trickle of blood from my eyes. "Because whatever it is, this game is growing old, and I'm done playing."

I hope to come across as self-confident even though I'm shaking in fear.

"You're an impatient little thing. But you're right. I'm tired of this cat-and-mouse game. A game you were bound to lose. You see, you cost me a lot of money when you ran. And you know how I hate to lose money," he scolds, waving his finger at me.

"So as I see it, you're indebted to me. And you're no good to me dead…so it's time to pay up."

I must have misheard him because he's surely not implying I go back to working for him like nothing happened, is he? If he is, then I'm just as good as dead.

"You're out of your fucking mind!" I shout, taking a step forward, about ready to beat the confident smile off his reptilian face.

My father, however, instantly stops my tirade when he pulls back Tristan's head, exposing his neck at a painful angle, the gun still pressed to his temple.

Freezing, I retreat and raise my hands in surrender, my eyes meeting Tristan's, who is wide awake. He looks dejected and desperate as he mouths, "I'm sorry."

I shake my head, giving him a weak smile because he has nothing to be sorry for.

"No. There's no way I'm doing that. I can't," I add, hating how weak I sound.

"Oh, stop being so melodramatic," Phil says playfully. "You'll go back to being my number one girl, and for the moment, we'll forget the idea of you spreading your legs."

Tristan's eyes widen at my horrible truth, and I don't blame him. It's an awful reality, and sadly, it's mine.

"For the moment?" I ask, wiping my eyes, refusing to allow my tears to break free.

"Yes," he replies with a smile. "See? I'm a reasonable guy. Besides, I wouldn't want you to throw another tantrum and shoot your daddy again."

Tantrum? Is he serious? This isn't some little issue I'm rebelling against. It was my life—my humanity.

But I can't go back to that.

Whether I'm a drug dealer or a whore, it all leads to my ultimate demise. My soul slips away with each deal I make.

"No," I spit one final time, shaking my head.

"Is that your final answer?" Phil asks, crossing his arms over his broad chest as he leans back against the oak desk.

"Yes," I reply with finality, my eyes flicking to Tristan, who concurs with my decision.

"Kill him," Phil says casually to my father, who cocks the

trigger.

"No!" I scream, diving for Tristan, but Phil pulls a gun from his waistband and points it straight at me.

"You move, and you're both dead."

The tears I've been trying so hard to keep away fall, and I openly weep, so afraid for Tristan's life.

What choice do I have?

None.

I can't allow them to hurt Tristan. And that's what will happen if I say no again.

Phil is a sadist, and he likes to toy with people to get a rise out of them, as their fear fuels his inner psychopath. But Phil tires quickly, and like all psychopaths, he loves power and control. So by saying no, I'm taking that away from him, something which he will ensure I pay for.

And by pay, I mean he will go after everyone I love.

He won't stop until every person I care for is dead. And he'll make certain their final moments on this earth are beyond painful, so when that time comes, they'll beg him to kill them.

"Okay," I whisper, sickened by my decision. I look at Tristan, begging him to forgive me.

"Mia, no!" Tristan roars, his head shaking uncontrollably. "No! Kill me! Kill me! Let her go, please, let her go. Kill me, but let her go."

"No," I spit, my heart breaking at his chivalry.

"I have your word?" I say to Phil, my eyes narrowing.

"Cross my heart," he replies, gesturing over his chest, and I scoff, as he doesn't have one. "Not a hair on this pretty boy's head will be harmed."

Satisfied with his response, I whimper, "Okay...I'll do it."

"No!" Tristan cries, futilely pulling at his restraints.

Thomas finds watching Tristan fight against the ropes, which bind his wrists to the arms of the chair, simply hilarious, so I snarl, "Untie him. I'm not going anywhere with you until I know he's safe."

Thomas looks at Phil, like the dog he is, obviously asking his permission before proceeding.

"Fine." He sighs, brushing a piece of fluff from his black suit jacket, not at all perplexed by the scene before him.

"Mia, no—don't. Not for me. Please, don't risk your life for me," Tristan begs, fighting Thomas, moving from side to side as Thomas attempts to untie his hands.

"I have to. There's no other choice. My life is worth sacrificing if it means you get to live. You deserve redemption, but I don't. I never did," I sadly confess, thinking back to all the horrible things I've done.

"No!" Tristan bellows, desperately trying to break free. "You're a good person, Mia. Please don't give up. I need you. We all need you!"

"Stay still!" Thomas roars, whipping him across the face with his gun.

"You said you wouldn't hurt him!" I scream, my eyes focusing on the trickle of blood pouring from Tristan's mouth.

"Oops." Phil shrugs, unmoved by Thomas's violence.

"I'm sorry, Tristan." I sob into my palm. "Please forgive me."

Both Phil and Thomas laugh at my helplessness while a tear trickles down Tristan's bloodied cheek.

"This is suicide," he cries, his voice cracking.

"It's the only way," I reply in a mere whisper, shaking my head.

Thomas bends in front of Tristan, pulling a knife from his boot to hopefully untie him. But when the door bursts open, startling the four of us, we all freeze to see who has barged in and, hopefully, saved the day.

"Mia, are you in here?" Cynthia asks but gasps when she witnesses the scene of pure bedlam before her.

Thomas slowly stands when he sees her, and his face softens. But just as quickly, it then contorts as if remembering a bitter memory, tainting any love he once had for his wife.

"Thomas?" she wheezes, her hand flying to her throat.

But suddenly, something strange happens.

I watch as Cynthia's horrified gaze lands on Phil. She stares at him, never blinking, and I realize that behind her stare, I see…recognition and betrayal.

But that's impossible, isn't it?

However, my fears are confirmed when she takes a small step toward him, whispering, "Phillip?"

For the first time in my life, I see something remotely human pass over Phil's features as he evenly replies, "Hello… little sister."

Sister?

This is her brother?

He is my uncle?

Just when I thought my fucked-up family history couldn't get any more messed up, this goes and happens.

"*Sister*?" I spit. "You've got to be fucking joking."

My sanity has slipped, and I don't see it returning soon.

There has got to be some mistake because this man surely cannot be blood. This man, alongside my father, used and abused me for his personal gain and had no misgivings of doing it again.

How can this be?

What have I done to deserve not one but two family members exploiting me in such a cruel and callous way?

141

Whatever patience I have been holding disappears, and I need to harm them both for every single thing they've done to me over the years.

I'm ready to kill him with my bare hands, but when I see an armed and bloodied Quinn, followed by a terrified Polly, who's holding a Colt in her shaky hands, I realize things are about to get messy.

The next few seconds are the longest of my life, but we all act on instinct, as survival is the only thing that matters.

The moment Thomas sees Polly, he swiftly raises his gun and fires.

However, Tristan rocks his chair and slams into him, which results in Thomas being knocked off balance and the gun slipping from his hands.

As Thomas trips, his temple hits the edge of the desk, knocking him out cold, and he slumps to the floor in a messy heap. Tristan's chair is tipped on its side, and he's flailing around, attempting to break free from his restraints.

Cynthia screams, but all I can focus on is Thomas's gun, which sits discarded under the desk.

I make a mad dive for it, scrambling to reach it despite the fact I hear a gun being cocked near my head. I am within inches from reaching it when a shot is fired.

I freeze for a nanosecond, and when I conclude I'm not dead, I grab the gun and turn, pointing it out in front of me.

"You little fuck, you shot me!" Phil yells, clutching the front of his shoulder as he drops to the ground with a thud.

I turn to look at Quinn, who's holding the smoking gun.

"Oh boo-fucking-hoo," he spits out, rushing to my side as I attempt to stand on my unsteady legs.

"Are you okay?" I sob, throwing myself into Quinn's arms and forgetting about my shakiness when I see his swollen eye and blood trickling from his ear.

"I'm fine," he breathlessly replies, crushing me against his chest and placing frantic kisses all over my temple and cheeks. His hands skim down my body, ensuring I'm not hurt.

"Looks like we got the wrong guy," Phil sarcastically says. "Or perhaps you would be far more useful spreading your legs, then?"

"Shut up!" I scream, tearing from Quinn's embrace and storming over to a snickering Phil, who has propped himself up against the wall, clutching his left shoulder.

"Looks like you'd make more money being a whore."

My body trembles in rage, and I stop inches from his feet, aiming the gun at his face.

"Go ahead and do it." He shrugs with a chuckle. "Your little redhead friend's life depends on it."

"What?" I gasp, my finger easing off the trigger.

What does Abi have to do with this?

"Well, when he," he says, flicking his head toward a seething Tristan, who has thankfully been untied and is standing near Quinn. "Up and left in a huff, we knew he was coming here."

"You knew I was here?" I gasp, startled to have my suspicions confirmed.

"Yes, of course we did," Phil spits, looking at me like I'm stupid.

"Then why?" I protest, my fingers clutching the gun. "If you knew where I was this entire time, why wouldn't you just kill me? Why did you drag this entire ordeal out?"

Phil tsks me, his hand pressing his bleeding wound. "Don't you get it? I don't want to kill you; I want to break you and all of those around you. I told you, Mia, you're very valuable to me."

Realization kicks in, but I don't allow him to elaborate because I don't want Quinn to know why he's kept me alive. Because if he found out that Phil intends to have me go back to my old ways, Quinn would kill him, no questions asked.

But the thing is, I need him and Thomas alive to clear our names. That's the fucked-up thing about this, which I've only just come to understand.

If we kill them now, how do we explain to the police that the people who we're accusing of the crimes we supposedly committed are dead in my mother's home?

Self-defense?

Sadly, that excuse won't stick.

Whichever way you look at it, we need them alive until Abi's dad can clear our names and expose Thomas and Phil for the vile human beings they are.

To the police, Phil is a hippy herbalist with a clean rap sheet, and my deadbeat dad is the father of a delinquent teen who looks totally guilty of the crimes she's been accused of. We need Abi's dad to come through and have solid evidence against them because who would a jury believe?

Me—a troubled teen and a high school dropout with a mile-long rap sheet?

Or Phil—the perfect social chameleon who pays his taxes on time?

Only when our names are cleared, and Thomas and Phil are rightfully accused and charged for the crimes they've committed, can we can dispose of these lowlife assholes.

But sadly, the only way for the police to charge them would be with their cooperation. And for that to happen, I need them both alive.

There's no loyalty here, and I know without a doubt one would rat the other out faster than the police can say "reduced sentence for being an informant."

And when that happens, when they're both found guilty, cementing our innocence, that's when I can deliver my own hand of justice.

The police can lead a blind investigation into their whereabouts, but they'll both be dead. And they'll be dead by my hand.

But now, because of Abi, their survival is all the more imperative.

"What have you done to her?"

"Nothing. Yet. I've had my guys trailing her and him," he says, jutting his chin out toward Tristan. "So like I was saying, when he up and left, he left her all alone to fend for herself."

Phil cackles, his voice hoarse after smoking way too many Cuban cigars throughout his life.

"You son of a bitch!" Tristan yells, lunging forward, but Quinn restrains him.

Phil snickers with a nonchalant shrug. "Not my fault you're in love with her. The way she was all over you on the balcony made me think it was him," he says, gesturing to Quinn, and the blood drains from my face as Quinn no doubt feels a stab of betrayal at his words.

"But hey, my bad, we beat up the wrong boyfriend."

I now realize they thought Tristan was Quinn. With the suit and masks, it does make identifying who's who a little difficult. But it looks as if Quinn has also taken a beating, but I don't have time to address that yet.

"Answer the question! What have you done to her?" I yell, waving the gun in his face.

"The moment I don't call in with my boys, they'll have their fun with her." I swallow the bile in my throat as he concludes, "Then they'll carve her up and bury her, piece by piece, where no one will ever find her."

"You're sick."

Phil shrugs like it takes no fucking genius to figure that out.

"Call them off!"

"No chance in hell." He laughs, shaking his head.

"Call them off!" I scream, lunging toward him and pressing the barrel to his temple.

"I don't think so."

I smack him across the face with the butt of my gun, refusing to stand silent to his insults a second longer.

"Oh, you're going to pay for that," he grunts, blood trickling from the wound to his temple.

"It'll be worth it to see you dead." I lightly adjust my finger on the trigger, ready to blow his brains all over the pristine wall.

My plans to allow him to live have just been made redundant. I would much rather figure out another way to prove our innocence and save Abi than have this motherfucker take another breath.

"Mia, no!" Cynthia yells, halting my movements.

"Please don't tell me you feel anything for this asshole," I spit, my eyes never wavering from Phil's.

"No, of course not, but you can't do that here. It'll ruin Chandler," she sobs, pleading I listen.

I have Hank's murderer within my grasp, and all she cares about is her fucking husband.

However, my voice of reason taps me on the shoulder by wrapping a warm hand around the gun I'm shakily holding.

"She's right, Red. They'll know it's us. It'll get complicated and sticky for all of us." Quinn never forces my hand, only providing the support I so desperately need.

I want to scream at Quinn, reminding him that this was our plan from the very beginning—to kill Phil and Thomas.

Yes, when the original plan was set in motion, it was going to be done so anonymously, tying us in no way to their murder. But now, everything has changed, and I know he's right.

When on the run, it was so much easier to orchestrate a plan where my dad and Phil ended up dead. But here and now, things are so different. Their dead bodies will lead directly to us, and it's not only Quinn and me who will pay the price, but rather, everyone in this room, in this house, will be a suspect.

It's all so complicated, and that's why Phil chose tonight. It's the perfect time to strike.

When we do this, it can't be in a house full of witnesses, who have already most likely heard the commotion and stray gunshot upstairs, which, when I turn, I see is embedded in Cynthia's leg.

"Oh my God, you got shot!" I cry, only just resisting the urge to go over and see if she's okay.

"It's just a flesh wound. I'm fine," she says, holding her hand over her bleeding thigh.

I suddenly become aware of my surroundings. My need for vengeance has blinded me to the people around me, and I hate that I allowed my humanity to slip.

Polly sits in the corner with her gun laid by her feet, white as a ghost. She has her legs drawn up to her chest and sits rocking, backward and forward, with her eyes closed. She hums an indistinguishable tune, but the harmony does nothing to conceal her fear.

My heart breaks because a sixteen-year-old doesn't need to see this.

Just because this is my normal, and this is my world, I

tend to forget this is far from being normal for others. I've just taken away Polly's innocence, and for that, I will never forgive myself.

"Let's go," Quinn murmurs, and I turn, confused about where we should go.

"Go?" I question. "What about them?"

I look at an unconscious Thomas and a nearly passed-out Phil.

"We leave them here, and we run," Quinn says slowly.

"No! We kill them both!" I stubbornly argue, shaking my head at the possibility of letting them live.

"Please, Mia, no, not here," Cynthia once again begs. "Chandler's career will be ruined. Please don't."

I despise that everyone is taking away my one chance at killing the two people who ruined my life. And the two people who killed Hank. This moment has been driving me for so many weeks, and now that I've been told no, I just can't accept it.

"We'll take them with us! We can keep them hostage until our names are cleared. Hell, it'll be worth going to jail to see them both dead. To see them pay for what they did to Hank."

As I think of Hank's last moments on this earth, my finger twitches on the trigger, ready to claim my retribution.

But Quinn softly squeezes my hand with his. "Let's go."

"Let her do it, Quinn! He deserves to die for what he did and for what he wants her to do!"

I spin toward Tristan, silently begging him not to disclose our secret.

He thankfully lets it go and turns his head away, clenching his jaw.

"Why can't they go with us?" I yell, knowing the answer.

"Because of the five hundred witnesses downstairs,"

Quinn calmly replies. "Someone will see us, and then we'll be in even more trouble. All of Abi's dad's hard work would have been pointless if we get caught. Abi's life depends on his survival, Red."

He's right, but I don't want to see reason.

"There's a back way? There's got to be a back way?" I beg, looking at Cynthia.

"Do you really think he'll go quietly?" She sniffles, and I look at Phil, who smirks menacingly.

No doubt he'll create a song and dance about being kidnapped. And if we gag him, we risk someone seeing us.

"So what, we just leave him here?" I ask, disbelieving this is even an option.

No, I refuse to accept this.

"Make the guests leave," I demand, though I know that would draw even more attention to our situation.

There really is no other choice.

But leaving them here without any consequence for what they did leaves a bitter taste in my mouth.

Sagging in defeat, I whisper, "He killed Hank. He needs to pay."

"And he will," Quinn states, slowly unwrapping my fingers from the gun.

"How do we know he won't cause a scene with the guests when we leave?"

It's my final plea.

Phil answers me this time. I almost forgot he was here. "Because, Mia, you know how I hate witnesses, and I don't have a problem with the lovely guests downstairs because they don't owe me millions of dollars, unlike you. No, my only problem is with you. And because of that, the people you love will pay for your sins.

"Those people downstairs can enjoy their Christmas, and I'll sneak out, undetected, like I was never here, as I too do not wish to draw attention to myself. I want you, Mia—only you. Those people aren't collateral, but everyone in this room is," he says, looking at every single person behind me.

"So you better run far, far, far away because when I find you, I won't be so generous."

I know he's baiting me, and it's working.

I'm thankful Quinn has removed the gun from my hands because I would have used it, punishing him for his threat alone.

"Polly, go downstairs and tell a few guests I've gone to bed with a migraine. Pass on my sincerest apologies for calling it a night," Cynthia says, breathing through her pain.

"Then they'll go home, right?" I ask, hopeful.

"No, Mia, they'll stay until the sun comes up. They don't care who's here. As long as there's food and brandy, they're oblivious to anything else."

"Rude, inconsiderate assholes," I spit under my breath.

"Polly?" Cynthia coos, and I turn to look at a broken Polly who is still rocking in the corner.

Quinn gives me a small smile before he turns and crouches down in front of a comatose Polly. I'm hoping he can help her pull this off.

Tristan takes his spot beside me, and every muscle in my beaten body cramps in protest, but I won't move.

"This one likes you," Phil leers, looking at Tristan. "You've got your hands full, don't you?"

He laughs while my temper rages.

How dare he think he knows me and talks to me like we're friends. I may be forced to leave him here, but there's no chance I'll go quietly.

"Listen to me, you motherfucker," I snarl, dropping to both knees in front of him. "You are a parasite, a bottom-feeder wishing you were a somebody, when, in reality, you're a nobody. You're a weak, pathetic loser." Phil clenches his jaw, as I know how much he hates being called a loser.

But I continue as his face turns a fiery red and the muscles in his neck pop out in anger.

"The next time I see you, I *will* kill you. You will pay for what you did to Hank, and so help me God, if you so much as touch a hair on Abi's head, you'll pay in ways unimaginable."

"Tough words, little girl," Phil says, but he backs up against the wall when I hover inches from his face.

"I've learned from the best," I state, displaying no fear. "Mark my words, this is the face of the person who is about to tear down your empire, brick by brick. You created a monster…Uncle."

Phil's nostrils flare.

"I won't stop until I destroy the one thing you love more than yourself—power. You'll watch it all crumble before your eyes, and then, only then, will I fucking kill you," I conclude, slowly rising to full height.

"You fucking little whore! I'll end you!" Phil screams, pounding his bloodied fist against the wall because he can hear the truth behind my words.

"Not if I end you first," I reply, reaching for his discarded gun behind the desk. I pistol-whip him so hard across the temple his head snaps back with a sickening thud.

Not expecting the blow, he bobbles his head forward, and the fact he's still awake pisses me off, so I drop to both knees once more, and I hit him again, and again, and again.

He's scarcely conscious, but I yank his hand away from his bleeding shoulder and dig my fingers into the bullet wound, which has him gasping for breath and then passing out cold from the pain. As he slumps to the floor, I barely resist the urge to pound him till he's a bloodied, beaten pulp on the ground.

Quinn bends beside me, whispering, "Enough, Red." His soft lips touch my temple. "C'mon, we've got to go."

My chest heaves from the force of my strikes, and my body hums with adrenaline, and although every muscle tells me to fight, I don't. I allow him to help me up and watch mutely as he places his suit jacket over my shoulders, cloaking my bloody, disheveled form.

I blindly watch as he leads me into our room, where he packs me a bag as I sit comatose on the end of the bed.

I guess now I really do look like a punk Cinderella slathered in blood and gore. But fairy tales are for children because this right here, it's real. Maybe I could write my own fairy tale, one with a modern twist of the girl who slays her own monsters and never looks back.

Ten

don't remember getting into a car and driving for three hours.

Nor do I remember walking into a cabin in the woods—Cynthia's secret holiday home—tucked away in a hidden nook of lush green bushland and remote open spaces.

And I certainly don't remember the bullet in Cynthia's leg being removed by a local, retired doctor friend, who swore his secrecy over what he saw.

But it happened.

I know it did because I watched it through someone else's eyes, and although those eyes belonged to me, I felt like a stranger within my own body.

How could I have left them there?

Yes, it made sense in theory, but practically, it made no sense at all. I wanted them dead, and I had that option, but we took this road instead, and now, we're on the run—again.

I'm curled on my side, barely clothed, in a bed with soft white sheets that provide me little comfort because all I can think about is how tonight changed me. I will never be the same person I once was. I terrified myself with my venomous words because I meant it all.

I meant every single awful word, and that's what scares me.

I don't want anger, violence, and revenge to be my fuel for survival. I just want to be normal, and this anger eating away at me is far from being normal. All my steps forward have just been erased, and now, I'm back at the starting line with no energy to finish the race.

I just want to sleep, but I can't. I'm too tired for rest, and I'm too tired to think. But my overactive mind won't switch off, and I doubt it'll do so anytime soon.

Wearily raising my head off the pillow, I see it's just after two o'clock in the morning, but it feels so much later.

I slump back onto the pillow, and my eyes take in the small room, lit by the bathroom light peeking out under the adjoining door. It's then that I realize the shower is running.

I can't believe we're back here, on the run, after foolishly believing we'd finally caught a break. When will this shitstorm end? When will it finally be over?

A little voice inside me whispers I can change that because I know what Phil wants.

I was stupid to think I could ever cut free from a life you never leave unless it's in a body bag. I'm never going to be normal because this fucked-up and crazy shit is starting to slowly become my usual once again.

The shower switches off, returning me to the here and now, and I want Quinn to hold me more than anything. I need him to make me feel safe and be the tether to my withering sanity, which slips away with every breath I take.

After a few minutes, the bathroom door opens, and I catch a quick glimpse of a naked Quinn as he turns off the bathroom light. I make no attempt to move and just lay still, listening to Quinn softly shift around the room, rifling through his bag and slipping on a pair of boxers.

His actions have me aware of my lack of undergarments.

I'm wearing a huge T-shirt, which I know is Quinn's because I can smell him on the material. He most likely showered me and bundled me up in his shirt before putting me to bed.

I don't remember that either.

The blankets are pulled back, and Quinn tiredly lowers himself onto the smooth sheets, no doubt his beaten body protesting every move he makes.

"You okay?" Quinn whispers, knowing I'm not asleep.

"No," I honestly reply. There's no point in lying because Quinn would see straight through me.

"It's okay to not be okay."

"My dad and my uncle both sold me out. How does one accept that and stay sane?" I state, not expecting any answers.

"Uncle?" Quinn asks. I forgot he wasn't present when the revelation from hell was revealed.

"Phil is Cynthia's brother. Therefore, that son of a bitch, sadly, is my uncle."

"Holy shit."

"Yeah," I blankly reply, feeling so numb that I actually ache. "It's just one thing after another. When will we catch a break?"

"I know." He sighs, bundling me up into his bare chest and kissing the top of my head.

We have so much to discuss, but I don't even know where to start. But there is one question I need to know—where was he?

When I was looking for him, where did he go?

"Where were you?" I ask, sinking into his warm embrace.

He remains silent for quite some time, and I think he may not answer, but my heart breaks once again when he does.

"The moment I left you, I was jumped from behind. I was so stupid because I let my guard down, and when I came to, it was because Polly slapped my cheeks, screaming at me to wake up because you were in trouble.

"They dumped me in the room next door to ours, so I grabbed what I could weapon-wise from our bags and searched for you. I was so worried about you. If anything had happened…" He adds, "I let you down. I'm so sorry."

"You have nothing to be sorry for."

"Yes, I do. I shouldn't have let my guard down, and thanks to my carelessness, you and Tristan got injured."

The mention of Tristan hurts my heart, and Quinn feels me freeze under his hold.

"He's fine; the doctor stitched him up. He'll be a little sore, but he's okay," he says, but I don't fail to pick up on his robotic tone.

I know his bitterness stems from Phil's misunderstanding about my reunion with Tristan being romantic. In reality, it was just two friends reuniting after being apart for so long.

Quinn needs to know that.

"What Phil said," I utter, but Quinn shifts, loosening his grip around me.

"It doesn't matter."

I wish it wasn't so dark because I can't see his face.

"Nothing happened between Tristan and me," I continue

because it does matter. "I hugged him, and to onlookers, I can understand how one could misinterpret our exchange as being romantic, but it wasn't. I was just so happy to see him."

Quinn softly pushes me away, sitting up against the headboard. "I don't want to talk about your reunion. Whatever happened, happened, and that got Tristan hurt. I mean, the fact they thought he was your boyfriend…"

The hurt in his tone is clear as day.

"Quinn—"

But he cuts me off. "It doesn't matter. Don't worry about it. We've got more important things to—"

I don't let him finish. I crawl up his body, wrapping my arms around his neck. "It matters, Quinn. *You* matter. You're everything to me. I'm sorry…for everything," I say, not even sure what I'm apologizing for because I'm damn sorry for the whole evening.

"Shh," he coos, resting his chin atop my head. "We just stick to the original plan, and we wait for Abi's dad to come through. I called her, and she's fine."

I feel awful for not even checking on her.

"You told her everything?"

"Yes. She'll be careful. She's a smart girl."

He's right. Now that Abi knows it all, I have no doubt she'll push her father even harder to prove our innocence.

"When will this end?" I whisper, closing my eyes and encircling myself around his body.

"Soon," he replies, but I know he can't guarantee that. "Besides, Tristan is here now, so that makes you happy, right?"

My eyes pop open. I have no idea what he means by that comment.

Yes, of course I'm happy that Tristan is here, but does Quinn think he was some kind of substitute while Tristan was away? Does he think I was using him until Tristan arrived?

I don't understand why there is jealousy between them. I mean, I don't think I've ever given Quinn a reason to think I want anyone other than him. Back home, I know he believed Tristan to be the better brother for me, but I never wanted Tristan.

It was always him. It'll always be him.

Deep down, I can't help but think this inexplicable jealousy has something to do with their childhood, which Quinn still refuses to fully discuss. The glimpses he has shared are painful, and I don't blame him for being so reserved about his past. I have firsthand experience with how a tainted past can pollute a bright future.

But whatever his history, I need him to know that he's all I want. All I need.

Reaching for the hem of my T-shirt, I pull it over my head and toss it behind me. I'm now totally naked and exposed in front of him. This is the only way I can show him that I need him and only him.

"Touch me," I boldly whisper, reaching for his hand and drawing it up to my bare breast.

My nipple hardens the instant his warm fingers encircle my flesh, and after the fucked-up night we've just had, it's nice to feel this one simple act of passion and honesty.

I remain still as he rolls his thumb over my nipple before his large palm cups my breast in one hand. He then lowers his lips and pulls at my nipple.

An unrefined groan echoes in my throat because it feels so damn good.

Arching backward, I thrust my chest forward, pushing more of myself into his mouth. My hips begin moving of their own accord, needing the delicious friction I feel from his growing erection. The moment my breast pops free, he cups the back of my neck and pulls me down to meet his eager, sinful lips.

We kiss like starved creatures, and the moment I draw his lip ring into my mouth, I know we've crossed the line of no return.

He reaches between us and begins running his fingers along my sex. I moan and buck forward, needing more.

I want him more than I've ever wanted him before, and I think back to my idea of what I wanted to give him for Christmas. The gift isn't much, but it's the only thing I can offer him that isn't stained and remains untainted by my past.

And that gift is me.

The moment his finger enters me, a guttural moan resonates in my chest, and Quinn's animalistic growl has my entire body undulating in desire and need.

But I need more, and I make that clear as I reach down between us, freeing his erection from the confines of his boxers.

"Make love to me," I whisper, biting my lip when I hear him hiss in response to my words.

However, he surprises me by sadly confessing, "I don't know how."

That's not entirely true as I've seen him.

I've caught him in the act, and although nothing was loving about it, he engaged in the deed with much passion and enthusiasm.

"But I've...seen you," I say, hating to taint this moment with that vulgar memory.

Quinn shakes his head. "Nothing about that involved love."

I don't understand what he's telling me.

"Red, I've...fucked plenty of girls." I cringe at not only the word but also the visual. "But making love," he continues. "That's totally uncharted waters for me."

What is he telling me? Has he never been in love?

"And you're not ready," he concludes, removing his finger.

How does he know if I'm ready or not?

Enraged, I reach for his hand and place it back between my legs. "I beg to differ."

He hisses but draws his hand away again because he's just as stubborn as I am.

"I don't mean that. I mean in here." He touches my temple.

Deep down, I know he's right, but I can't help but think he isn't ready, either.

I bite my lip, feeling stupid, vulnerable, and shy. I also feel slightly rejected. This isn't the first time Quinn has said no, and it's a blow to a girl's ego.

"If you don't want me, just tell me."

Quinn's heavy breathing rattles in his chest as he reaches for my hand, placing it between us so I can feel how hard he is.

"You know how much I fucking want you. Listen to me because I'm only going to tell you this once. I don't know how to make...love." He says the word with such distaste that I suddenly wonder if I read this wrong.

Feeling a little self-conscious, I attempt to shift off him, but he stops me as he grasps my chin between his fingers, pressing a soft kiss against the corner of my mouth.

"I don't know how to love, Red, because I've never been in love. I can fuck you," he confesses, and I shiver at his coarseness because it's a total turn-on. "But love? We're both virgins when it comes to love."

"You've never been in love?" I ask in case I've misconstrued what he's just confessed.

"No," he replies, and I don't miss the touch of sadness behind his response.

"But someone has loved you, right?" I ask because I want to believe that we're all loved by at least one person in this world—even me.

However, when Quinn remains quiet, I feel my heart breaking.

We all need love, whether we crave it or not, because it's nice to know that someone cares enough to keep us in their thoughts. It's human nature to want to be loved. But to feel unloved? I can tell you now that nothing is more heartbreaking than feeling unworthy of being loved.

I don't know whether to be insulted, so I remain quiet as I attempt to process his confession. I may be a virgin when it comes to sex, but my feelings for Quinn? There is absolutely no doubt in my mind that I love him.

But now, the question is, what does he feel for me? Is it something like love? Or at least like? I need to know.

"Do you think you could?"

"Could what?"

"Fall in love."

He doesn't respond but commences kissing down my neck and chest, resting over my fluttering heart.

"You make anything possible," he finally whispers, the metal of his hoop tickling my heated skin. "God knows I don't deserve your love, but I want it…so very much."

He slowly lowers me onto my back, his body hovering over mine.

Just as I'm about to tell him that he has it, that he has me, he professes, "Let me love you the only way I know how."

He licks down my body, his barbell leaving an impassioned

trail as he descends farther down my torso.

He twirls his tongue inside my belly button, and I arch off the bed in preparation for what's to come. The moment he reaches the apex of my thighs, I buck upward, and Quinn's hot breath warms my sex.

"I love how you smell," Quinn says, shifting closer and breathing in deeply.

I freeze because this is the first time he has used that word to express his feelings.

Before I can process another thought, however, he continues. "And I love how you taste."

He licks at my entrance with his skillful tongue.

My back bows, and my eyes roll to the back of my head as this sensation, mixed with his words, will have me coming in a matter of seconds.

But he's relentless.

"I love how much you want me," he says against my clit and quickly flicks his barbell across my heated flesh.

"I…I love how much you want me," I parrot breathlessly, surprised I'm able to construct a coherent sentence as he sinks his tongue into me.

"I love how I make your heart race," he hoarsely says, sliding his hand up between my breasts and resting it over my heart.

I mewl the moment he begins playing with my nipples, keeping in time with his tongue as he devours me down below.

"I love the sounds you make when you're close to coming." He kisses over my clit, and as if on cue, I purr in response to his touch.

He slides his hand back down my body, and his finger now joins his mouth as he opens me up to him and invades my body like never before. His fingers, mouth, and tongue drive me over the edge, and I can't help the feral moan that rips from my throat because this feels beyond incredible.

Quinn is wrong when he says he doesn't know how to love because this, right here, is driven by pure love. This selfless act is guided by love, and although he doesn't know it, I feel adored by Quinn every moment of every day. I have from the first moment I met him, and I'll make sure I show him that from now on.

But now—now I want to come.

"Oh fuck." I groan a little louder than expected as it echoes off the small cabin walls.

"Shh." Quinn chuckles from between my legs, his warm breath sending tiny goose bumps over my entire body.

But I'm anything but quiet as I cry, "Holy fuck!" at an ear-splitting level when he twirls his barbell around my center.

Quinn chuckles once again, and before another string of profanities can come tearing from my throat, his hand softly covers my mouth, muffling my cries.

However, I can mute my impassioned screams in another way, a way that benefits us both.

I open my mouth in a silent demand of what I want. Quinn obeys, slowly inserting the two fingers he had snugly inside me moments ago. They taste like me, and as I moan around him, Quinn growls, burying his head deeper between my legs.

But his fingers are not what I want in my mouth.

As hard as it is to pry myself away from him, I wiggle out of his hold, and before he has time to protest, I push him onto his back and turn around so I'm positioned up near his head. We're instantly on the same page as he scoots me backward and yanks my legs over each side of his head. Just like that, I straddle his face.

The moment his tongue makes contact with my sex once again, I lean forward, yank his boxers all the way down, and take him into my mouth, sucking with a desperate need to consume him whole.

"Fuck," Quinn mumbles, and as his voice vibrates throughout my entire body, my release is so close that I can taste it.

I suck harder, taking as much as I can into my mouth, and at this angle, I can appreciate how thick and large he is. I swallow as deep as I can go, and as he hits the back of my throat, I try not to gag.

The sensation has Quinn swelling in my mouth, so I do it again because I want him to explode in an earth-shattering release.

Licking him from base to tip, I reach down and stroke his shaft as my mouth encloses his head, tasting his pre-cum.

He flicks over my clit, and the barbell feels like a cold, hot spank. It's my undoing.

I come so loudly with my hips fucking his face, but I don't let him go and continue sucking. Seconds later, he joins me, coming hard and loud in my mouth, and I love every second of it.

It takes me minutes before I'm able to unwrap myself from around his body, and when I do, I feel pleasurably numb. I curl myself into him as he throws the blanket over our naked bodies, cuddling me into his side.

I am finally on the cusp of sleep, but Quinn's heavy words have me opening my eyes, giving him my full attention.

"With you, Red…this feels like it."

"Like what?" I whisper so softly, I'm afraid he may not have heard me.

But his reply lets me know he's heard me, loud and clear.

"Like love. Because this…with you, it feels…something like love."

I can't stop the smile from spreading from cheek to cheek because it's nice to know that the one person who loves me is…Quinn.

Eleven

I wake before Lucky and Quinn but don't have the heart to wake either of them.

Quinn's confession last night nearly broke me, and it makes me even more determined to find out about his past. If we move forward, I need him to trust me with his secrets because once they're revealed, they'll no longer be secrets but a part of his past.

Silently slipping out of bed, I dress in my jeans and Quinn's sweater. Just before I open the door, I stop and inhale the collar, loving his scent.

I close the door behind me and look down the long hallway. I have no idea where to go. An old wooden staircase is to my right, so I venture downstairs, hoping to stumble across some well-needed coffee.

Downstairs is small but cozy, and it's everything I would

expect a holiday home to look like. The small fire warms the floorboards, and my cold feet instantly thaw out with the heat. I take a quick look around the living area and see a few family photos sitting on the mantel.

Curious, I pick up a silver frame and see the faces of a juvenile Polly, a happy Cynthia, and a handsome man, who I presume is Chandler. Standing in front of the cabin, they smile broadly while holding a fish and looking proud of their catch.

They look so normal, but I can't help but wonder if there lies an unhappy, broken soul behind Cynthia's smile with a shitload of baggage, just like me?

After the events of last night, I decide to go easy on her since she's the only family I have. She and Polly came through for me, and if it weren't for Cynthia looking for me and Polly waking up Quinn, I hate to think where Tristan and I would be.

Every time I envision Tristan beaten, bruised, and begging for my life, a fierce anger overtakes my senses, and I need a moment to calm down. But I'm not here to dwell on the past. I'm here to focus on the future and be pleased about showing Thomas and Phil that I'm a different girl than the one they once knew.

The smell of coffee reaches my nostrils, which is exactly what I need.

I gently replace the frame on the mantel and hum in delight when I enter the kitchen and see a coffeepot brewing. I have no idea where anything is and feel incredibly nosy going through the cupboards, but I strike it lucky when I find the mugs above the stove.

I fill the mug to the brim with much-needed coffee, and my body instantly unwinds the moment I take a small sip.

Cradling my mug, I look outside the window above the sink.

The rain clouds imply it will be another wet day, but as I look through the lace curtains, I see a beautiful lake in the backyard, and the gloomy weather complements the murky waters. The stunning landscape extends farther than my eye can see.

A dense green forest complements the lake, and suddenly, a bare-chested Tristan emerges from the woodlands, casually jogging.

I quickly avert my eyes as his track pants sit quite low on his narrow waist, revealing an impressive body. I feel wrong looking at him because he's barely clothed. But I find my gaze straying back.

I watch him cool down by doing overhead stretches, highlighting the length of his muscled body and ripped abs.

He's far enough away that he can't see me, but I still feel like I'm doing something wrong.

Just as I'm about to look away, a voice causes me to yelp and spill my coffee all over Quinn's sweater.

"Who are you spying on?" Polly asks on a yawn.

"Spying? I'm not spying." I quickly scoff, wiping the hot coffee from my top.

"Sure." She peers over my shoulder and playfully moans. "No wonder you were spying. He's gorgeous. Black eye and all."

"Coffee?" I ask, needing to change the subject.

"Sure," Polly replies, taking one last look at Tristan before giving me a small smile.

I pour her a cup, and we stand silently staring out the window.

Every so often, my eyes drift to Tristan, who has thankfully thrown on his T-shirt, and as he sits, wincing when stretching out his hamstrings, I know that last night impacted us all.

"I'm sorry about last night."

Polly sighs before slowly turning toward me, and it's the first time I've really paid any attention to her appearance.

The bags under her eyes rival mine, and her hair is the same as last night, just a little messier as wisps have come undone and fall across her face. She's in ripped sweats and an oversized black sweatshirt and I almost don't recognize her as the girl in red from last night.

That reality makes me unbelievably miserable, and again, I feel the need to apologize.

"Polly, what you saw last night…I really am sorry you had to witness that. If I could take it back, I would. But I can't, so all I can offer you is a shoulder to cry on or something," I awkwardly say, clearing my throat as I'm not good with this whole consoling crap.

Polly gives me a stiff smile as she brushes her hair off her face. "It's fine. I'm not going to cry. I know it wasn't your fault."

"No, it's not fine. That bullshit you saw? That's my reality, not yours. I would never wish that upon anyone. I wish you were never exposed to such violence because that shit—it changes a person. I mean, look at me."

I hate the truth behind my words.

"I am looking at you, Mia, and all I see is a strong, powerful woman. You didn't waver once, and you weren't at all scared. You were like a fucking superhero," she says in admiration. "I can only dream of standing up to someone the way you did."

"I was scared," I confess. "But not for me. I was scared for you. I was scared for everyone else in that room."

Polly nods, taking a small sip of her coffee as she turns to look out the window. "And that's what makes you nothing like them," she whispers, and I know who she's referring to. "I've come to realize that you're not the bad guy. I mean, I've met the villains in this story, and I now understand why you are the way you are."

I don't know what to say.

"Truce?" she asks, turning to face me and timidly extending her hand.

I stare down at her hand, mouth agape, not knowing if her peace offering is genuine. But going with my gut instinct, I slowly reach forward and slip my hand in hers. We shake limply, both uncomfortable with the sisterly moment, but a part of me wants to pull her in for a hug.

Thankfully, the back door opening has us quickly dropping our hands, and we turn to look at a flustered Tristan as he enters the kitchen.

He pauses when he sees us both standing awkwardly and goes to turn back the way he came. "Oh shit, sorry," he apologizes as he pushes open the screen door.

"Tristan, don't be silly," I quickly say, reaching forward and latching onto his bicep. "We were just having coffee. Want one?"

"Um, yeah, sure," he replies, giving me a dimpled smile when I nod, gesturing it's okay to stay.

Letting his arm go, I pour him a cup and try not to flinch when I look at his black eye as I pass him the coffee. He happily accepts, jumping up to sit on the edge of the counter while cradling the warm mug in his hands.

Polly takes a seat at the kitchen table and swiftly fixes her hair by brushing it back off her face and fastening her long bangs with a bobby pin.

"So," Polly asks with a flirty smile, "who are you?"

The way she looks at Tristan makes me feel weird and

uncomfortable. I don't know why, so I figure it's just too much caffeine and too little sleep.

"Hey, I'm Tristan," he replies, giving her a small wave as he sips his coffee. "I'm Quinn's brother."

Polly nods with a flirtatious smirk. "I'm Polly, Mia's sister."

The fact she admitted she's related to me without gagging surprises me, but I can't seem to get over how it bothers me to see Polly outright flirt with Tristan.

As I watch their exchange, I can see that Polly is attracted to him. But I can't read Tristan's body language, as he seems to give me subtle side glances when I remain quiet, deep in thought.

"Mia, what do you think?"

I have no idea what she's just said, as I have been miles away.

"Sorry, what?" I ask, turning to guiltily look at her while Tristan chuckles.

"Should we have a Christmas dinner tonight?"

"Sure, that sounds cool because oh my God, it's Christmas today. Merry Christmas," I add, feeling like a total scatterbrain.

"Merry Christmas," Polly says, quickly jumping up and giving Tristan a hug.

Tristan hugs her back while throwing me a cheeky smile over her shoulder because he knows she's crushing on him.

As she pulls away, she looks at me, and we stand awkwardly, not knowing if hugging is moving too fast in our recent truce status.

"Merry Christmas, Polly," I say, giving her arm a light pat.

Polly seems almost as relieved as I am and nods. "Merry Christmas to you, too."

There's an uncomfortable silence before Tristan jumps down from the counter, giving me a slight grin.

"Merry Christmas, Mia."

"Merry Christmas, Tristan," I repeat nervously because I know Tristan is about to pull me in for a hug.

It's just a hug, I tell myself, *and this is just Tristan. What is the matter with me?*

I step forward, and he opens his arms, wrapping them tightly around me and resting his cheek atop my head. Burying myself in his warm embrace feels nice, and I finally relax, scolding myself for being so silly because this is Tristan, my friend, and hugging him is natural.

"Kids," a curt voice unexpectedly says, which has me instantly pulling out of Tristan's arms and backing up against the counter.

I blindly reach for my coffee mug, suddenly needing something to do with my hands as Quinn strolls into the kitchen, wearing nothing but black sweatpants that sit so low that they reveal his defined V. His disheveled hair is flicked up rebelliously, and the brightness of his vivid green eyes, combined with his wild tresses, has me gasping for breath.

A smug smile pulls at his full lips as he leisurely advances toward me.

I freeze, about ready to pass out from lack of oxygen. I prepare for a kiss but am rudely disappointed when he slowly reaches over my shoulder, making sure to skim my sweater as he gets the coffeepot.

"Morning, Red," he huskily says, meeting my wide eyes.

I grunt in response, and he steals my mug from my limp hand, making sure he runs his fingers over my knuckles.

"Brat or should I say brats," he teases as he blatantly checks me out while pouring himself a cup of coffee before turning around to face them.

"Merry Christmas, Quinn," Polly gushes, jumping up and

giving him a hug.

Suddenly, the already small kitchen just got a whole lot smaller.

"You too, kiddo," Quinn replies, affectionately returning her hug. I wonder when they became best friends.

It could have been when she was saving my life.

"Merry Christmas, jerk," Tristan says, playfully bumping his shoulder into Quinn when he can finally pry himself out of Polly's clutches.

"You too." Quinn laughs, throwing his arm around Tristan and pulling him in for a warm hug, but I don't fail to see him flinch when he sees the damage inflicted on Tristan's face.

My eyes fill with tears, which I quickly brush away, as I don't want to look like a total crybaby watching their heartfelt exchange. It's just so good to see them together. I know Quinn has missed his brother, and I have no doubt Tristan feels the same.

Once they pull apart and Quinn playfully messes up Tristan's hair, he turns to me with a lopsided smile that lets me know I am in trouble.

"Merry Christmas, Red," he hoarsely says, pulling me softly toward him by the drawstrings on my sweater until we are inches apart.

"Merry Christmas, Quinn," I reply with a hitch to my voice as I stare into his bold eyes.

"So have you been naughty? Or nice?" he asks with that damn smirk.

"A bit of both," I reply, licking my suddenly very dry lips.

Quinn's eyes follow the movement, and his mouth tips up into a grin. "I think you've been a little naughtier than nice."

He taps the end of my nose with his finger before pulling away with a wink.

"So you up for a big Christmas dinner tonight?" Polly asks, gazing at Quinn's impressive physique, her eyes lingering on his nipple ring.

"Sure, sounds fun," he replies, absentmindedly scratching his ribs with a yawn.

Mentally slapping myself and refocusing on the here and now, I ask Polly, "What are we going to eat? I mean, we should try to keep a low profile and not go into town just yet."

Polly nods but looks awfully happy, so I know she's thought this through. "Have you seen the size of that pantry?" she says, pointing at the cupboard that takes up half the wall. "We could feed the whole country for a week with the stuff in there."

I turn to look at Quinn because he's gone awfully quiet, and I notice him staring at Tristan. Tristan must notice it too because he quickly looks away, uncomfortable under Quinn's sharp-eyed stare.

But that isn't a deterrent for Quinn because he stalks over to him and grabs his chin, turning his face from left to right, examining the damage those bastards inflicted on him.

I'm surprised Quinn didn't do this sooner, but when the small beam of sunlight hit Tristan's face at the right angle, the serious damage seems highlighted under the gentle rays.

Quinn grinds down on his jawbone but keeps a level face. "You okay?"

I now understand his distress.

The seriousness of our situation has hit him, and seeing Tristan's face is just a reminder of what could have happened. When the god-awful truth is painted in swirls of black and blue, it becomes very hard to ignore.

But Tristan scoffs, "Dude!" and swats his hand away, embarrassed by Quinn's brotherly concern as he shrugs off his injuries.

"You look like a bad motherfucker, little brother," Quinn teases, but the strain around his eyes reveals just how concerned he is to see Tristan beaten and bruised.

But he doesn't push or make a big deal about it.

This whole situation is still so raw, and I don't think any of us wants to start picking at the open wound just yet.

Tristan reads our concern but quickly brushes it off. "I'm gonna hit the shower." He turns to leave, obviously not comfortable with discussing this.

His announcement has Polly rising and promptly following him upstairs to no doubt spend whatever alone time she can with him.

With the room cleared, I'm now left alone with a pensive Quinn.

We don't say anything and just stare, appreciating each other.

Granted, I have a lot more to appreciate, seeing as my subject stands before me, basically nude. The daylight, however, reveals his injuries, and although they aren't as severe as Tristan's, the cut above his right eyebrow and the light bruising around his cheek suggest he also took a decent beating.

As my gaze drops to his ribs, I can see his torso took the brunt of his attack, and I clench my fists, infuriated that he got hurt. I'm also angered that I didn't notice this sooner.

"I'm okay, Red," Quinn says, gently reaching forward and unclasping my fist.

Raising my eyes to meet his, I notice a small clump of hair sticking to his brow. Curiosity gets the better of me, and as I brush it back, Quinn hisses and pulls away, not wanting me to see. But it's too late because hiding under his hair is a massive raw gash.

I gasp, horrified that he's so badly hurt, and I didn't even know. "You are not okay!" I affirm, pulling my hand away. "Does it hurt? Do you need stitches? Have you dressed the wound?"

I attempt to examine it once again, but Quinn ducks out of the way.

Suddenly, I painfully remember slamming my hips not so gently against his face, and I cringe, hoping I didn't add to his injuries.

"Don't you dare apologize." He grins, reading my concern.

"But I…sat…on your…face," I state, almost dying of embarrassment. "You should have told me you were hurt."

Quinn smirks as he pulls me toward him, pressing my chest to his. "Red, it would have hurt a lot more if you didn't sit on my face."

I feel my cheeks instantly redden at not only his comment but also the vivid memory currently replaying in my mind.

My eyes drop to his torso, and I can't help but examine his tattoo, and in the light of day, it's even more stunning than I remember it.

Quinn can see me looking at it as he's propped up against the counter, leaning backward, but he doesn't shy away from my gaze.

"It's beautiful," I say, gesturing to his ink with my finger as I raise my eyes to meet his.

"Thanks," he replies, running a hand down his side. "Jim Morrison is awesome."

"Huh?" I counter, cocking an eyebrow, and Quinn chuckles at my puzzlement.

"It's a Jim Morrison quote."

"Oh," I reply, disappointed, as I thought there was a

hidden meaning behind it for some reason. "Does it hold any significance to you?"

After last night, I need him to know that whatever his fate may be, he'll always have my love.

He sucks on his hoop and weighs up how best to answer me, which makes me think he's thinking up a plausible lie that'll shut me up.

No such luck.

"I think we all get tattooed for a reason. Each piece has its own story and usually holds some significance for us to get it permanently inked on our skin. A forever reminder of why we got it in the first place."

"Nope, no significance here," he replies casually, but I don't buy it. "You look disappointed."

Of course I am because, deep down, I know he's lying to me. But I don't have time to answer him because Cynthia hobbles into the kitchen, ending our discussion.

"Good morning, you two," she says with a strained smile.

Her condition has me quickly forgetting the tattoo issue, and I swiftly reach for a chair, pulling it out so she can sit.

"Thank you, Mia," she says, hissing in pain as she lowers herself onto the seat.

"I'm gonna hit the shower," Quinn says after a moment of silence.

Once he's washed out his mug, he kisses my forehead lightly and leaves us alone, giving us some privacy.

I stare at Cynthia, and as I see her worn and tired body sag in exhaustion, the anger and hate I feel toward her slowly fade. She's not the enemy, and in a way, she's just as much a victim as I am.

The fact she left me with my dad and uncle has changed the story, as maybe, just maybe, she thought she was doing the right thing.

"I'm so sorry, Mia," she whispers, disturbing my thoughts.

With a heavy sigh, I reply, "You need to tell me the truth. The fact that Phil is your brother...you owe me the truth."

"You're right. I left you because..." She pauses, her lower lip trembling. "I left you"—she looks at the floor—"to save your life."

A tear spills from her red-rimmed eye.

"How? How does that make any sense?"

"Because your father was going to kill you if I took you with me," she sobs. "I left you, Mia, because if I didn't, he'd kill us all."

Her revelation hits me like a sucker punch to the gut, and I clutch the countertop for support. "What do you mean?"

Cynthia wipes her teary eyes before she begins her tale. "I loved your father, I really did. But he never wanted kids, which was something he never told me. But I thought that would change when I got pregnant with you."

I give her my full attention, not wanting to miss a moment of her story.

"Throughout the pregnancy, your father never changed his mind. He showed no interest and pretended I wasn't pregnant. He just refused to accept he was going to be a father. If I had known how strongly he opposed being a parent, I never would have married him. He changed, Mia. He wasn't the man I once knew.

"Halfway through my pregnancy, I converted the spare bedroom, which was Thomas's study, into your nursery, and I spent hours in there making it perfect. I thought if I could show him how this wasn't a curse but a blessing, he'd come around, but sadly, he didn't.

"He simply ignored me, and when I asked him to come

to my doctor's appointments or shopping, he just acted as if neither of us existed. After a while, I just accepted his detachment, disillusioned by the fantasy that he would eventually come around."

She takes a big breath before she continues. "One Friday evening, I was putting together the crib I purchased for you, and Thomas came home, smelling of cheap beer and even cheaper women. He found me in the study and looked around the freshly painted pink walls like he'd stepped into a dream. The look in his eyes scared me," she says, shuddering at the memory.

"He demanded to know where all his things were, and then, everything just exploded. I questioned where he was because he was obviously with a woman, as the cheap lipstick mark on his collar was a dead giveaway. But he was enraged, and the more I pushed him, the worse he got.

"All he seemed to care about was where his things were. In a rage, I lied and said I had thrown them all away. They were in storage, but I was just so mad that that's all he cared about."

An ominous feeling begins building within me, and I know what she tells me next will break me.

"I began yelling at him, and my anger toward him came boiling to the surface. I told him that I couldn't be with him if he wouldn't accept you into our lives. He got so mad," she whispers, wringing her hands.

"The look in his eyes was so cold, so detached, and I knew then that he would never accept being a father. I told him I would stay with my mom until I figured out what I wanted to do. But he didn't take too kindly to that suggestion, and when I tried to leave, he stood in my way. I fought him, which was silly, but I was just so angry with him. I never thought he'd fight back."

"What?" I gasp, covering my gaping mouth with a shaky hand.

She sadly nods. "When I told him I was leaving and he couldn't stop me, I felt so elated for the first time in so long. But I only got as far as the hallway because he grabbed me and threw me against the wall in a drunken rage. I don't remember the pain because all I could focus on was the red pool of blood staining my white tennis shoes."

I blindly fall into the empty seat next to Cynthia before my unsteady legs collapse from under me.

She continues her story, appearing as if she can't stop now that she's unbottled the truth. "I drove myself to the hospital because your father was too drunk to drive. I ignored his tears and apologies the entire time because all I could focus on was you. I couldn't lose you because you were all I had. After this, there was no way I was staying with Thomas.

"We arrived at the hospital, and I was on autopilot as I calmly walked into the ER, leaving a trail of blood behind me as I asked to see a doctor. Everything is a blur from that moment forward because I slipped in and out of consciousness, but that Friday night, I nearly lost you, Mia."

She sniffles, meeting my wide eyes.

I wish I could speak, but I can't, so I only nod, silently begging her to continue.

"They performed an emergency C-section to get you out because you were dying. The whole time, Thomas cursed you, saying it was your fault, as I too almost died from internal hemorrhaging.

"You were so little when they pulled you out, and you weren't crying, so I thought you hadn't made it. But the moment I heard your tiny cry, my body gave out in relief, and I passed out. I came to the day after, demanding to see you, but Thomas said you were in the NICU, and the doctors weren't sure if you'd survive.

"I demanded to see you, and thankfully, Thomas complied. He lifted me into a wheelchair and took me to see you. The moment I saw you through that glass window changed my life. You were a part of me, Mia, and I promised never to allow anyone to hurt you again."

"What happened? Because you lied," I reply, my throat raw as I try to keep my tears at bay.

Cynthia sighs, rubbing her brow. "I know, and I'm so sorry. You stayed in the hospital for weeks, and I visited every day. The day I finally got to hold you was the best day of my life. You were so tiny, but you were perfect because you were mine, and that's when I decided on your name. Mia. It seemed fitting.

"During this time, Thomas slowly accepted you, but it was too late. You had almost died because of him. But as each day passed, the old Thomas Lee returned, the man I loved and married, and my illusion of playing happy family became a reality."

Cynthia watches me scoff, and she nods. "I know, Mia, but I was young and stupid, and I was also afraid. A single mom at age nineteen scared the living daylights out of me, and I wanted to provide my baby with what I never had. A mother and a father. Because, like you, in a way, I never knew my father. He left when I was too young to remember, and it was only me, my mom, and Phillip."

I see the way her voice quakes when she mentions Phil. But he will have to wait because I need her to finish this story.

"So what happened?"

"When the doctors said it was okay for you to come home,

I only agreed to go back on the proviso that your father attend counseling. He promised he never meant to push me. That it was an accident, and he would change, and he did.

"The next eighteen months were the happiest of my life as we became a family. But the day Phillip was released from prison was the day things changed."

"Phil was in prison?"

"Yes. Phillip was always a troubled teen. I blame my father for his behavior. Anyway, he was incarcerated for possession of a large number of ecstasy tablets. Phillip stated they were for recreational use, but the judge didn't buy it. He had over five hundred tablets on him when the police arrested him."

My face pales as I begin to digest what Cynthia just said.

This means that Phil started out being a drug pusher, just like me. That motherfucker imposed the same life sentence on me. And even though he knew the risks, he didn't care. He had no qualms about forcing his eight-year-old niece to follow in his footsteps.

Cynthia sees my pain and softly places her hand on my knee. But I pull out of her grip, not wanting any comfort.

She nods, understanding my actions. "Because it was his first offense, he went to jail for five years. The man who went into Statesville Penitentiary was not the same man who came out. Prison changed Phillip, and instead of teaching him a lesson, it only taught him to become a smarter criminal.

"I knew your father looked up to Phillip, he always had, but once he was released, Thomas worshipped him. It was like Phillip represented what he wanted—freedom.

"Not long after, they became very close, and Thomas started going out all night with Phillip and not returning until the early hours of the following morning. He slept all day and partied all night, and the man I loved was once again lost to me.

"A few months after your second birthday, I made the decision to leave your father. He missed your birthday when he promised he would attend. In secret, I made preparations to see an attorney, and that's where I met Chandler. He was an intern at the law firm, but I lied and didn't tell him why I was there.

"There was an instant attraction because Chandler was everything your father once was—kind, caring, and in love with me. After the hardships I had with Thomas, I was vulnerable, and in a moment of weakness, I sinned, breaking my marital vows."

I can't help myself as I turn my lip up at her in disgust.

"It was one time, Mia," she says, seeing my disappointment. "But I paid the ultimate price for my infidelity, as I got pregnant with Polly. I had known Chandler for only a month and was pregnant with his child. I was so ashamed, and I also knew your father would know the child wasn't his because we were no longer intimate."

I instinctively rub my chest. This story is causing my heart to hurt.

"Chandler was moving to Canada, and he asked me to come with him because he wanted to keep the baby. He said he loved me and wanted to marry me. But—"

"But what?" I know this is where my history is about to turn cruel.

"He didn't know about you," she whispers, ashamed.

Suddenly, the wheels in my head begin turning, and Cynthia can see me piecing it all together.

"I was weak, Mia. I know it's no excuse, but I was broken and beaten. Your father had broken me."

"No, it's not an excuse," I spit out.

"I know, and I'll forever regret my decision. Your father overheard me talking to my mother and put two and two together. He confronted me, and I told him everything. I didn't know how he would respond, but what he said next was the last thing I ever thought he'd say.

"He told me he would give me a divorce and wouldn't cause me any problems. He would let me go and pretend he never existed."

"But…?" I prompt because this all sounds too good to be true.

"But I was to leave you with him. I said no, absolutely not, but he said if I wanted a chance at a normal life, then I was to forget you and he ever existed, and if I didn't…"

"What?"

"He would find us and make us all pay. Me, you, and Polly."

"What?" I gasp because there's no way I heard her correctly.

There is no way she left me there with a deranged lunatic, knowing full well that he was willing to hurt his three-year-old daughter to spite her.

"How could you leave me? With an obvious psychopath!"

"I know, Mia." She sobs. "I made a mistake."

"Mistake? Running a red light is a mistake. Mixing your colors with whites is a mistake. Leaving your daughter with her maniacal father is not a mistake. It's a fucking tragedy!"

"I know, I know." She sniffs, losing her composure as she covers her face.

"Why did he want me?" I ask, straightening my spine. I will not collapse, not yet. I need to know how this story ends.

"To hurt me," she replies, wiping away her tears. "He wouldn't allow me complete happiness. By holding on to you, he made sure I would never forget him. A piece of me would always be missing, and he would always have the upper hand."

"I wasn't a damn bargaining chip!"

"I know," she confesses, nodding. Her eyes search mine, hoping I will absolve her of her sins. "Please forgive me."

"He made you choose, and you chose another life. A life that was simpler without me in it. How can I forgive you?" I ask, my voice quivering in rage but also in utter defeat.

Cynthia silently cries as she lowers her head, her shoulders trembling with every tear she sheds.

"So what happened?" I ask, needing to hear the god-awful truth before I pass out.

"I left you because of Phillip. He loved you, Mia."

I'm unable to contain my disbelief.

"He may have been a shitty brother, but he loved you," Cynthia affirms, believing her bullshit lies.

"Loved me? He turned me into a drug dealer!" I shout because surely, she's gone insane.

But she only nods, begging me to believe her. "Don't you remember? He used to play catch with you."

"He never played catch with me," I spit out, but then memories I've tried so hard to repress come charging forward, and I blanch.

Suddenly, vivid memories of Phil, not my father, playing catch on the front lawn assault my senses, and I hold the table for support.

"No, it can't be him," I deny, but I know what she says is true, as faint flashbacks of Phil being kind to me rise to the surface.

"That's the only reason I left you. Phillip promised me he would look after you, and I knew your father loved you in his own way."

"Loved me? Do you realize how crazy you sound? He used me to get back at you! And then Phillip made me his drug mule!"

"I never thought he'd hurt you," Cynthia says, her desperate eyes beseeching me to believe her.

"Well, he did."

"I didn't know. Phillip promised me."

"Yeah, well, Phil is a fucking liar!" I yell, kicking back my chair.

"Mia, please, let me explain. There's more," she says, standing and attempting to latch onto my arm to stop my retreat.

But I pull out of her grasp before I detonate and take her down with me. "I've heard enough."

"I know you're angry with me…"

"Angry?" I sarcastically chuckle. "I'm a little more than just angry. I know I asked for the truth, but I just need time. And space. I need to get my head around this and not see you as being the bad guy because right now, from where I stand, you're worse than them.

"Your selfishness and your cowardliness is the reason I'm so fucked up. It's the reason I wanted to kill myself every day of my damn life!"

My harsh words slap her across the cheek, and she recoils, the hurt evident on her face. "I'm so sorry," she whispers, tears running down her cheeks.

"Yeah, so am I." I shoulder past her, shoving open the back door before I suffocate.

I take off into a quick sprint, desperately needing to get away from the truth I so longed for. But I now realize I preferred the illusion of my past because hearing the truth has not set me free. It has only made me angrier and all the more hostile toward someone I was starting to open up to.

"Idiot," I mumble as I slow down to a walk after charging off into the dense woods like a raving lunatic.

My heavy breathing is the only thing I can hear, and it's refreshing to know I'm out here on my own because I need time to digest Cynthia's confession.

I did ask for the truth, but I was so not ready for her to divulge the sins of her past and for them to be so earth-shattering. I know there's more to the story, but I've heard enough for today. This will put my curiosity to rest for now, and I'll think twice before asking for the truth again.

Not once did I fathom my past could be so messed up.

But the more I learn, the less I want to know.

I turn around before I get lost and slowly make my way through the woods. Just as I'm about to push through the clearing, I see Polly sitting on the top step of the deck, puffing on a cigarette. Next to her sits Quinn, and for some reason, I mask my steps and creep toward them, hoping to remain unseen.

I can't hear them, but I can sure see them. I clearly see Polly lean into Quinn, and he lightly pulls her into his side for a loose hug.

However, I surprise myself because my jealousy doesn't have me charging toward them in a fit of rage. I can see their embrace is purely platonic.

No doubt the whole house heard Cynthia's and my exchange downstairs because I wasn't exactly quiet. But Polly has a right to know as this involves her, too.

It involves us all.

Hearing a branch snap behind me, I quickly spin around with my heart in my throat. I let out a relieved breath when I see Tristan and Lucky a few feet away.

"Hey," he says, his cheeks pink from the cool breeze.

"Hey, yourself," I reply with a small smile as I crouch down to pat Lucky between the ears.

"Was just taking this little guy out to do his business," Tristan explains, but I can tell by the strain around his eyes he heard my exchange.

"So you heard?" I ask, not even bothering to clarify what I mean.

"Yeah." He guiltily nods. "Sorry, I wasn't eavesdropping."

"It's fine. I'm sure everyone in Antarctica probably heard," I solemnly reply, scratching Lucky under the chin.

"You okay?" Tristan asks, the concern clear in his voice.

With one last pat, I rise to full height, meeting Tristan's troubled eyes.

The morning lights draw out the warmness in them, and I can't help but admire their beauty. However, his beaten face drowns out the color, and my anger escalates.

"I will be," I confess, taking a step toward him as I examine his bruised face more closely. "I'm so sorry for what happened back—"

"Shh," he says with a small shake of his head. "It's not your fault."

"Yes, it is," I reply, looking at his battered face. "You got hurt once again because of me. I just can't seem to stop hurting you, can I?"

"Hey, stop that. This isn't your fault."

But it is, and I lower my eyes, feeling ashamed.

"Were you really going to sacrifice yourself for me? Would you have gone with those assholes to save me?"

"Of course I would," I reply without thought. "There is no way I would allow them to hurt you."

Tristan's eyes soften. "So you see, this isn't your fault. You always put everyone first. Stop blaming yourself."

Tristan's kindness is touching, but talks of sacrificing remind me of the bargain he was so willing to make. "You can't ever sacrifice yourself for me again. People like Thomas and Phil don't believe in nobility and would have killed you without a second thought."

"I don't care," he stubbornly retorts, shaking his head.

"Well, I do. I refuse to allow another person I love to get hurt."

The small space between us becomes incredibly tiny when my brain registers what my mouth just said.

"Well, neither will I," he whispers, his eyes focusing on mine, and I can see he means every word.

I should be pulling away, but I don't.

I stand motionless and allow him to hesitantly brush away a strand of stray hair from my face. But I quickly take a step back, breaking our moment. I don't fail to see the flicker of disappointment behind his eyes.

"Please don't tell Quinn about what Phil and Thomas asked me to do," I say after a moment of uncomfortable silence.

"Why?" Tristan asks, and I'm thankful the awkwardness disappears.

"He's got enough to worry about. I don't want to add to the shit pile."

Tristan nods but doesn't look too happy. "He's smart, Mia. He'll figure it out."

I sigh because he's right.

But if I can stop Quinn from worrying about this one thing, then I'll do whatever it takes.

"But you've got my word. I won't tell him."

"Thank you."

"Anything for you," he whispers, surprising me with his statement.

Suddenly feeling heated under his intense gaze, I nervously brush a piece of hair behind my ear. Why am I so edgy around him?

This is just Tristan.

Tristan, who is my friend and Quinn's brother.

Unexpectedly, my heart races as my friend hesitantly draws his hand toward my face and lightly rests it on my cheek. I don't know what to do because it doesn't feel wrong or weird. It feels…normal.

"Mia…" Tristan sighs, and as faint as it is, I feel him trace a line over my cheekbone with a shaky finger, which has my skin breaking out in goose bumps.

"Mia, I—" he presses, gazing at my mouth.

I need to pull away because some part of me knows we've crossed some invisible line, but I can't. I don't know why.

However, the voice of reason suddenly sounds, and I yelp at the intrusion.

"Everything okay?" the stern voice asks, and I quickly pull out of Tristan's embrace, gingerly meeting Quinn's demanding gaze.

I'm suddenly hit with a serious case of guilt even though I've done nothing wrong. But deep down, I know that's not entirely true because something weird is happening between Tristan and me.

I just don't know what.

"Fine," Tristan quickly says, trying to fill the uncomfortable void.

Quinn's eyes never leave mine, and I avert my gaze, which makes this scenario look all the more suspicious.

But Quinn knows, and Tristan's comment suddenly takes

on a whole different meaning.

"*He's smart, Mia. He'll figure it out.*"

Sadly, I think he already has.

"Well, I'm starved," Tristan says. "I'm, um, going to get some breakfast."

When neither Quinn nor I move, Tristan clears his throat.

"Okay, well, I'll catch you later." And he's gone, leaving me alone with Quinn.

We remain silent, the strong breeze howling around us. I know I should say something, but what?

As much as I hate to admit it, Tristan being here has changed the dynamic between Quinn and me.

And I'm afraid to find out why.

Polly has insisted we continue with the charade of this Christmas dinner, and as I slip on my sweater, I have a bad feeling about tonight's proceedings.

Quinn has been missing for most of the day, and I've let him be because if he wanted to be found, he would have made himself known.

This morning has played on my mind, and as hard as I try to deny the shift between Tristan and me, it's there. It's not romantic; it's just…different. Something has changed, but I just can't figure out what.

Sighing, I sit at the foot of the bed to tie my laces but peer up when the bedroom door opens. Quinn sways in, notebook under his arm, and by his clumsy entrance, I dare say he's drunk.

I stand, looking at him, waiting for him to explain where he's been.

However, he brushes past me and silently digs through his backpack, ignoring me.

"Where have you been?"

He doesn't turn around as he replies, "Out."

His clipped response surprises me, and I try to keep the hurt from my voice. "Did I do something wrong?"

Quinn rips the T-shirt off his head and turns to face me, chest bare. "Nope. Everything is fine. Perfect."

"Quinn." I sigh, but he shakes his head, his messy hair spilling over his brow.

"It's fine. I'm fine. It's all fucking fine," he heatedly replies, quickly putting on a shirt.

Before I have a chance to respond, he charges out of the room, making sure to slam the door shut behind him.

What was that?

Groaning, I fall onto the bed and stare at the ceiling, dreading this dinner even more now.

The phone chiming in Quinn's backpack has my already jumpy body jarring in shock, and I quickly dive off the bed, searching for it.

"Hello?" I breathlessly say when I find it but am greeted with static. "Hello?"

"Mi...a," the broken voice says.

"Abi?" I question. Her voice is all jumbled as if we have a bad connection. "Abi, is that you?"

"Mia...can you...hear me?" she asks through a cloud of static, but I can hear that it's her.

"Abi, we must have a bad connection. Hello? Hello? Shit," I curse, pulling the phone away from my ear and looking at the screen.

The screen reveals I'm no longer talking to anyone, and I desperately try dialing Abi's number, but all I hear is a beeping, which informs me I have no cell service.

"Dammit!" I curse again, running around the room, hoping to find a signal as I raise the phone in the air, but I have no luck.

I yank open the window and extend my arm out and up, hoping to get something, but still nothing.

What good is an untraceable phone if it doesn't have a signal?

I fruitlessly move the cell from side to side for a few minutes, and just as I'm about to give up, the phone beeps, indicating I have a text message.

> You must have no service where you are, but good news. We're almost there. Dad said we're DAYS away from this being over. You'll be home before you know it, and everything will go back to normal. Can you believe that?! I can't wait to see you again. I really miss you. I'll text when I have news. Miss you!
> Ps. Sorry about Tristan :(He just left without telling me!
> Pps. Merry XMAS! Love you! x

As I read her message over and over, I find myself needing to bask in the news that this may finally be over. My freedom, *our* freedom, is within reach, and I don't know what to do.

I don't want to celebrate prematurely, but I can't stop the small smile that spreads from cheek to cheek. This is the best news we've had in a while.

However, as I read over her message one last time, I can't help but think that when we all return home, things will never go back to "normal."

Tossing those thoughts aside, I decide to go downstairs

because this news will surely get Quinn out of his bad mood. However, the moment I descend the stairs and head for the den, I wonder if I've stepped into an alternate universe.

Polly is coaxing Tristan to come dance with her in front of the fire, while he sits rigid on the sofa, politely declining. She then turns her attention to Quinn. He's sitting on the recliner, watching TV while drinking a beer.

"Come dance with me, Quinn," she pouts, seductively moving in front of him, hoping to persuade him.

My eyes narrow, and when he stands up in an attempt to humor her, I use that as my cue to enter.

My gaze meets his, silently demanding he explain what's wrong. He arrogantly tips his beer my way in salute before downing the whole bottle.

Polly and Tristan turn to see what's captured his attention, and when they see it's me, they both give me puzzled looks. I only shrug in response because I'm just as clueless as them.

"Okay, dinner is served. Come sit," Cynthia says, gesturing to the table, which is filled with a Christmas feast to feed a small army.

"Smells great, Mom."

"Thanks, honey," Cynthia distractedly replies as she's looking at Quinn because he's still glaring at me.

"Mia?" she asks with a hint of confusion.

Giving Quinn one last look, I turn to meet her worried eyes.

"Thanks. It does smell great," I say, trying to forget our screaming match only hours ago.

I take a seat across the table from Polly, and Tristan is the next to move. When he pulls out the chair near me, I try not to cringe, as I have a sneaking suspicion that Quinn is acting insane because of Tristan.

He's made it more than obvious he's jealous of our friendship, but I just wish he would talk to me about it instead of acting like a two-year-old.

His boots thud on the wooden floor as he pulls out the chair next to Polly, who gushes, elated that Quinn is sitting near her.

This dinner is already giving me heartburn.

"I hope you enjoy it," Cynthia says, sitting at the head of the table.

We politely reach for what's closest and start filling our plates. We do this in silence, and I know Quinn closely watches every movement I make.

I don't understand his problem, but whatever is his deal, I wish he would quit. This dinner is awkward enough.

Flicking my eyes to meet his, I silently demand he tell me what's wrong, but he leans back in his chair and sips his beer, giving nothing away.

Ignoring him, I pass Tristan the ham.

"Thanks."

He's either ignoring Quinn, or he's totally oblivious to his hostility.

"So, Mom," Polly says, tearing her bread roll in half. "Have you spoken to Dad?"

That captures the entire table's attention, and we all turn to watch Cynthia pale. "Not yet, honey. I'm hoping tomorrow. You know we have no cell reception or a phone line out here."

Before I have a chance to tell everyone I received a text from Abi, Quinn decides now is a good time to speak. "I'll drive into town."

"That would be great, Quinn, thank you. By now, I'm sure Chandler will be beside himself," Cynthia says with a strained smile.

"You think?" Polly scoffs, reaching for her drink.

"Of course he is."

"Well, why isn't he here, then?" she demands, narrowing her eyes.

I watch their exchange with interest, as I have no idea where this is headed.

"Because he's in Europe. You can't expect him to magically appear overnight," Cynthia replies, the strain in her response clearly evident.

Suddenly, Polly's fork smashes down onto her plate, and I jolt at the abrupt, loud noise. "He should have been here in the first place. It's Christmas! But no, of course work comes first. Just like it always does."

"Pollyanna! Watch your tone," Cynthia snaps, her mouth agape.

"No, I won't sit here quietly while you defend him. He should have been here to protect us."

I lower my eyes, ashamed they needed protecting in the first place.

Tristan sees my regret and kindly reaches for my hand, squeezing it softly. Sadly, this simple gesture sets off a clusterfuck of events.

"Pollyanna, go to your room!" Cynthia demands, standing up and thumping her fist on the table, which surprises me because I've never seen her this angry before.

"No!" Polly screams, jumping up and stomping her foot. "You can't just send me to my room. I'm not a child anymore. I won't censor my thoughts because they hurt your delicate feelings."

Tristan squeezes my hand once again when I let out a small sigh because I feel remotely sorry for Cynthia.

The gesture is purely innocent, but in a room filled with

crazy, angry people, Tristan's hand may as well have squeezed my boob.

"How 'bout you keep your hands to yourself, Tris?" Quinn barks from across the table.

Tristan apprehensively loosens his grip, but he doesn't let go.

"She's a big girl and doesn't need you to hold her hand."

"What the fuck is your problem?" I retort, my last tether of patience snapping as I glare at Quinn.

As he clenches his jaw, I stupidly say, "I think you and Polly need to chill the fuck out."

The moment it's out, I know that comment will bite me in the ass.

"I'm not going to chill out. We wouldn't be in this mess if it weren't for you!" Polly yells, pointing her finger at me. "So fuck you."

I rip my hand out from Tristan's grip, who looks hurt that I've broken our connection. "How about you stop being a spoiled brat for one second and—"

"You destroyed my life!" Polly cries.

"Polly, that is enough!" Cynthia cries, horrified.

But Polly ignores her as she kicks back her chair and stalks over to me.

Tristan is up in an instant, ready to protect me. He stands in front of me, acting as my human barricade.

But Quinn adds fuel to the already out-of-control fire as he snarls, "She doesn't need your protection, Tristan."

"But she does yours?" Tristan spits back, turning to glare at Quinn.

"Stop it!" I yell, looking across the table at Quinn, who looks ready to explode. "What is the matter with you? Stop being such a jerk."

"You're the jerk!" Polly suddenly screams, advancing forward, but Tristan remains my bodyguard.

"Excuse me?" I gasp, leaning to the left so I can look at her without Tristan's broad back in the way.

"You heard me," she replies, stopping inches from Tristan's chest. "It's so damn obvious that these two"—she gestures back and forth with a finger between Tristan and Quinn—"are in love with you, and you're just stringing them both along. How about you choose one and put the other out of his misery?"

How. Dare. She.

There is no truth to her lies, but as I look at Quinn, I can see that he might actually agree with her. And the fact that Tristan hasn't piped up in my defense is a sure sign that he doesn't entirely disagree with her.

I don't understand; how did I end up being the bad guy?

The bad guys are the ones who did this to us. They're the ones who forced us to run, and now we're stuck in this cabin of confessions where I'm the monster. Well, fuck them all.

"Choose one?" I spit out, pushing past Tristan, who tries to put a reassuring hand on my shoulder, but it's too late.

I shrug him off as I continue scowling at Polly.

"You want me to choose one so you can have the other?" I sneer, getting into her face, totally ignoring her personal space.

She gasps, taking a small step back, obviously frightened by my rage.

But she can go to hell.

They all can.

"Well…fuck you all because I choose me. You can have them both."

I shoulder past her before I say something else I'll regret.

Twelve

"**W**hat am I doing?" I whisper to my only friend in the world.

Lucky whines before leaning forward and licking my cheek in support.

"Thanks, boy," I coo, resting my head on his mane.

This is so fucked up.

Actually, it's beyond fucked up, and at the moment, I would happily turn myself over to my dad to escape this situation.

Polly is lucky I didn't knock her damn teeth out.

I'm not stringing Tristan and Quinn along.

Or am I?

I'm baffled when thinking back to the feelings I felt for Tristan in the woods because I don't know what that was. I've never been in love with one, let alone two boys before, so maybe I am stringing them both along?

Throwing the pillow over my face, I scream into it, needing to get some of this rage out before I see Quinn.

I've been in hiding for about two hours, hoping the time away will give me the willpower to not want to kill the inhabitants of this house. So far, it's not working.

A knock on the bedroom door only adds to my irritability.

"Mia?" Tristan asks from outside my door.

"What?" I reply, throwing the pillow to the ground.

When he remains silent, I shout, annoyed, "What do you want, Tristan?"

"It's Quinn." That's his simple reply, and I quickly sit up as he's got my full attention.

"What about him?"

"He's going to drive into town."

"What? *Now*?" I snap, jumping off the bed and charging toward him.

As I open the door, Tristan's pale complexion has me softening a fraction.

"What's going on?"

"After you stormed off, he lost it, and I thought he was just going to blow off some steam. But he's adamant he's driving into town to call Chandler, as he needs to get the hell away from here."

"Hide the keys," I order, though I know that won't stop a determined Quinn.

Tristan runs a hand through his hair, also looking worse for wear. "We have, and that's held him off...until now."

At that precise moment, the car engine roars to life, startling both Tristan and me.

"Shit," I curse, pushing past Tristan and flying down the staircase.

As I shove the back door open, I'm blinded by bright headlights. Giving my eyes a moment to adjust, I shield them and run madly toward the car.

"Get out!" I spit, reaching for the handle, but the door is locked. "Quinn, get out of the car!"

I glare at him, but he won't look my way and only stares vacantly straight ahead through the windshield.

"Quinn!"

But his only response is him stepping on the gas and loudly revving the engine, drowning out my pleas.

"Listen to her. You're in no state to drive. Get out before you hurt yourself."

Tristin's comment only infuriates Quinn further. "I'm fine. Now move."

I really wish he would stop saying he's fine when he's clearly not fine.

"What has gotten into you?" I yell, bashing on the window in frustration because I have no clue what the hell is wrong with him.

As Quinn's mouth tips up into a sinister smile, I feel the tiny hairs on my arms prickle in panic. "You really want to know?"

"Yes, you asshole, tell me!"

"You," he snarls, his foot revving the gas. "You're taking over every fiber of my body, and I'm drowning."

I take a step back, startled by his confession.

But when he doesn't elaborate and simply turns to stare blankly out the windshield once again, I snap.

"What have I done?" I cry, fruitlessly attempting to open the locked door. "Talk to me!"

"Mia, leave him," Tristan says, pulling my hand away from the handle. He can see this is a losing battle.

I cringe at his unintended inept comment but sag against him, utterly defeated because Quinn is being an absolute dick.

As Tristan wraps one arm loosely around my shoulder, the gesture doesn't go unnoticed by Quinn, and he quickly turns, scowling at our union.

But that was Tristan's intention all along because as soon as Quinn is distracted, Tristan suddenly shoves me out of the way, and out of nowhere, he smashes a rock straight through the window.

He must have grabbed the rock when I was pleading with Quinn, as he too saw that there was no way we were getting Quinn out without excessive force.

Quinn is just as stunned as I am, but it's game on as Tristan reaches into a hole where the window once was and yanks Quinn out.

I'm pushed to the ground in the scuffle and watch in absolute horror as Quinn and Tristan are about to kill one another and anyone who stands in their way. They circle each other like two caged fighters, ready to brawl till the bitter end.

But I can't allow that to happen because, unlike those fighters, who are mere strangers, these two are brothers.

And they are blood.

"Stop!" I scream, thankfully finding my feet and storming toward them.

But the Berkeley brothers are in sync with the other, and they both charge, facing the other head-on.

My pleas fall on deaf ears as Tristan throws the first punch, landing Quinn square in the jaw. Quinn's head snaps back with a sickening crack, and I cover my mouth, stunned. Tristan takes another swing, splitting Quinn's lip open, and blood instantly pours from the wound.

I've seen Quinn fight before, and this fight is purely one-sided. He's accepting each strike, almost embracing it, like it's punishment he deserves.

As Tristan hits him a third time, blood trickling from a wound to his eye, I know this has to stop.

"Fight back!" Tristan yells, clenched fists raised.

But Quinn shakes his head, wiping his bloodied mouth with the back of his hand. "No."

"Fight me!" Tristan implores, ready to strike, but I reach for his arm, holding on tight.

"Enough, Tristan. Enough."

The contact stuns him, and his muscles slacken under my hand.

"Enough," I say one last time, and thankfully, he listens, dropping his bloodied fists to his sides.

But Quinn just refuels the fire by spitting, "Dad was right. You are pathetic, getting everyone to fight your battles."

"Quinn!" I reprimand, but I don't have time to elaborate as my body vibrates, but it's not me who's trembling. It's Tristan.

I know I have roughly five seconds to defuse this situation because if I don't, Tristan will do something he'll regret for the rest of his life.

It happens in a heartbeat, and I foresee every move.

I release Tristan's arm, and spinning around quickly, I slap him—hard.

He stands stunned as he cradles his reddening cheek, but before he has a chance to speak, I charge over to Quinn, who also looks stunned, and I give his cheek the same treatment as Tristan's.

His hand also flies to his cheek, and as he opens his mouth to no doubt yell at me, I yank on the scruff of his collar and drag him across the grass.

He comes willingly because he knows better than to

provoke me when my temper has exploded. I won't see reason. I don't know where I'm going, but I do know that I need to separate the two brothers and talk to Quinn.

Is he drunk or just plain crazy to provoke Tristan that way?

Maybe he's both.

Either way, I need him to tell me what the hell is going on.

I'm thankful when I see a small, secluded boathouse ahead because I'm about to implode from my raging adrenaline.

Quickening my step, I kick the door open and pull Quinn in, releasing my hold on his collar as I slam the door shut behind me.

"What is the matter with you?" I scream as I turn around and stalk toward him.

"I think you're the one with the problem," he says, moving his jaw from left to right. "Tristan really does fight like a pussy compared to you."

"This isn't funny, you asshole!" I yell, barely refraining from slapping his face once again. "Tell me what the hell is going on."

"Why don't you ask Tristan?"

"And what the hell does that mean?"

But I know exactly what it means.

Quinn is jealous. But this stems way beyond jealousy. This has got to do with his past.

"Why didn't you fight Tristan?"

Quinn only shrugs, not answering my question, so I decide to make him answer. "What, you're jealous? Is that it?"

But he remains silent, crossing his arms over his chest in defiance, which enrages me further.

"I think you are. I think you're so damn jealous, it's making you act like a crazy person. But why? Have I ever given you any reason not to trust me?"

Quinn lowers his eyes, my words hitting hard.

But still, he remains silent.

"I know I haven't. So why do you feel threatened by him?"

"Drop it, Red," he hisses, meeting my eyes with a look of fury.

As cruel and mean as this may sound, I need to pick at this sore till it bleeds open. "No, on the contrary, I think we're finally getting somewhere. So no, I won't drop it. Start talking."

"There's nothing to say," he snarls, furiously wiping his bloodied lip, angered by my persistence.

"Like hell there isn't. I understand this whole situation is getting too much, and being cooped up here together is too much, but there's something more. Tell me what it is."

But he stubbornly shakes his head.

Suddenly, I have a sickening thought.

What if he's finally had enough? What if he wants out? What if he's finally seen me for what I am and realizes I'm not worth it?

Is that it?

Has this got nothing to do with Tristan after all, and the only problem he has is with…me?

"Stop it," Quinn abruptly says, walking over to me and lightly gripping my biceps. "Whatever you're thinking, stop it."

"You've had enough, haven't you?" I whisper, the words hurting more than I thought humanly possible. "You want out."

"Red, no!" he cries, demanding I believe him.

"Then what's wrong? I don't understand what I've done. Is it Tristan? What Polly said—you don't believe her, do you?"

His silence cements his thoughts.

"You do? You think I want him? You think I...love him?" I gasp, pulling from his embrace as I feel like I'm about to be sick.

His eyes drop briefly before he raises them and sadly meets mine. "I think a part of you...does. We both know he's the better choice. He—he loves you," he says, his mouth dipping into a frown. "And he deserves you. What we've been doing...it's wrong."

"What? No. Quinn, no," I beg, my heart slowly shattering.

Is he breaking up with me?

"Yes. But I'll make it easy for you," he says, his voice dripping with regret. "I'll leave you alone. And when this gets sorted, and we're finally free, I promise you, you'll never hear from me again."

"No!" I cry, tears stinging my eyes. "I don't want that."

"You don't know what you want," he replies with a sad smile. "With Tristan, it'll be easy, and you deserve that. You both deserve that. And I owe him this. To sacrifice the only thing I've ever—"

He pauses before taking a deep breath.

"To sacrifice the only thing I've ever loved is the right thing to do. I will happily sacrifice my happiness for his because the two people I love more than anything in this world will be happy. Together. He deserves happiness. And so do you, Red. So do you."

He lowers his head, his long hair masking his tears.

I stand frozen, not knowing what the hell to say. But as I piece through what he just said, I know I have to fight because he doesn't get to decide this. He doesn't get to decide my fate.

"Self-sacrifice is not honorable; it's the coward's way out. And you don't look like a coward to me, Quinn. I know you aren't. You've fought beside me every step of the way, and now you're giving up. You're giving up because of some unrealistic notion that you get to play God and have a hand in my fate. In Tristan's."

But as he stands rigid, unresponsive to my pleas, I know only one thing I can say will make him understand. "I don't want Tristan. I want you. I love…you. No one else, only you," I whisper, afraid I've shared too much.

Suddenly, I'm rewarded with the response I so desperately craved, and the sight before me is one I will remember for the rest of my life.

Quinn locks his eyes with mine, and I can see that this changes everything.

And there's no turning back.

"You love me?"

"Yes, Quinn. I love you. Before you, I only ever wanted to exist in the darkness. But now, you are the light in my forever darkness."

However, his stunned expression has me concerned that he may not feel the same way.

"Do you…love me?"

Taking a step toward me, he clutches my cheeks in his palms. "Love you?" he questions, his eyes searching every inch of my face. "I love you so fucking much that it hurts. You've possessed me, but I've never felt so alive."

Before I have a chance to reply, he swoops forward and slams his mouth to mine.

He owns me; every part of me is his, so I happily surrender and let this moment overtake us both.

This kiss drowns with urgency, but it's also draped in love because we are both open and honest for the first time ever, both stripped bare for the other to see. And what I see is simply beautiful.

I yank at the messy strands of hair curling at his nape, and he groans into my mouth, relishing in the hard pressure. He wraps me in his arms and enfolds me into his embrace so tightly, I can scarcely breathe. But who needs oxygen when Quinn Berkeley is your life source?

But I want more, so I mold my mouth to his, kissing him fiercely and demanding his tongue. I whimper when his barbell finally caresses me deliriously slow, but it's still not enough.

I need more.

His hard-on has me craving more, and suddenly, I know that there's only one thing that will ever be enough.

And when Quinn backs me up toward a sofa in the corner of the room, I know he feels it, too.

Lowering me onto the soft cushions while never breaking our connection, I know this is what he was waiting for. This is perfect. This is our something like perfect.

His gentle movements are filled with passion and desire, and I feel it all. My body is so in sync with his that I feel every breath he takes. But after his lips burn a pathway down my throat and come to rest at my frantic pulse, I feel him pull away.

"Why did you stop?" I breathlessly ask, looking up at him, my body begging him to continue.

He slowly sits back on his heels, and as my eyes drop to his crotch, I know it's not due to lack of excitement.

"If we do this, then you need to know it all. And if you still"—he pauses—"and if you still want me after you've heard it all, then I'm yours. I'll forever be yours."

Sitting up, I place my hand over his heart. "I'll always want you."

I lie back down, resting my head on the armrest and

giving him my full attention.

Quinn nods before lowering his head. He's still on his knees before me as he commences his tale. "I did something terrible. Something I wish I could take back. But that's the fucked-up thing. I can never take back my sins."

I listen, remaining silent, not wanting to interrupt this long-overdue confession.

"I wasn't always a bad kid. I loved my mom. I knew that she stayed with my dad 'cause of us. I knew she sacrificed her happiness for us. But the day he hurt me…"

His fingers gently pass over his brow, and I remember Tristan revealing that their father once hit Quinn so hard he split his forehead open.

At the time, Quinn was ten.

"Something inside her snapped," he continues, lost in thought. "She kicked him out and threatened to go to the police if he didn't leave. Of course, he left, and things were okay for a while. Mom worked so hard, but she never once complained. The only downside of not having Dad around was we didn't have an adult to look after us, not that he ever did much anyway.

"So I grew up fast, and I became the man of the house.

"Things were good, and I loved that it was just Tristan and me when Mom was at work. It was him and me against the world, you know?"

I nod, indicating I'm listening because I have a feeling things are about to get real.

"Then one day, just after my fourteenth birthday, my mother came home and told us our uncle Brandon was coming to stay with us."

"Uncle?" I softly question.

Quinn nods, finally lifting his eyes to meet mine. "My

uncle Brandon, he was my father's brother—his younger brother, and he'd just got discharged from the Army because he got hurt in combat. The moment I met him, I just knew something wasn't right. The way my mother fawned all over him and made a big deal that he was finally home was weird.

"I mean, she never got this excited to see Dad, and she was married to him. But I shrugged it off and didn't think much of it because I liked him. Uncle Brandon had a welcoming smile, and his smile would especially grow big whenever he looked at Tristan.

"So, of course, I liked him because anyone who liked my brother was a friend."

The dread forming in the pit of my stomach begins churning, but I nod, as I need to know what happens next.

"Uncle Brandon, he looked after us when Mom was at work. At first, I wasn't too happy about it, as I liked our family as it was. But after a while, I came to realize I was missing out on a load of fun stuff because I was babysitting Tristan all the time.

"So I began hanging out with my friends more often and leaving Tristan in the care of Uncle Brandon.

"Uncle Brandon ended up moving in, and I'd never seen Mom so happy. And her appearance changed, too. She wore makeup, bought new clothes, and started getting her hair and nails done. I really didn't understand why, but she was happy, so I didn't question it," he says with a shrug.

"Uncle Brandon coming to live with us was the worst thing that ever happened to me." He sighs, chewing on his lip ring. "He started acting like my dad, bossing me around and telling me to be nicer to my brother. By this stage, I was fifteen, and I started to rebel. I despised being told what to do, so I started hanging out with my friends more, who were just as messed up as me.

"But it was better than staying at home with Uncle Brandon, who thought he had a say over what Tristan and I did. Tristan and I grew apart. My uncle favored him over me, and in a way, it pissed me off.

"Tristan was happy he finally had a father figure in his life who treated him how a parent should treat a child. But me, I hated his guts. He and Uncle Brandon could both go to hell.

"I told Mom that I didn't like him and wanted him to leave, but she said he was a part of our lives now and wasn't going anywhere.

"I was hurt. I mean, I was her kid, and it felt like she was choosing him over me. So I started staying out late and snuck home when everyone was asleep, but they didn't care. I ended up skipping school a lot, and when I wasn't causing trouble with my friends, I hung out with…Hank," he confesses, and I bite my lip, holding back my tears.

Quinn looks at me, and I nod, silently telling him I'm okay with him continuing.

"Hank knew I was skipping classes, but because he was friends with my grandma, he let me hang out there 'cause he knew things weren't great at home. I told him everything, and he told me that sometimes, we must make sacrifices for the people we love."

I choke back a sob because, true to his word, Hank did that for me.

Quinn reaches forward to brush away my tears. "I'm sorry, Red," he whispers. "I didn't mean to upset you."

Shaking my head, I lean into his comforting touch. "You didn't. You just reminded me of what a kind, gentle man he was."

Quinn nods, his eyes growing soft. "He was. Night Cats

was my sanctuary, and talking to Hank, knowing he was there for me, and knowing I had someone to talk to, was my salvation."

I barely hold back my sniffle, but Quinn allows me to grieve, as I know we're both brokenhearted over the loss of a beautiful man.

"I remember it was a cold day," he softly continues, removing his hand from my cheek. "But it was like any other day. I skipped school and headed to the motel to hang out with Hank, but he wasn't there. I then remembered he was out of town for some car show, and I knew all my friends were at school because they were getting their asses kicked by their parents for skipping.

"My mom didn't seem to care, and my dad, well, I only really saw him every now and again around town. But he never came to see Tristan and me, and I always wondered if he knew Uncle Brandon lived with us.

"I decided to head back home and play some video games, as Mom would be at work, and Uncle Brandon would probably be there too because he started helping her out during the day. I remember coming home and thinking something wasn't right. But I ignored it, grabbed a beer, and went to my room.

"However, I had to pass my mom's room, and suddenly, I had that feeling again. I felt like I wasn't alone."

Quinn nibbles on his lip ring, his eyes in a distant place.

"I remember stopping dead in my tracks, waiting in the hallway for any signs that someone was in the house, and that's when I heard it," he confesses, swallowing past the lump in his throat.

"I heard the faintest whimper coming from inside her room. I waited, thinking it was my fucked-up mind playing tricks on me, but then I heard it again—louder this time. I panicked and charged into her room, using the beer bottle as my weapon, ready to attack whoever was hurting my mom. But what I saw, it made me sick."

Quinn takes a deep breath while I'm on tenterhooks, waiting for him to continue. I don't have to wait long.

"My mom was on her knees, getting right royally fucked by my uncle Brandon."

"What?" I gasp, my hands flying to my mouth as I sit up in shock.

Quinn nods, his jaw clenching in anger. "Yes. I just stood there, not knowing what to do because surely what I was seeing couldn't possibly be true. The moment she opened her mouth, guilt and excuses came pouring out, but I didn't want to hear it.

"She was fucking my uncle, my dad's brother, while she was still married to my father. I know they had long separated, but he was still my dad, and I saw what she did as the ultimate betrayal to not only him but also to me and Tristan.

"Even though Dad was a deadbeat, he was still my dad, and I knew what she was doing was wrong, and so did she. I could see it in her face.

"I ran from that house and stayed with my grandparents for the night, as they were back from their six-month vacation. The next day, Mom came over, guilty as all shit, begging for forgiveness. She said that what I thought I saw, I didn't, and to forget it. But I couldn't. And I never did. But we never spoke about it again, and I never told Tristan."

This story grows more awful by the minute, but sadly, I know the worst is yet to come.

"After that, I looked at her in a different light. She was my mom, for fuck's sake, and she wasn't meant to be the bad guy, but both she and my dad were a huge disappointment. So after that, I really rebelled.

"I was just so angry all the damn time. I rebelled against any form of authority—school. Police. Work. Uncle Brandon, but most of all, my mom.

"I hated her for pretending everything was fine when, in reality, it wasn't. She saw how out of control I was getting, and when she tried to discipline me, I just threw her infidelity in her face. After a while, I think she just gave up.

"Uncle Brandon, he tried to discipline me too, but when I threatened to ruin his little charade and tell Tristan what I saw, that shut him up immediately.

"As much as I hate to admit this, Red, I hated my brother," he confesses, looking utterly ashamed. "I hated him because he was the perfect son. And that's how Uncle Brandon treated him, like his goddamn son. And he treated me like a piece of shit.

"I resented Tristan when, really, he just wanted to belong.

"When I turned sixteen, I was out of control. I was failing school and on my last warning, but I didn't care. I stopped seeing Hank, the only good adult in my life, a decision I wish I could take back," he says with regret.

"I got sent home for lighting firecrackers in the girls' locker room and was expelled.

"I decided to drop past the diner and tell my mom the good news. I wanted to let her know what a great job she did at raising a delinquent, but I should have just gone home.

"As I snuck round the back to have a cigarette, I saw her with him again, and I just lost it. They were only talking, but in my eyes, they may as well have been fucking. The first punch caught them both unawares, and after that first strike, years of anger just exploded out of me, and I couldn't stop.

"Mom tried to pull me off, but I could only focus on the anger because it felt so fucking good. The way my fists felt connecting with his face made me feel liberated. How sick is that?" he spits out, shaking his head in disgust.

"How did you stop?"

"I only stopped when she told me who he really was," he replies, the pain slicing across his face.

"Who was he?" I ask, my voice wavering in fear.

He takes a deep breath and confesses, "He was Tristan's dad."

"What?" I gasp, not understanding what he was saying.

Quinn nods sadly. "Yes, he was my uncle but also Tristan's dad.

"She met my dad in college and decided to give in to his endless pleas to go out on a date. They had been seeing one another for a few weeks, and that's when she met Brandon. She said it was love at first sight." Quinn scoffs.

"Brandon apparently felt it too, but he stayed away because she was his brother's girl. He wasn't interested in a family feud. Their attraction grew and grew, but she swore they never did anything. She said she always loved Brandon, but because of his commitment to the Army, she couldn't stand in the way of his number one love—his country.

"Brandon went away for a few months to train in Texas, and they wrote to one another the entire time. He told her he wanted her to leave my dad and marry him once he returned. They were sick of hiding their feelings for one another and would tell my dad they had fallen in love."

"What happened?" I ask because that obviously didn't take place.

"Well, my dad was pushing my mom to drop out of college and take over at the diner for my grandparents. He saw that diner as an easy meal ticket. In my mom's head, I think she believed this was her way out, too.

"When Brandon came back, she and him could work here and live happily ever after, financially sound, so she dropped out.

"One night, Dad came banging on the diner door, demanding my mom let him in. She was sick of him, and his drinking was steadily becoming an issue. But she promised Brandon she would wait for his return before she broke up with my dad because Brandon wanted to be the one who told him.

"They had a huge fight because although my father was a drunken idiot, he wasn't stupid, and he knew something was wrong. He demanded to know what, but she never told him, as she had promised Brandon, and she didn't want to get him into trouble.

"When he wouldn't let it go, she did the only thing she could do to shut him up—she slept with him. On the dirty kitchen floor of that diner is where I was conceived."

I can feel my mouth moving wordlessly because I don't know what to say.

But Quinn shakes his head, not wanting my sympathy.

"When she found out she was pregnant, her hopes of playing happy family got shot to hell because she knew Brandon would never marry her now. Marrying your brother's ex, who is pregnant with your brother's baby, is fucking messed up, and in the end, Brandon chose his family over her.

"He never returned to South Boston after she wrote to him and told him she was pregnant. He said the honorable thing to do would be to marry my father because the scandal of her being pregnant before marriage in a small town such as ours, well, you can just imagine the gossip. So she did.

"She married him and was fucking miserable until, of course, Brandon came home. She told me the moment he returned, they both felt it. Her love for him was still as strong as the day he left, but things had changed.

"Brandon was married, and his wife was expecting their first child. This broke my mother, who was unhappily married with a son she never wanted, so she did everything in her power to make Brandon want her again. She seduced him, and because all men think with their dicks, he fell for her seduction. They finally consummated their fucked-up love, and that's when Tristan was conceived."

My mouth is still hanging open, as I don't know what to say. I thought my family history was fucked up, but this, holy crap, this shit is messed up.

"Deep down, I think she meant to get pregnant, hoping he would choose her and her baby over his new family, but he didn't. After all was said and done, he returned to Texas to his wife and legitimate child."

"So he knew she was pregnant with Tristan?" I finally say, thankful I can speak.

Quinn nods. "Yes, but he didn't care. This broke my mom, and she stayed with my father because she would prefer to be miserable than alone. And also, being a young, single mom with two kids in a small country town really doesn't do any favors to one's reputation.

"Deep down, I think my dad knew Tristan wasn't his. I mean, he only had to take one look into Tristan's eyes and see Brandon's eyes staring back at him. But he never said anything, as denial is bliss. And besides, he had an easy ride being married to my mom. He gambled away our money and drank himself silly.

"But something inside my mom snapped the day he hit

me. She finally grew balls and left him, and everything was going great until Brandon decided to come back home and fuck everything up. He divorced his wife and granted her full custody of his son, Mason."

My mouth once again parts in shock, and Quinn sadly nods. "Yes, Red, Tristan has a half brother."

"Oh, Quinn."

"I don't want your pity."

I quickly nod, understanding the feeling all too well. "So what happened?"

"Well, as messed up as life is, what I walked into was my mom and Brandon discussing their future—a future that didn't include me. My mom was finally going to get her wish and be married to Brandon, and together, they would run the diner—her dream finally come true.

"Tristan, of course, was a part of this fairy-tale ending, and they were going to tell him that Brandon was his real father."

"So where did that leave you?" I ask, almost afraid of his answer.

"It left me to rot in some Army boot camp for delinquent teens. Brandon convinced my mom this was for the best as she could no longer help me, and my only future would be a military one. Otherwise, I would end up in prison or worse still, end up like my father.

"She tried to reason with me that this was for the best, and she was only doing this for me. But I knew she was only doing this for herself. I was the last piece tying her to a past she longed to escape because she never wanted me.

"She was never mean to me and tried her best to be a good mother, but I know when she looked at me, she saw my father, and she also saw her wasted youth. And now that she was given a second chance with Brandon, she wasn't letting anyone stand in her way—not even her son."

"What did you do?" I question, knowing Quinn would never stand for this.

He sighs, running a hand through his hair. "I did the only thing I could do."

"And what was that?"

"I told my dad," he confesses, and the room suddenly begins to spin. "I knew that it was wrong, but I was so fucking angry. Why were they the lucky ones? Why were they allowed a second chance, and I wasn't? It wasn't my fault that my mother was a coward.

"I never asked to be born, so I just didn't care.

"When I told him, he reacted just as I thought he would, with a shotgun pressed to my temple, demanding where they were. This was exactly the response I had hoped for. I wanted my father to scare the shit out of Brandon, hoping he would leave and maybe, just maybe, Tristan, my mom, and I could go back to the way things were. But I was a stupid kid."

"Why?"

"Because there was one person in this whole fucked-up mess who was purely innocent."

"Tristan," I gasp, and Quinn nods.

"By telling my dad the truth, I only just confirmed what he thought to be true. And when he dished out his revenge, he was going to make sure Tristan paid for my mother and Brandon's mistake.

"I couldn't allow that to happen, so I lied and told him they were at the diner. Dad left, shotgun in one hand and a bottle of bourbon in the other, intent on revenge.

"I knew I didn't have long, so I stole a car and sped to my house, needing to warn my mom. Tristan was at my grandparents' for the night, which made me feel slightly better, so I knew it was now or never. I told my mom and Brandon what I had done, and then I gave my mother an ultimatum. She chooses me or him."

I close my eyes, now understanding all the times Quinn opened up to me about his mom.

Everything begins to make sense.

I now understand his heartbreaking cries for forgiveness when he was dreaming that night in the truck. His confession at the diner right before Justin attacked me; it all makes sense because I know who his mother chose.

"If she chose me and Tristan, then I would call Dad and tell him it was all a lie, and I would suffer the consequences. But if she chose him, then I would call Dad and tell him where they were.

"Brandon knew he was in trouble because he had seen my dad's temper firsthand, so he decided to give my mom his own ultimatum. She could leave with him right now, and they could start a new life where no one knew them—no one would ever know the sins of their past.

"Or he would do all that without her.

"He couldn't face his brother, knowing what he had done, so he took the coward's way out.

"I could see her mulling over the offer, and I could also see his offer was becoming more appealing than mine when Brandon upped the stakes. He said they would take Tristan with them and be the happy little family they were always supposed to be."

"What about you?" I ask, tears stinging my eyes.

"They didn't care. But there was no damn way they were taking my brother. And in a sick way, I was jealous. Why did he get a chance at a normal life, and I didn't? But my mother knew my father would never stop looking for them until he found them and made them pay for their betrayal.

"She could never live a happy, normal life while always looking over her shoulder, in fear my father had found her. And I knew that, too. So I upped the ante.

"She was to leave Tristan here with me, and Grandma and Grandpa could look after us until I turned eighteen, and then I would look after Tristan myself. I also told her I would never tell my grandparents why she left and spare her the shame of them knowing she cheated on her husband and had an illegitimate child with his brother.

"If she did this, then I would call my dad and tell him I made it all up. I would tell him that I drove her away because she couldn't deal with me any longer. She knew that if I did this, then she would finally be free of him."

"What did she do?"

Quinn takes a moment, mulling over the past. "She chose him. She left us behind because she was selfish and weak. But the worst part is, I gave her that ultimatum. I jeopardized my brother's happiness because of my selfishness," he confesses, and I've never seen him look so heartbroken.

"She left us. She abandoned us when it got too tough. She chose a better life without us in it. But I stuck to my word and called my dad, telling him I had made it all up, and then, they left. They left because I lied, giving my mom and Brandon the perfect alibi.

"I couldn't believe she actually left, and I stood in my living room for minutes, trying to process what the hell I had done. The only thing that snapped me back into reality was when a car's headlights shone brightly through the window because I thought it was them. I thought she had changed her mind. But she didn't.

"Those headlights belonged to Sheriff Davidson because he was arresting me for stealing a car.

"I didn't care because being arrested probably saved my life. I knew my dad would have beaten me within an inch of my life for lying to him and for being the reason why my mother left. I got six months in juvie thanks to my prior convictions while my grandparents looked after Tristan."

Holy shit, my mind is reeling, but I nod because I know there's more.

"Six months is a long time when all you've got is time. So I promised myself, then and there, that I would be the best brother I could possibly be to Tristan. I took away his happiness because he could have been happy and lived a normal life. But I took it all away because I was jealous."

"Quinn, uprooting a teenager and taking him away from his brother and his friends probably wouldn't have made him happy," I say, hoping I don't anger him.

But Quinn shakes his head, his jaw clenched tight. "But I took that choice away from him. He was thirteen; he would have made new friends and forgotten all about me.

"I have lived with my decision every day since. My selfishness caused my grandparents unnecessary pain because they never understood why their only daughter took off without a trace. I hurt my dad even though he doesn't deserve any sympathy. I hurt my mom. But most of all, I hurt the only person who never looked at me like I was a loser. Never questioned me because I was his older brother, and I fucking betrayed him in the worst way possible.

"So whatever Tristan wanted, he got. I would never again deny him a moment of happiness. My grandparents split when I was eighteen, leaving me in charge of the diner and making me the rightful owner. I didn't want it, but Tristan did. So I gave it to him."

So technically, Quinn is Tristan's boss.

Holy shit, him scoffing when I called him the boss now makes perfect sense.

"But there was one thing I couldn't give Tristan." Quinn's eyes sadly search mine. "And that was a girl. All the girls I messed around with weren't good enough for my brother. They would forget his name the minute they got what they wanted, and Tristan deserved better than that."

"But you deserved that?" I unhappily question, hating he thinks so poorly of himself.

"I deserved worse," he replies, taking a deep breath.

"Quinn—"

But he shakes his head, cutting me off.

"I knew Tristan wanted a girlfriend. My brother is a hopeless romantic, but I love that about him. I love he sees the world through his rose-tinted glasses because I don't.

"The single girls in our town, well, excluding Tabitha, they're all the same. But then...then you arrived. The moment he saw you, I knew that he liked you."

Thinking back to when I first met the Berkeley brothers, I can't help but smile. I never would have predicted that precise moment would alter my life in a way I never thought possible.

"I tried so damn hard to stay away from you and to honor my promise to make Tristan happy. But the more I pushed you away, the harder you fought, and the more I fucking wanted you. You don't understand how many times I had to stop myself from—" He pauses, chewing on his lip ring as he gazes down at my body.

"Why me?"

"You don't realize how special you are," he replies, slowly moving toward me. "What's in here"—he presses his hand to my heart—"I want to possess. I want to own, but I don't deserve you. I never have."

His words bring tears to my eyes, and there is only one thing I can do to show him he's more than worthy of my love.

Pulling out of his touch, I slowly reach for the hem of my sweater and pull it over my head.

Quinn follows the movement but makes no attempt to move.

Next, I slip off my tank, and his eyes continue to watch me as they smolder with desire.

"I'm just like him," he whispers, his eyes filling with tears. "I'm stealing my brother's girl. I'm turning into the man I've grown to hate."

Everything suddenly comes crashing down, and Quinn's reasoning for staying away from me becomes crystal clear.

Quinn doesn't want to be like his uncle, taking me away from Tristan.

But the thing is, I was never Tristan's girl—I've always been Quinn's.

And I always will be.

I don't allow his words to discourage me as I lie back down and carefully unzip my jeans. As I wriggle out of them, raising my hips to slide them off, Quinn stops me by placing a hand on my hip.

"You still want me?" he asks, astounded. "After everything I just told you? This doesn't change your mind?"

Sitting up, I slowly reach around and unhook my bra, allowing the straps to glide off my shoulders, and we both watch as the lacy material lands in my lap.

As Quinn bites his lip, his eyes zeroing in on my nipples, I lean forward and place my trembling palm on his cheek. "This changes everything."

Quinn blinks, and the fear is reflected in his tender eyes. "I'm sorry I'm not the man you thought I was."

"No, you're not," I confess, and Quinn lowers his head, ashamed.

"You're more." I cup his cheek and coax him to look at me.

"What?" he gasps as he searches my face for answers.

"You're everything I want. What you just told me shows me who you really are."

"And who's that?" he asks, beseeching me to give him the answer he's been searching for his entire life.

Slowly clutching the hem of his shirt and slipping it over his head, I gently rub my finger over the hoop in his nipple.

As I watch his skin break out into goose bumps, I whisper, "You're you, Quinn. Nothing's changed. And that man, whether he believes it or not, is a good man. And he's the man I will want with my last breath."

I bend forward, kissing his trembling lips.

Quinn willingly returns the kiss, and I gently slip my hands between us so I can unbuckle his belt, making my intentions clear.

"Red, stop," he pants, pulling his hips away. "I don't have a condom."

But I wouldn't have this any other way.

With his confession, I want no more barriers between us. I just want it to be Mia and Quinn.

"I don't care," I whisper, lying down and slowly slipping off my black underwear.

Quinn watches the movement, and I can see his inner turmoil.

But I'm so sick of what's right and what's wrong. I'm sick of abiding by other people's rules because all I want to do is live.

And this, right now, is the most I've ever felt alive.

Some may call it irresponsible, but I call it living. And after living my entire life in darkness, I've finally found the light.

I don't plan on getting lost in the dark ever again.

Reaching forward, I run my fingers along his ribs, tracing his tattoo. "We make our own fate." I now finally understand the meaning behind his ink. "Let me be yours."

And that's all it takes as I watch his resolve slowly slip away.

When he slides off his jeans, I nervously gulp because seeing him naked is a sight that takes my breath away.

"This might hurt a little," he whispers, lowering his warm body onto mine.

"It's okay," I reply, wrapping my hands around his neck as I open my legs to allow him to slip inside.

"I'll go slow."

I nod, my body trembling in fear but also in need.

"You're so beautiful," he whispers, kissing my chin while I feel him slip a finger inside me, testing to see if I'm ready.

When he slips in another, he knows that I am.

"I don't deserve you," he says, his long hair caressing my cheeks as he nips at my jaw. "But I want you. I've wanted you from the first moment I saw you."

The way his fingers sink into me has my hips rising in wanton need, but it's not enough.

I want more.

I reach between us and grip his shaft.

He groans, drawing his hips toward my touch. He senses my need and slowly removes his fingers, replacing them with the tip of his cock. I feel the first slice of pain as he gradually eases into me, and he freezes as I hiss, my muscles familiarizing themselves with the delicious intrusion.

"Keep going," I whisper as the burn subsides.

Quinn kisses my trembling lips as he slowly pushes deeper into me but stops. "This is the part that'll hurt the most," he says, his voice shuddering under the pressure of holding back.

Closing my eyes and taking a deep breath, I will my body to relax. "Don't stop."

I raise my hips, encouraging him to move because I want this.

I want him.

"I love you, Red." With one sharp, quick movement, he's sheathed inside.

"Holy fuck," I moan, my body bowing.

"I'm almost there," he pants, controlling his breathing.

I'm not sure if I can fit any more of him inside me without splitting in half, but as Quinn reaches down and begins rubbing over my clit, my fears are quickly forgotten. I slowly rock, following his touch and his rhythm, and before long, I'm hungrily raising my hips, wanting him to go in deeper.

"You okay?" he gasps, his heated breath tickling my ear.

"Yes. Just don't stop."

"Never." He places a gentle kiss on the tip of my nose.

He sinks in and then pulls out, and I almost cry, needing him back inside. But with one quick thrust, he's finally all the way in.

He pauses, allowing my body to adjust.

"Can I move?" he asks, his voice strained.

I nod.

I'm thankful the movements start slow and controlled because my body couldn't take anything harder.

I wrap my arms around the back of his neck and whimper into his mouth as he kisses me deeply. I focus on his mouth and the way his tongue circles mine, and not on the pain between my legs. It doesn't hurt in the traditional sense, but it does feel foreign.

But as I slowly find my rhythm, slow and controlled isn't enough.

"Faster," I breathe out.

But Quinn shakes his head. "I'll hurt you."

He sucks his hoop into his mouth, concentrating on his guarded strokes.

"No…holding back," I gasp, and arch my back, silently begging him to let go.

"Fuck," he curses, attempting to pull out, but I grip his hip.

"Let go," I say, hoping I don't regret this tomorrow. "Show me you love me, as I do you."

I reach for his nipple ring and give it a gentle pull.

"You are incredible."

And then, then he begins to move.

At first, my body screams as he sinks in deep and hard, but the moment he bends forward and captures my nipple into his wet mouth, those screams turn to mewls of utter pleasure.

The speed, the friction, the depth, all of it increases, and so does a tiny bundle of nerves in my belly, which slowly awakens as he strokes me with expert precision. The faster he moves, the quicker it rises.

"Oh my God," I gasp, as I never imagined it could feel this good.

"You all right, baby?" he pants, kissing the corner of my parted mouth.

"Yes," I moan, my hips meeting his, thrust for thrust.

I'm so close, I can taste my approaching climax, but I can

sense Quinn isn't there just yet.

So doing what feels natural, I hook a leg around his waist and push down on his firm ass cheek with my foot, pushing him into me at a deeper angle.

"Holy shit," he groans. "You feel amazing."

He kisses me fiercely, devouring my lips as I revel in the way his body molds to mine.

We fit perfectly, and as I begin to find my rhythm, I gather a little more confidence and lose myself to this experience I will remember for the rest of my life.

I arch my neck, moaning when Quinn bites the side of my throat. He isn't gentle, and I like that it feels like he's marking me because I know he is intent on leaving a mark. So I decide to leave a mark of my own.

I score his flesh with my fingernails as I run them down his back.

He hisses against my throat, biting harder before driving into me with deep, delicious strokes.

I can feel him everywhere; he is ingrained into every fiber of my body, and I want to stay like this forever.

Our bodies move in unison—the perfect combination, straddling the line between pleasure and pain. Quinn grips my hip, encouraging me to meet his thrusts as he slams into me over and over again.

He fucks with passion and love, the most perfect combination.

Before long, my body grows lax, and I surrender to Quinn as he takes control.

"Ready?" he asks but doesn't wait for me to reply as he withdraws before flipping me onto my stomach.

He sinks into me once again, fucking me harder.

This angle is so intense that I reach overhead, gripping

the arm of the sofa as I need an anchor before I drift away.

He holds my hips, fucking me hard, so hard, my body jars upward with the force. But I like it. I like that his movements reflect how badly he wants me.

He bends down and grips my chin, coaxing me to look over my shoulder so he can kiss the ever-living fuck out of me. When his barbell strokes me in a way that coincides with what he's doing to me down below, the knot in my belly tightens.

"Lift your hips, Red," he orders, and when I do, he fucks me so hard and so deep, tears sting my eyes.

We continue kissing while Quinn quickens his strokes. My ass is high in the air, but I'm still lying on my stomach. Every time Quinn pulls out, he does so slowly, allowing me to feel every hardened inch of him, only to then slam back into me.

The more he does this, the more enjoyable things become.

My body welcomes his delicious strokes, and as I bounce back to meet his passionate thrusts, a string of profanity leaves Quinn.

He grips my hips and commences fucking me hard. The sound of our flesh slapping together and pleasured moans spilling from us both is fucking hot, and I know I'm moments away from coming.

"Tell me you love me," he hoarsely orders, his strokes wilder, his grip tighter.

"I love you, Quinn Berkeley," I answer breathlessly.

"I love you too. This changes everything. You belong to me. And I"—he scoops a hand under my belly, coaxing me to my hands and knees—"belong to you."

His possession is what I want because I feel every word.

He continues sinking into me, gripping my ass and spreading me wide. I lose myself to this feeling of completeness, and when Quinn reaches around and plays with my clit, I let go and come with a guttural groan.

Tears sting my eyes as I arch my back, my body milking every tremor. I still bounce back however, taking everything Quinn gives as he continues to pump into me, drawing out every last vibration.

"Fucking beautiful," he hums before pulling out, and I feel his warm jets on my ass.

I collapse into a loud, messy heap, too sated to move as I close my eyes, basking in my post-orgasmic bliss. My lungs feel like they're about to explode, and my heart kicks against my rib cage, threatening to break free, but I wouldn't change this feeling for anything.

After a few moments, I feel a light flutter on my back and turn over my shoulder to see Quinn cleaning me up.

We both watch one another closely, and where I thought there would be embarrassment or shyness over what we just did, I find nothing but love. And we don't speak for minutes because there are simply no words.

Thirteen

It's dawn when I finally rouse, sore but sated. The delicious burn between my legs is a wonderful reminder of what Quinn and I just did.

Flickers of our naked bodies becoming one overwhelm me, and I clench my inner thighs as I'm turned on all over again by the memory alone. I never thought it could be that way with someone, and I'm afraid that now that I've experienced this, I won't be able to stop.

I'm addicted to Quinn, but after tonight, I'm a full-blown junkie waiting for my next fix.

"You okay?"

My body hums the second I hear his voice, and my memories magnify, spreading animated warmth over my entire body.

"I'm good," I finally reply, turning to face Quinn, and he

looks fucking epic.

His hair is wild and freshly fucked, and his eyes are all sleepy and heavy. But it's his mouth that has me mesmerized. The way it tips up into a dimpled smirk tells me he's been thinking the same thoughts as me.

Brushing a fallen piece of hair off my brow, he smiles.

"How long have I been asleep?" I ask with a yawn.

"A couple of hours. You looked so peaceful. I didn't want to wake you."

"You do realize that's creepy, right?" I tease. "You've just upped the stalker ante to full-blown creeper."

I like that there's no awkwardness between us because, for me, this only brings us closer.

"What's the matter, Berkeley? No comeback?" I squeal when he pushes me down quickly, catching me unawares.

Pinning my arms about my head and securing my wrists in one hand, he begins tickling me with the other.

"Quinn!" I say, laughing so hard I almost choke. "Truce!"

"I don't think so." He continues torturing me until I wheeze and gag.

"You're so mean." I breathlessly laugh when he releases my wrists.

"Oh, Red, I can be so much meaner."

We're both breathing rapidly from our impromptu play fight.

It's only now that I'm not squirming and begging for him to stop do I realize I'm lying under a very naked Quinn, my very naked chest pressing against his. But any shred of modesty was lost when I stripped bare in front of him as he bared me his soul.

And I like that.

I like that my messy, chaotic, unusual life has this one

scrap of normalcy—it anchors me to my humanity. It keeps my hope alive that I'll finally find my normal one day.

Quinn can read my thoughts as he places a tender kiss under my ear. The loving touch sends a shiver down my spine, but Quinn mistakes my pleasure for pain.

"Are you cold?" he asks, rubbing my upper arms.

"I'm okay." I smile, touched by his concern.

"We should get back inside anyway," he says after a moment of silence.

He's right. I don't even know what time it is or how long we've been out here.

We quickly get dressed, and I can't help but watch the way Quinn puts his clothes on. Something so simple shouldn't get me hot, but it does.

"Who's the creeper now?"

I am so busted, but I just shrug in response.

As I'm about to do my laces, Quinn drops to his knees before me and does them for me. "It'll be okay. I'll do all the talking."

"I just feel…weird?" I say, and Quinn chuckles, placing his hands on my upper thighs.

"Is that a question or a statement?"

"I don't know."

I feel so stupid for behaving this way, but I don't want to hurt Tristan. And I know I need to apologize to everyone, but I don't want to. Polly said some fucked-up things, and I think she should be the one to apologize.

But I'll be the bigger person because this house is small enough without adding any more uncomfortableness.

"What are you going to say to Tristan?"

Quinn sighs, running a hand through his hair. "I'm pretty sure he knows what happened. I mean, we were gone for a really long time. But I'll be honest and tell him the truth."

I nod and wonder if that truth will include telling him about his dad.

"Not yet, Red," Quinn says, reading my thoughts. "I'm not ready for two ass kickings in one day."

"Well, three." I gently run my finger over his bruised lip.

Last night, his injuries were the furthest thing from my mind, but now that I'm not riddled with lust, I can see Tristan got in some good shots. I hope I didn't hurt him while I was mauling his face, but he didn't seem to mind.

"I love you," Quinn says softly, and I gasp. Hearing it for the first time after last night and in the bright light of day makes it real—makes us real.

"I love you," I reply, running my finger over the cut above his eye.

Quinn rises and reaches for my hands, pulling me into his chest. "Remember, let me do the talking."

"I'll be quiet," I agree, but Quinn smirks.

We walk toward the house and enter through the back door, but when I hear giggling, I arch a questioning brow as I turn to look at Quinn.

He only shrugs.

As we walk into the kitchen, we're both unprepared for what we see. Quinn and I stop and stare, unsure of what to do as we witness a very shirtless Tristan chasing a very scantily dressed Polly around the kitchen table, the kitchen sink spray in hand.

They haven't noticed us gawking at them, and Polly giggles. "Stop it. I'm wet enough."

Her comment has me nearly gagging on my tongue, and I step forward, enraged. "What's going on?"

They both spin toward me, surprised they have company.

The moment Tristan meets my eyes, I know he knows.

Suddenly, I feel really, *really* shitty, and it shows on my guilt-ridden face.

"Tristan, we need to talk," I choke out after a moment of silence, my wavering voice betraying my nerves.

"So much for keeping quiet," Quinn utters behind me.

I ignore him as I turn my attention toward a soaked Polly. "Polly, can you go upstairs for a minute? We need to talk to Tristan," I say, hoping she doesn't decide to be difficult.

"Yes, I do mind," she replies, boldly crossing her arms over her bust.

"Well, too bad," I bark back, my patience wearing thin.

"It's fine, Mia. She can stay," Tristan says, which surprises me.

Polly cocks a challenging brow my way. But I don't take the bait.

"Fine."

How do I exactly tell him I chose his brother? To be fair, there was never a choice to be made. It was always Quinn.

"I...um," I mumble, feeling my cheeks explode in a burst of red.

Quinn reaches for my sweaty palm and interlaces his fingers through mine.

The moment I feel his touch, my heartbeat slows, and I take a small breath. However, that breath gets caught in my throat as I watch Tristan's eyes drop to our union. I automatically try and drop his hand, but Quinn holds on tight.

"Tristan, look—" But Quinn pauses, as Tristan's eyes are still glued to our hands, and he looks absolutely furious.

I'm about five seconds away from running out the door, so I suddenly blurt out, "We had sex."

Why my mouth filter malfunctioned and exploded into

an uncomfortable mess right this second is beyond me, but now that it's out, we've gotta roll with it.

However, Quinn closes his eyes and runs a hand down his face, softly groaning. No doubt he wishes I would just stick to my word and shut the hell up.

Polly bites back a chuckle. No doubt she loves watching me squirm.

"Tristan," I quickly say. "I'm sorry."

Once again, I've put my foot in it because Quinn turns to look at me, cocking an unimpressed eyebrow and letting go of my hand.

"No, I'm not sorry it happened," I quickly amend, reaching for Quinn.

But when he and Tristan groan in unison, I decide now is a good time to shut up.

"It's fine. I'm happy for you. No need to explain."

He gives a casual shrug.

Both Quinn and I know he's not fine, nor is he happy for us.

"Tristan—" Quinn sighs, but Tristan holds up a hand.

"Save it, Quinn. You got the girl. No need to gloat," he bites back, pushing off the counter.

"I wasn't going to—"

"I don't want to hear it."

Polly decides now is a great time to butt in and add to the shitstorm. "You got the girl too, Tristan," she says, running a fingernail down his chest and flicking his belt buckle.

"Excuse me?"

"What? You think you can have them both?" Polly smugly asks, turning to glare at me.

"Excuse me?" I repeat, as it's better than the alternative of fuck you. "For your information, I don't want them both."

For fuck's sake, I need to stop.

Right.

Now.

Tristan snickers, and I quickly backpedal, but I know it's too late. "Tristan, I love you as a—"

"If you say brother, I will seriously stab myself."

Quinn takes a step toward his brother. "I love Mia," he says with such strong resolve, I can't help but melt. "We never planned for this to happen, it just—"

Quinn pauses, turning to look at me with nothing but adoration in his eyes.

"Tristan, I've loved her for a long time," he softly concludes, and I almost fall flat on my face.

He's loved me for a long time? This is so not the time to swoon, but wow…

However, I remain composed because Tristan looks like he's about to snap.

"How long?" he asks, taking a steadying breath.

Quinn clears his throat, averting his eyes, revealing his guilt.

But Tristan presses. "Since you've been on the run?"

However, Quinn only stands motionless, his eyes transfixed to the floor.

"What? Before then?" Tristan asks, his voice betraying his shock but also his pain.

"Before," Quinn softly replies with a nod, finally looking at Tristan.

"What?" I gasp, silently begging him to meet my eyes.

But he avoids my questioning stare.

"Oh please, can I vomit now?" Polly snickers, sticking a finger down her throat.

I internally count to ten to stop myself from sticking my

whole fist down there and focus on Tristan.

"Tristan?" I question, as he's gone deathly quiet.

He flicks his pained eyes my way. "And you want him?"

As much as this is going to kill me, I nod. "I do. I'm sorry."
Thankfully, Quinn understands this time around.

Tristan runs a hand through his hair, pulling at it in
frustration. "Well, fuck me."

My heart breaks, and I stop myself from reaching out to
him because I know my touch is the last thing he seeks at the
moment.

"Why do you care?" Polly suddenly yells, turning to face
Tristan. "You kissed me last night! I thought you liked me."

Quinn groans and leaves behind an angry Mohawk as he
fists his hair in frustration.

"Seriously?" He sighs, pointing at a pouting Polly. "You
wanna know what she is?"

I allow him to finish because I'm quite certain his
description of her will be a lot nicer than mine.

"She's trouble, Tristan. She's sixteen!"

"I'm seventeen in two days!" Polly pipes up defensively.

"Same shit! You're still a kid!" he yells, and Polly shuts her
mouth right away.

"I don't need to listen to this shit, 'cause from where I'm
standing, you're in no position to tell me what's right and
wrong," Tristan snarls, and Quinn flinches, devastated by
Tristan's intentional stab.

Polly reaches for him, but he violently shrugs out of her
grip and storms outside.

I move to take off after him, but Quinn grabs my forearm.

"Let him cool down. I'll talk to him once he's blown off
some steam."

I look at the door, biting my lip as I really want to go talk to him. But I nod because Quinn knows his brother better than I do.

Quinn turns dangerously slow toward a cowering Polly. "And you," he snarls. "Stay the fuck away from my brother. He's got enough shit to deal with, and he doesn't need your melodramatic crap to add to the shit pile."

Polly's mouth gapes open, and I fight the urge not to smile.

Polly sees me silently gloating, and her eyes turn cold. "This is all your fault," she says between clenched teeth. "You've ruined my life."

A tad overdramatic, but I don't have time to rebuke as Quinn quickly snaps, "No, you spoiled brat, you've ruined your own life by being nothing but self-absorbed and only thinking of yourself. You talk to her like that again, and I'll show you what a ruined life looks like."

He latches onto my hand, and we leave the room, headed for our bedroom.

He sits on the edge of the bed and cradles his head in his hands.

He's not okay. And neither am I.

We just told his brother, who might be a little bit in love with me, that we had sex and that Quinn has loved me since… when? When was the exact moment he felt it?

I know there was never a precise event or moment for me—I think I've always been in love with him. But that love, it grew into…this.

Stepping forward, I run my fingers through his hair, giving his head a light rub. "Hmm…that feels good."

"Thank you for sticking up for me."

Quinn raises his eyes, looking completely confused.

"You know, with Polly," I explain, and his mouth forms an O in understanding.

"She had it coming."

"I thought you liked her?"

"I guess I had a little soft spot for her."

"Why?" I ask, my voice dripping with disgust.

"Her situation reminded me of—"

Tristan, I internally finish.

Of course he would have a soft spot for her.

She is, after all, my half-sibling. Just like Tristan is Quinn's. I still can't get my head around that and doubt I ever will.

I can't help but wonder when Quinn will tell Tristan the truth. But this is his decision to make, and I know it's one he won't make lightly.

"I should find Tristan."

"Do you want me to come with you?"

"No, I better do this alone. I should have done this a long time ago."

I nod in understanding because I know he's referring to us being honest in the first place.

But what we were doing, and who we were back then, doesn't even skim the surface of how far we've come.

I wish I could take away Tristan's pain, but do I regret finally telling him the truth?

No, I don't.

"I just wish this was all over," Quinn says, looking utterly exhausted.

His comment reminds me that I have yet to tell him about Tabitha's text message.

"It will be," I say with a smile and stalk over to the dresser to fetch the phone. "Abi messaged me."

"She did?" Quinn pipes up, standing and storming over to me. "Holy shit, I forgot we had this phone. We can call Chandler."

I'm still tinkering around on the cell, but it won't turn on. Suddenly, I know why. "Dammit, the battery is dead."

Quinn reaches for the phone and tries pushing a few buttons, but he quickly confirms my fears.

"What did Abi say?"

"She said we're days away from this being over. We're nearly free," I reply, reaching for Quinn and placing my hand on his cheek.

"Thank fuck." He sighs, leaning into my touch. "The fact we no longer have a link to Abi is a problem, though."

I look at him, as we both know what needs to happen.

"I'll go into town tonight, give Chandler and Abi a call, and hope one of them can give me some good news."

I hate how fatigued he sounds.

"It'll be over soon." I smile, but we both know that soon can't come soon enough.

As much as I hate that Quinn has to do this on his own, he's right. I'm probably the last person Tristan wants to see at the moment. I'll most likely make things worse, so I told Quinn to come find me when he's done.

That was two hours ago.

I fight the urge to go looking for him because I know this can't be rushed.

However, I'm bored out of my mind and antsy as hell.

There's no way I'm going to talk to Polly because after today, she can go to hell. I've tried my best, but I've accepted the fact that we will never see eye to eye. And messing with Tristan was the last straw.

I know she doesn't like him, and Tristan deserves better

than that.

Kicking off the bed, I decide to take Lucky for a walk, and if I happen to stumble across Quinn in the process, then so be it. Reaching for his lead, I vaguely hear a small whimper coming from the room next door—Cynthia's room.

I have no idea how she is after our dinner from hell, and I feel a little guilty for not thinking about her till now. So, with that thought in mind, I decide to check on her.

As I reach her door, I hear the whimper again, and I know she's crying.

Not knowing if I should intrude, I decide to knock. She can always send me away if she doesn't want the company. I rap lightly on the door, and the crying stops. I wait, not knowing if I should knock again or run in the opposite direction.

Before I have the chance to make a decision, the door opens, and I shrink back at Cynthia's appearance. She looks like shit, and I instantly feel awful because I seem to be the reason behind her constant sorrow.

We stand, staring at one another uncomfortably, and my heart softens when I see how exhausted she is.

The bags under her eyes reveal she's had many sleepless nights, no doubt tossing and turning, thinking about our dire situation.

"Are you okay?" I ask, barely audible.

"I'm okay, Mia. I'm just…tired," she confesses, and I think she means she's sick and tired of dealing with my mess.

"I'm sorry, Cynthia," I say, biting my lip, as this is difficult for me to say.

When she remains silent, I continue. "I know this has been hard on you, so I promise, once this is all over, I'll leave you alone. I don't expect anything from you. I mean, you told me what I wanted to hear, and I appreciate it," I say, realizing that although my past sucks ass, I would never trade the truth for lies.

When this is finally over, all I can hope for is to move on from my past, a past that has shaped me into who I am. And no matter how cruel or how shitty it may be, it's my past, and I'm going to own it.

I won't allow it to define me because I'm sick of living in the past. I have a new future ahead of me now, and that future includes Quinn.

Cynthia snaps me out of my thoughts. "Mia, I don't want you to leave me alone unless you want that. What I told you about your past, it's not something I'm proud of. If I could take it all back, I would. If I could erase your pain, I would. But I can't.

"The only thing I can do is hope that you will give me a second chance. God knows I don't deserve it, but I want you to be a part of my life. I'm not naive. I know we'll never have a normal mother-daughter relationship. But maybe one day, we could just have a...friendship. I'd like that a lot," she finishes, and I stand with my mouth agape, as this was not what I expected.

After how I've treated her, I thought she would be glad to see the back of me. But here she is, extending the olive branch, and fuck me, I want to accept it.

I don't know what's changed, but I don't want to keep fighting with her.

I, too, am not naive, and I doubt I'll ever get to the stage where I'm comfortable enough to call her Mother.

But maybe one day, I could call her my...friend.

"I'd like that too."

She nods, brushing away a stolen tear. "Did you fight with Pollyanna?" she asks, and although the subject matter is a crappy one, I'm thankful she changed the topic.

"Yeah, you could say that," I reply, thinking which fight, as I seem to be fighting with her constantly.

"Polly is just like her father—headstrong and stubborn," she says, but cringes when she mentions Chandler.

"Quinn said he'll call him tonight. We really need to get the hell out of here."

"What about your friend?" she asks with a hopeful look in her eye.

I know she doesn't want to involve Chandler in my mess.

"I didn't get a chance to tell you before, but Abi sent me a text message. Sadly, the battery is now dead, so we can't use it. But anyhow, she said we're close. It's only a matter of days until we're free," I say, unable to keep the relief from my tone.

"And what happens when you're free?"

Giving her question some thought, I answer the only way I know how. And that's with honesty and hope.

"I start living," I reply, and my heart weeps for that possibility to become a reality real soon.

Cynthia nods but quickly excuses herself, as she no doubt feels the same way.

Sitting on the porch swing and overlooking the peace in front of me is calming.

The past few…forever has been grueling and tough. My life hasn't been easy, and I wish I could forget some parts.

But other parts, even the shitty parts, that I look upon now and realize they've shaped me into the person I've become. My life has never been normal, in no way, but if I could have it all back, would I?

If I turned out to be the spoiled little brat Polly is, then I think I would take my life as is.

If I never endured what I did, then I would have never ended up in South Boston, and I would have never met Hank or Tabitha or Tristan or Quinn.

I know that's selfish because since my arrival, my past has impacted each one of them gravely, especially Hank. And although I wish we'd met under different circumstances, I'm still glad we met.

They will always be my family of misfits, and no matter what happens, I'll never take back a moment spent with them, especially Hank.

What Quinn told me about Hank just makes me love him all the more.

He was also drawn to the misfits, as I believe he saw Quinn and myself for who we really are—two lost souls just wanting to belong. He opened up his home to Quinn and me, and I'll be damned if I let his death be in vain.

The past couple of days have been about cleansing both my past and Quinn's, and we've both exorcised our demons for the time being, but now, now it's time to get serious and figure out our plan of attack.

Yes, we may be closer to gaining our freedom, but I still plan on dishing out my revenge on Phil and Thomas. That fact hasn't changed. I just need to figure out how, when, and where.

So first things first—we need to make contact with the outside world.

It's been just over five hours and there's still no sign of Quinn. I'm not worried, as I know this can't be rushed. No doubt Quinn will put the entire truth out there and allow Tristan to process it in whatever way he can.

My heart still aches when I remember the look on Tristan's face when I told him it was Quinn I wanted, not him. There would never be an easy way to do it, and I think that's why Quinn waited so long to tell him.

I understand his notion of not wanting to hurt Tristan, but maybe a part of him had hoped I would just give up on him, just like everyone else had, and go for the easy option. But the heart wants what the heart wants, and I've never been one to take the easy option when it comes to life.

Rubbing my chest, I decide to start on my plan of attack and stop thinking about the Berkeley brothers, as they're giving me heartburn.

I searched for some paper and a pen to write down my ideas, but when I found Quinn's sketch pad, I took that instead. It sits in my lap, and although I shouldn't, I want to see what's inside.

I don't know if this is the equivalent of reading someone's diary, but either way, it's happening.

However, as soon as I open the first page, I slam it shut. I feel like I'm intruding on Quinn's personal thoughts. But curiosity gets the better of me, and I slowly reopen it.

The opening picture is one of the first deadbeat motels we stayed at when first on the run.

Quinn's drawings are unlike anything I've ever seen before. His attention to detail and the way he captures small elements that most take for granted take my breath away. As I run my finger over the charcoal lines of the motel's roof, I trace over a small bird perched on the roof's peak.

I never noticed the bird in real life, but now, now I'm sad I didn't pay more attention, as it's simply beautiful.

After staring at the picture for quite some time, I flip through the pages, enthralled by what I see. It's like I'm reliving our journey thus far because Quinn has captured almost every aspect of our travels.

Cars we've stolen, diners we've eaten at, places we've been to, and people we've seen.

As awful and ugly as being on the run has been, seeing it through Quinn's eyes has made me realize that Quinn has seen the beauty in it, too. This here, this is our past, and I can't stop a tear slipping down my cheek.

Quinn and I have been through so much, but we've been through it together. This experience brought us together, and for that, I'm thankful.

Wiping away my tears, I turn to the next page, and what I see has a fresh set of tears forming.

Tracing over the executed, long lines and the expert, perfected strokes, I outline over the carbon copy of me and Hank. I know this was done from memory alone, as all these pictures were sketched after Hank's death. But Quinn has captured his crooked smile, weathered hands, and most of all, his kind eyes like he only saw him yesterday.

A sob gets caught in my throat because I can almost feel his hand on mine and smell his unique scent, which always smelled like home, and I can also hear his kindness as he bends down to whisper something in my ear.

This sketch had come to life before me, and I can clearly picture that memory as I pluck it from time. It was Thanksgiving—Hank's last day on earth.

It seems so long ago, but looking at this awakens memories I didn't even know I'd made.

"Merry Christmas."

Quinn takes a seat near me, his shoulder touching mine, and I know I should give back his book, but I can't. I can't close this page on Hank because as each day passes, I lose a piece of him, and before long, I'm afraid my memories will fade.

But I sniff back my tears and ask, "Merry Christmas?"

Quinn silently nods as he reaches over and gently rips out the page.

I gasp, terrified that he has torn the drawing, but let out a sigh of relief when he offers me the picture.

Flipping it over, I see that Quinn has written something on the back.

> For in that sleep of death, what dreams may come.
> All my Love, Q x

"It's *Hamlet*," Quinn explains as I stare at his handwriting, on the verge of another breakdown.

"It's beautiful," I reply, my lower lip quivering as I think about its meaning and how perfect it is.

We can only hope that in death, Hank found peace. And whatever dreams he had, I hope they're coming true because I have to believe that there is more out there than…this.

I don't realize I'm crying until I feel Quinn's gentle touch on my cheeks as he wipes away my tears.

"I'm sorry I made you cry."

Raising my eyes, I shake my head because although I'm crying, they aren't all entirely sad tears. They are tears of the living.

When I think back to a time when I refused to cry, it's now a bittersweet feeling to allow myself this one reprieve and not scold myself for that weakness. Because now I know these tears make me human.

And they make me normal.

Climbing onto his lap, I straddle him, making sure to place the drawing on the swing beside me out of harm's way. Wrapping my arms around his neck, I rest my ear against his chest, listening to the steady beating of his heart. A heart I love so very much.

"Thank you," I whisper, closing my eyes, his heart a soothing balm to my blistering soul. "Best Christmas present—ever."

Quinn chuckles, and the sound spreads goose bumps over my whole body. "It could never compare to what you gave me," he says seriously, and I shudder at the memory of me giving myself over to him. "But I wanted to give you something from my heart, too."

I can't stop myself as I sit up and smash my lips to his. He's taken off guard but catches up quick enough as he returns my frenzied kiss with enthusiasm and warmth. I'm in control, however, and Quinn allows me to take what I need from him. And right now, I need him naked and soaked into every pore.

We quickly make our way into our bedroom, and the moment the door closes, he cups the back of my neck and kisses me fiercely.

When his lip ring bites into me, my already wanton body is soaked with desperation, and I can't get his clothes off fast enough. Rearing back, I reach for the hem of his T-shirt, nearly ripping it in half as I pull it off his body. His chest heaves, turned on by my aggression.

Snapping the top button of my jeans open with ease, I cry out the moment his fingers sink into me.

He quickly pulls back, afraid he's hurt me, but I latch onto his forearm, demanding more.

"Are you sore?" he whispers, his finger slowly testing my limits.

Arching backward and rotating my hips to get a deeper angle, I moan, "Yes, but it's a good pain. So good."

Nothing else matters when I'm with Quinn. And when I'm with him in this way, everything else just…slips away.

I need to be skin to skin, so I clumsily reach for my shirt and pull it over my head while still riding Quinn's fingers. The moment I remove my lacy bra, Quinn groans in the back of his throat and latches onto my nipple.

"This is mine," Quinn hisses, his fingers increasing the speed and pressure while I bite my lip, tears stinging my eyes. "Tell me you're mine."

I understand why he needs to hear this. We both need to know we belong to the other as we've never belonged before.

"I'm yours. Always."

With a smirk, Quinn pushes me onto the bed, but a soft rap on our door interrupts us.

"Um…Mia?" Cynthia mumbles through the door.

"Hi," I say, making it clear that if she wants to speak, it's through the door.

"Is this a bad time?"

Quinn shakes his head when he reads I'm about five seconds away from telling her to come back in an hour.

"It's fine. Everything okay?" I say as we quickly compose ourselves before I open the door.

She doesn't seem to notice my flushed cheeks as she has other pressing matters to deal with. "Have you seen Polly?"

"Um…" I look at Quinn, who shrugs. "No. We haven't seen her."

"Oh dear."

"What's the matter?" I ask, sensing a whirlwind of chaos about to form.

"I t-think…um."

"What's going on, Cynthia?"

Meeting my eyes, she wrings her hands in front of her as she whispers, "Polly is missing."

"Missing? Why do you think that? Maybe she just went out for a walk?" I suggest, which is improbable, as I haven't seen Polly do any kind of walking since I've met her.

But I try and stay positive before I go jumping to conclusions.

However, Cynthia shakes her head, determined she's gone. "I checked her room. It looks as if it's been ransacked."

My hand flies to my throat, as her comment worries me. "Ransacked? You don't think—" I say, leaving the sentence unfinished, as there is no way Thomas and Phil have been here undetected.

Cynthia quickly shakes her head. "No, I don't think... that. I think she's run away."

Quinn is the first to speak up. "There's no way someone like your daughter would run away. No offense," he adds with a strained smile.

"Then where is she?"

"Maybe in true Polly fashion, she's just thrown a temper tantrum, trashed her room, and gone to harass Tristan?" I offer, as it's a plausible scenario.

Speaking of Tristan, I look at Quinn, silently asking where he is. "When I left him, he said he was taking a walk...to clear his head."

The way his mouth dips into a tight frown pulls at my heartstrings.

"Maybe you're right, Mia," Cynthia concedes, but her tense voice tells me otherwise.

Pushing past her, I storm down the hallway into Polly's room. This little brat has once again become the center of everybody's universe.

Cynthia is right—the place does look like it's been ransacked, but Quinn also has a point. Someone like Polly wouldn't last one minute out there alone without her damn lip gloss or moisturizer. And let's face it, where would she go?

We're out in the middle of nowhere.

"I'm worrying over nothing, aren't I?" Cynthia asks, needing reassurance.

Just as I'm about to comfort her, Quinn confirms her fears. "No, I think you're right, Cynthia," he says, storming over to Polly's desk.

"Exactly. Hang on, what?" I amend when I hear his unexpected response.

But he ignores me as his intelligent eyes scan over a discarded newspaper, his fingers running down the page.

"What?" I raise an eyebrow, asking him to explain.

But all my questions are answered when Quinn shoves the newspaper under my nose, allowing me to see for myself.

"She wouldn't?" I gasp, looking at him and shaking my head.

But as he nods, I know that she so would.

"I'm going to kill her." I sigh, snatching the paper from his fist.

"What's going on?" Cynthia asks, clearly confused by our exchange.

"Your daughter decided that going here," I say, pointing at the ad, "would be a good idea."

I hand her the newspaper so she can see for herself.

"No," she says, her eyes wide as they scan down the page.

"Yes," I retort, my jaw clenching.

"There is no way she would think going here, where there are thousands of people, thousands of witnesses, would be a good idea."

But as Quinn and I stare at her, incredulous to her naivety, she knows we're right.

"I really don't think a lot of thought was put into her decision, Cynthia," Quinn snaps, and I groan.

"Oh, Pollyanna." Cynthia sighs, covering her face with her hands as she shakes her head.

I curse under my breath as I look at the ad circled in purple marker for the "End of Year Rave," which is happening tonight in town, where thousands of people will be in attendance.

And no doubt my father, Phil, and half of Canada's police force will also be there.

"A rave? Seriously? Do these things even exist anymore?" I ask, angrily tying up my boots. "How lame."

Quinn nods as he reaches for his jacket. "I know, it is fucking lame, but I don't think people go there for the music."

Looking up at him mid-lace, I shake my head, disgusted.

So not only do I have to attempt to remain invisible to the police, who have no doubt memorized my face, I now have to look for my bratty sister among drug-enhanced delinquents.

And to add to the mile-high shit pile, I have to be on constant watch for Thomas and Phil.

Groaning, I finish tying my laces and stand up. "Let's get this over with."

But Quinn reaches for my arm, stopping my retreat. "Are you going to be okay?"

I know by okay, he means am I going to lose my shit by being around my past. "Honestly, I am so desensitized at the moment that nothing shocks me anymore," I reply, tucking my hair underneath my baseball cap.

A black baseball hat and some tacky, fake tattoo sleeves, which I found in Polly's room, are my only disguise for the evening.

We're so screwed.

Quinn stills my fingers as I irritably stuff my thick, stubborn hair into the sides, but it keeps slipping out.

"Nothing?" he questions with a playful smirk, rubbing his thumb over my knuckles.

And just like that, my homicidal tendencies get taken down a notch, and I let out a pent-up breath. "Well, almost nothing," I reply, running my finger along his bottom lip, instantly missing his piercing.

"It'll go straight back in," he says with a smile as he sees me frown.

We both agreed that Quinn's lip piercing makes him too recognizable, and after what happened at the ball, we can't afford another blunder like that, especially tonight.

"That'll never come out." He grins, referring to his tongue piercing as I make sure he's left that in.

"Oh yeah? Why's that?" I ask, suddenly feeling heated from head to toe as he slowly pulls my cap off.

"Because I wouldn't be able to do this." He lowers his mouth to mine, kissing me wildly.

I sag into him, and although I miss the feel of his hoop, I love how his barbell is the only piece of metal dominating my mouth.

Moaning when his tongue duels with mine, I almost forget we have someplace to be, but a swift knock on the door has us breaking apart, reminding us of our duties.

"Hey, it's Tristan," he says after a moment of silence.

I hurriedly reach for my discarded hat, and Quinn quickly

wipes his mouth as he opens the door.

"Hey," Quinn says, looking awfully guilty.

"Hey. Cynthia told me about Polly," Tristan replies as I stand behind the door, adjusting my cap.

Quinn nods, and Tristan continues. "I want to help. I feel like it's my fault."

Typical Tristan, always taking the blame. But there is only one person to blame.

"It's not your fault," I say, stepping out from behind the door and into Tristan's vision.

He flinches the minute he sees me, and my heart breaks at his cold response.

But I play it off as I shrug into my coat. "This is all on Polly. The only person to blame here is her."

Thanks to Tristan smashing a rock through the driver's window, I'm now freezing my ass off.

My teeth are chattering, and no matter how high I turn up the heat, the cool breeze just blows it away. But I'll have to endure it because no way in hell am I sitting in the back with a scowling Tristan.

This car ride has got to be the longest in history, and it doesn't help that I'm about to catch pneumonia as Quinn speeds down the deserted road as he heads into town. As I reach for the heating and attempt to turn it on high, I realize it's already there.

"Shit," I mumble, slumping back into my seat and rubbing my arms.

The silence is killing me, and I can't sit still. Not only is it warmer when I move but it also gives me something to do.

Quinn has been quite cold and distant toward me, and I know this has to do with Tristan.

It disappoints me that although Tristan knows about us, we still have to behave like we're not together. I thought once he knew, we could be open about our relationship, but obviously, I thought wrong.

Tristan hasn't spoken a word to me.

He seems to be totally fine with Quinn, but if I so much as breathe in his direction, he turns his lip up in disgust and looks the other way.

I pull the lapels of my coat over my face and sink into the hood.

Lost in my frostbite nightmare, it takes me a second to realize Quinn is pulling over.

Turning to face him, I barely contain my shudder when the cool breeze slaps my cheeks, but by the hard set of his jaw, I know that won't be an issue for long.

"Get in the back," he commands, gesturing to the back seat with his chin.

"I'm fine," I lie, stubbornly crossing my arms. I would rather freeze to death than deal with Tristan right now.

But Quinn reaches over and unfastens my seat belt, indicating this conversation is not up for discussion.

I'm not a child, and I most certainly won't be bossed around like some mindless girlfriend.

However, as a bug the size of a flying saucer comes flying into the car, most likely seeking shelter from the minus-zero conditions, I quickly kick open my door and storm over to the back door and yank it open.

Tristan looks out his window, but I can see his mouth tipped up into a small grin—asshole.

Slamming the door shut behind me, Quinn puts the car

into drive, and we're back onto the highway, hopefully bug-free.

I hate to admit it, but it is a lot warmer back here, and my frostbitten nose and fingers thank me for making the change. But my queasy stomach is definitely not thanking me since Tristan's aloof behavior makes me uncomfortable.

He still won't face me as he gazes out the window, and I can't stop myself as I ask, "Are you mad at me?"

He slowly turns and looks surprised that I've addressed him.

I'm not the one with the problem here, he is, and I hate that he won't talk to me about what's going on. It'll be a hell of a lot easier if he just vents or screams at me, but this silence, it's killing me.

And it's also pissing me off.

He sighs as he runs a hand down his face. "No, I'm not mad at you," he replies, but by the angry look contorting his features, I dare say that's a lie.

"Then what's up? I'd prefer it if we just got everything out into the open, instead of you looking at me like I'm the Antichrist," I say, my voice slightly lowered as I don't want Quinn to hear.

He's had his turn to talk to Tristan—it's now my turn.

"I'm sorry for looking at you like you're the Antichrist."

I smile because it's nice to hear him making a joke.

"I just…you and Quinn, I…" But he leaves the sentence open, and I can see him mulling over the right thing to say.

"Tristan, I never meant to hurt you," I say and bravely reach out to touch his thigh.

He pulls his leg away quickly, and the movement saddens me, as it was never this way between us in the past.

However, I let it go. I know he needs time to process this

revelation, so I'll give him all the time he needs.

"Just know that I adore you, and I value your friendship very much. I just want things to go back to the way they were."

When Tristan flinches, I know that's not probable.

"Things will never go back to the way they were."

I lower my eyes, realizing I've sacrificed my friendship with Tristan by choosing Quinn.

"I know, but for what it's worth, I'm sorry I hurt you," I whisper, meeting Quinn's knowledgeable gaze in the rearview mirror as he watches our exchange.

Tristan only scoffs, not believing me, and as he turns to look out the window, I realize that Hank was right again. We do have to make sacrifices for the people we love.

I just hope I'm worth it.

The rest of the journey is traveled in silence until we're finally here.

I can't wait to get this over with, as being out here makes me nervous. I've already spotted a few patrol cars, and I hate to think how many police are in the actual venue.

Quinn senses my apprehension as he stands in front of me and gently rearranges the bill of my cap so it conceals more of my face.

"You going to be okay?"

"I'll be fine," I reply, placing my hood over my head, looking like a total gangster.

"You stay close to me, all right?" he says with a nod. I roll my eyes because we've had this discussion five times already.

But I humor him. "Yes, Quinn, I know. Let's do this already and get the hell outta here," I say, turning on my heel, as I've procrastinated enough.

We've parked the car about three blocks away, hoping it remains undetected by the police.

This whole situation is incredibly risky, and one wrong move will mean game over.

So we make sure we blend into the shadows, heads bowed, and remain invisible to partygoers. But the closer we get to the venue, the harder it will be to remain anonymous since there are so many potential witnesses here.

We make a quick beeline for the entrance. The venue is a run-down warehouse in a sketchy industrial part of town. I have no doubt they chose this particular location so they don't run the risk of any noise complaints.

As we wait in line to enter, I look over at Quinn.

He gives me a reassuring nod, but it's all for my benefit. He no doubt understands how quickly this can turn to shit. After everything we've gone through, everything we've fought for—after tonight, it just may all go up in flames.

Shaking those thoughts aside, we pay the cover charge and enter.

The minute we're inside, I only just refrain from covering my ears as the music assaults my eardrums and vibrates in the pit of my stomach. But this is only the beginning of what's to come because the farther we venture, the louder and more crowded it becomes.

The vast mass of tangled bodies on the dance floor exceeds three thousand people, not including those above us, milling on the second level.

"Shit," I curse. There is no way we'll find Polly without splitting up.

Quinn looks at me and shakes his head, reading my thoughts. I look at Tristan, who bites his lip. He realizes this will be much harder than we originally thought.

The strobe lights, flashing glow sticks, and the thumping bass make it virtually impossible to see or hear a thing, so we're left with no other option. It will be every man for himself.

"I'll go upstairs!" I say, cupping my hand over my mouth as I scream into Quinn's ear.

He, of course, shakes his head, grabbing my arm to stop my retreat.

I yank out of his grip. I don't like this any more than he does, but what choice do we have?

Tristan intervenes and points at the upstairs balcony, gesturing with his head that he and I go up there together. Quinn clenches his jaw, but he finally nods, and I let out a sigh of relief.

"You watch her," Quinn warns Tristan, who nods as he grabs my upper arm.

It pisses me off that they think I need a babysitter, but I let it slide because we're wasting time arguing.

Turning to leave, Quinn quickly latches onto my bicep and spins me around before smashing his lips to mine. I'm taken off guard and cannot return his affection because this kiss isn't tender. It's dominant, and it's a warning.

"You stay close to Tristan, Red," he cautions, his eyes burning into mine. "We meet back here in twenty minutes, okay?"

He looks at Tristan, who has turned his head, no doubt disgusted by our exchange.

Tristan, however, nods and reaches for my hand as he leads me through the hordes of people.

I turn over my shoulder to look at Quinn, and the pained expression on his face reveals just how unhappy he is that we're in this situation. I know he fears for my safety. I give him a strained smile, but he doesn't return it. I watch as he turns to push through the gyrating bodies on the dance floor, ready to start his search.

Focusing on our mission, I try to adjust to the intermittent lighting as I can barely see a few feet in front of me. Tristan's hand tightens in mine when I get wedged between a couple who want me to be a part of their dancing duo.

I keep my head bowed, not wanting to make eye contact, and slide out between their sweaty bodies when Tristan gives me a gentle tug.

Giving him a small smile, we fight our way through the dense crowd until we finally reach the staircase.

Tristan leads, but my hand sits securely in his the entire time, as I know he's taken Quinn's words to heart.

As we reach the top step, Tristan thankfully lets go of my hand. It's slightly less crowded up here, but I still stay close as we begin our search. There is a fluorescent-lit bar to our left with a few lounges and tables and stools, and I know this is where people come to make out or to score drugs.

My eyes follow the movements of a young wannabe gangster with baggy pants, a white tank, and a blue bandanna hanging from his back pocket as he works the room, seeking out his prey. My stomach roils, and I feel sick that I know his kind so damn well because I am his kind—a fact I wish I could change.

Tristan follows my line of sight and quickly places his hand on my cheek, turning me to face him. His gentle eyes soften as he wordlessly tells me that I'm nothing like that gangster, but I am.

I shrug him away as unwanted tears well in my eyes.

"I'll check the girls' bathroom!" I yell into his ear as I stand on tippy-toes to reach his tall frame.

He nods, and I'm glad he doesn't insist on waiting outside because I need some time alone. Being in this environment brings back too many unwelcome memories, ones I wish I could permanently erase from my mind.

Pushing my way through groups of people, I finally make it to the bathroom and escape inside, grateful to be alone. It smells like vomit and piss, but I take a minute to center myself and focus on what's important so we can get the hell out of here.

After checking every stall and coming up empty, I brace my hands over a sink and bend low, taking a deep, calming breath, which makes me feel slightly better. Turning on the faucets, I splash some water onto my heated cheeks and look at my face in the mirror.

I look tired and drained, but I tell myself to man up and get back out there.

A girl in a one-piece tube dress comes stumbling out of a cubicle, wiping her white powdered nose with the back of her hand. My blood instantly boils, and I tell myself to get out before I give her a lecture about using drugs.

Kicking open the door, I find Tristan leaning up against the wall waiting for me.

"Anything?"

"Nothing," he says with a firm shake of his head.

"You?"

"Nothing. Let's go find Quinn."

We make our way back downstairs.

If possible, the crowd has doubled, and I cringe. Finding Quinn will be a nightmare. Tristan senses my dilemma and reaches for my hand, giving it a reassuring squeeze.

Regardless of how he feels toward me at the moment, he can't help but come to my rescue during times of crisis. He will forever be my knight in shining armor, and I know I don't deserve it, but having him on my side makes me stronger and makes everything seem like it'll be okay.

"There he is!" Tristan yells, gesturing with his head to our far right.

Standing on tippy-toes, I see Quinn scanning the crowd looking for us, and no doubt Polly, as his search looks to have been unsuccessful also.

Tristan suddenly places me in front of him so I'm wrapped in the safety of his huge body. He then proceeds to push his way through the swarms of people, using both hands to clear a path in front of us.

This method proves to be successful as people move, and I stay enclosed in his warmth, feeling safer than ever before. When we finally reach Quinn, he eyes our connection with distaste, but he doesn't say a word and only looks at Tristan.

"Find her?"

Tristan's chest rumbles against my back with his reply. "No."

They continue talking while my eyes scan our surroundings, desperate to find Polly.

Suddenly realizing I'm still engulfed in Tristan's arms, I take a small sidestep and almost fall over my feet when I do.

Over Quinn's shoulder, I just make out the side profile of Polly as she secretly talks to the scumbag dealer I saw upstairs. My anger is suddenly amplified, and if I've ever been this mad, then I don't remember when because right about now, I'm on the cusp of murdering her.

Shoving past a stunned Quinn, I practically run to where she stands, shouldering anyone who stands in my way because I'm focused on my mission, and that mission is to kill my sister. I'm about two feet away when my fists begin to twitch, and I give in to my urge and smash my fist into the dealer's face.

He staggers back, stunned, as it was a blind attack, and

although I'm not proud of my actions, it sure as shit felt good.

His hand flies to his jaw, and I take great satisfaction in seeing his lip bleed, but it's not enough, and I launch forward, taking another swing.

He reads my attack this time and dodges my punch, but he doesn't stand a chance.

I raise my leg and slam my kneecap into his groin, watching as he collapses to the floor. Just as I drop down to one knee, my fist raised and ready to strike, a pair of hands wrap around my middle and lift me off the ground, stopping my attack.

I kick my legs, bucking wildly as anger clouds my vision, and I won't stop until the writhing, moaning sack of shit at my feet is dead.

"Red, stop!" Quinn snarls into my ear, but this time around, his voice of reason fuels my fury. I attempt to headbutt him, but I only make contact with heated air.

"Let me go!" I yell, kicking out and scratching at his hands, hoping he lets go.

But he doesn't, and his grip around me only intensifies, foiling my plans of finishing what I started.

My eyes narrow on the slumped figure in front of me, and as I watch him cup his balls, crying out in pain, the seriousness of what I've just done hits hard.

Everything slows, and suddenly, I'm transported back to when I was him.

I'm the one dealing to naive kids who want nothing but a good time.

I'm the one dealing to children, accepting their dirty money, when I knew what they had to do to get it. Little did they know, every hit was slowly edging them toward the point of no return.

And I was responsible for their fall. I'm responsible for it all.

I'm going to be sick.

Quinn must feel my stomach roil as his grip suddenly loosens, and he lowers me to the ground. The moment my feet touch the floor, I pound on the concrete and dry heave in the corner of the room. Nothing comes up as I haven't eaten all day, but I force myself until I'm gagging and retching, wanting to make the pain go away.

This whole situation has me thinking about what Phil proposed to me to do.

But tonight proves that there's no way I can go back to that life without it doing severe damage to my already fragile mind. I'm as good as dead if I'm caught by them because Phil knows being kept alive and going back to a life I'm trying so hard to forget is far worse than being dead.

That thought is the mental slap I need.

We need to get the fuck out of here because of the scene I've just caused.

No doubt the police are on their way, and if Phil and Thomas are here, I have just waved a big red flag.

Taking a deep breath, I straighten up and turn to meet Quinn's gentle eyes.

I focus solely on them because if I see the chaos I've caused, I don't think I'll make it out of here in one piece.

"We gotta move," he says, his eyes pained when he sees my tears.

Nodding quickly, I reach for his hand, and we push through the circle of nosy bystanders who watch our escape with wide eyes. No one stops us, and even if they did, I know Quinn would kill anyone who stood in our way.

It takes us minutes to get outside, and as we both hear the

sirens echoing in the distance, we quicken our pace, fleeing the crime scene as quickly as we can.

The moment I burst through the exit, the cool breeze slaps some sense into me, and I realize we have to go back in for Tristan.

"Tristan!" I yelp, violently tugging my hand from Quinn's and turning to go back inside.

But his voice stops me, and I've never been so glad to hear him address me.

"Mia, I'm here," he says and throws his arms around me, suffocating me with his embrace.

I hold on tight, burying my nose into his shoulder, and as I feel his frantic heart beating against mine, I realize he must have grabbed Polly and fled when I was having my meltdown.

Pulling out of his embrace when I've calmed down somewhat, I seek out the person who has created this clusterfuck of events.

The moment she sees me hunting her down, she has the audacity to laugh. And if I didn't know any better, I'd say she looks fucking high.

"Red," Quinn implores, latching onto my arm to stop me from delivering my reckoning.

But I shrug him off and storm over to her, ready to rip out her hair.

"Are you fucking high?" I roar, clutching her biceps and shaking her wildly.

She only laughs in my face, and her untroubled attitude enrages me to breaking point.

"You selfish little bitch!" I scream, my fingernails digging into her skin. "What is the matter with you? Do you know what you've done? Do you even care?"

I vaguely hear Quinn telling me to let her go, but I can't

because I'm not in control of my actions right now.

All the pain, rage, frustration, anger, hurt, everything comes bubbling to the surface, and there's no way I'm going to let her go. She needs to understand that every action has repercussions, and her self-centered actions have cost us all.

"You think this is funny?" I spit, infuriated when she just continues to cackle, thinking this is all some big joke.

I know that's probably the E she took, but I'm about to smack the ecstasy right out of her.

"You make me sick," I snarl, letting her go as I shove her backward. "You think this is all a game? This is our lives you're fucking with! Give me one good reason why I shouldn't just leave you here and let you fend for yourself when the wolves come."

Polly's eyes widen, and she quickly shuts her mouth when reality kicks in. "I didn't think."

She hiccups, her high slowly fading.

"That's your fucking problem. You never do! You think Phil and Thomas will go easy on you because you're a kid? You think Phil cares that you're his niece? He will have absolutely no qualms about exploiting you and breaking you down until you beg for a reprieve. And by reprieve, I mean be his fucking slave! He doesn't care, Polly—trust me, I know," I spit, getting into her face as I watch her lower lip tremble.

"He didn't care that I was a virgin when he organized for some asshole to take away my innocence," I painfully reveal, and Polly gasps, a wavering hand covering her mouth.

"I didn't know," she whispers, tears stinging her eyes.

"Of course you didn't! You've got your head so far up your ass, reality has been replaced by your fantasy world where you think the universe revolves around you. Well, you need a reality check because shit is about to get real! You think it's fun to get high?" I snarl, gripping her cheeks in my fingers and pursing her lips like a goldfish.

She struggles to pull out of my hold, but I only squeeze tighter until she whimpers under the pressure.

"You want me to show you what happens when you get high?" I threaten, letting her go.

She quickly shakes her head, but it's too late.

Taking a step backward, I jam my finger into my chest. "You'll turn into me! I watched my father shoot up, snort, fucking ingest drug after drug, and although I never once touched the shit, I felt like I was high for my entire life because surely, this messed-up reality, this reality which was mine, had to be some drug-induced coma.

"But it wasn't. It was my reality. Don't let it be yours," I say, and sadness overtakes my rage. "You're sixteen. You've got your whole life ahead of you.

"Stop wasting it, and just be a kid and…live. Be happy. Do what I couldn't do, Polly—live. Live for me and be free," I cry, tears sliding down my cheeks.

She breaks down as she slumps onto the cold ground, sobbing into her hands.

Whether she's coming down or whether my pep talk knocked some sense into her, I'll never know. But whatever the cause, I can only hope she'll never get high again.

I wake incredibly hot, but I'm too tired to move.

I don't know what time it is, or where we are, but I know the warm body lying beside me belongs to Quinn.

No doubt he put me to bed after I passed out. I've been out for the count ever since my breakdown.

I know tonight has changed things, and although Polly is mostly to blame, so am I.

My actions brought us nothing but unwanted attention, and if Phil and Thomas were in attendance, then they've probably seen us. I don't know if we've been followed, but either way, I know what needs to be done.

My eyes flutter open, adjusting to the darkness, and I wish I could stay this way forever, but it's time to face the harsh light of day.

"Are you awake?" I whisper, not wanting to disturb him if he's still asleep.

But he isn't, as his mind is probably unable to switch off. "Yeah, Red, I'm awake."

"I'm sorry about tonight, Quinn. I shouldn't have lost my cool. I'm such an idiot," I groan, rubbing a hand down my weary face.

"Hey, stop that," he says as the room is suddenly lit up by the bedside lamp.

My eyes take a moment to adjust, and as I look at the man I love with my entire being, my heart breaks.

He looks utterly exhausted and drained.

His eyes have lost their customary spark, and his mouth dips into a dismayed frown. I just wish this would end.

"So you think they saw us?" I ask, not stipulating who "they" are.

Quinn sighs, running a hand through his messy hair as he sits up. "I really don't know. If they were there, then probably—I mean, we caused quite a scene."

"You mean me," I correct as I lean up against the headboard.

"No, we," he firmly emphasizes. "I never should have allowed you to come. I never should have allowed you to be subjected to that."

And by that, he means my old life.

All along, he knew.

He knew I wasn't ready. I pay no attention to his alpha comment because I am my own person and can make my own decisions. But in this circumstance, I think he may be right.

"I can't go back to that life, Quinn," I whisper, my lower lip trembling.

The events of tonight have proven to me the one thing I always knew: I can never go back to my old life.

This revelation only reiterates what I have to do—Phil and Thomas must die.

"And you won't." He quickly pulls me into his lap, crushing me to his chest, and I go willingly, as there is no place I'd rather be.

I don't tell him that if my father and Phil catch me, and I'm given an ultimatum, then I'll have no other choice but to go back to the one thing that will finally break me.

Quinn has dealt with enough of my shit, and I know that this would break him.

This would only fuel his revenge, and I'm afraid he won't wait until we're free. I'm afraid he'll go out and find them, consequences be damned.

"We don't know what my future holds."

Quinn breaks our embrace, pulling me away at arm's length. "Our future," he states. "They'll never hurt you ever again. I'll kill them both before they have a chance."

He knows just as I do that this story ends in violence, bloodshed, and murder. There is no compromise because you can't negotiate with people like my father and Phil.

"We didn't call Abi," I suddenly gasp, only just realizing this fact.

Thanks to Polly's antics, our plans to contact the outside world have been put on hold.

"We've always got tomorrow," he replies, pulling on his hoop, and I smile when I notice he's put it back in.

Deep in thought, I run my finger along his plump lower lip, realizing that tomorrow can't get here soon enough.

"I just want it to be over. I don't know how much more I can take," I confess, lowering my eyes, ashamed of my weakness. "I'm slowly losing my mind, and even though we're so close to obtaining our freedom, I've never felt so trapped. When our clemency finally arrives, what happens then?"

He ponders my question as he runs a finger across my cheek. "We do whatever it takes to survive," he replies after moments of silence. "I promise you'll get the life you deserve."

But that's the million-dollar question—what life do I deserve?

From where I stand, everything bad that has happened is just the karma train collecting passengers.

"You're a good person."

"Am I? Because at the moment, all I can think about is killing my father. If that's not a bad person, then I don't know what is."

"You're a survivor. Sometimes, two wrongs make a right."

I mull over his response because he's right.

There is never a right time to kill somebody, but in a circumstance such as this, what other choice do I have?

I could let the police deal out their own hand of justice, but no doubt Phil knows a lot of dirty cops. He would buy and bribe his way out, not paying for his crimes. Not paying for what he did to Hank. And I can't live with that.

"There is always an exception to the rule, and this is one of those times," Quinn whispers. "Just like you are an exception to my rule."

"Your rule?" I question, arching an eyebrow.

Quinn nods, his eyes smoldering as he tugs on his hoop. "Yes. I promised myself that I'd never fall in love because I didn't deserve that happiness. But with you, I didn't have a choice. You own me heart, mind, body, and soul. I am yours."

Tears sting my eyes because I feel everything he feels, too.

To be so deeply in love with another and have that other person love you in return is wonderful.

When you've never been loved before, experiencing this kind of love, this all-consuming, obsessive, infatuated kind of love, then it makes up for all the loneliness, because nothing could ever compare to being adored by Quinn.

"I love you, Quinn Berkeley," I say, leaning forward and nuzzling his cheek.

"And I love you, Mia Lee."

I gasp, as it's the first time he's addressed me in such a way.

Right now, I just want to forget about everything and lose myself in Quinn. But I know he'll probably refuse, as what happened between us in the boathouse was a one-off thing until we can visit a pharmacy.

Quinn reads my train of thoughts loud and clear. "Don't do that."

"Do what?" I question, pulling back in confusion.

"You know what," he replies with a lopsided smile. "Do you know how hard it is to not strip you naked and fuck you until we both forget our troubles?"

"I'd say very hard," I playfully tease as I peer down at his erection.

Quinn moans in his throat as he flops down onto his pillow, frustrated.

Placing his hands behind his head, he stares up at the

ceiling, and suddenly, I see his lips moving.

"Are you…counting?" I ask with a smirk as I shuffle down next to him.

"Shh," he replies, his lips continuing their muted murmurs.

"What are you doing?" I chuckle, running my fingers along his tattoo and watching his skin break out into tiny goose bumps.

"Not helping," he grits out between clenched teeth, his eyes squinting shut.

His strange behavior fascinates me, so I won't quit until he tells me what he's doing.

Listening closely, I hear him reciting his…times tables?

"Quinn, are you doing math?"

Abruptly stopping, he opens his eyes and turns his head toward me. "Yes, I'm doing math."

"Um, why?"

"Because it reminds me of my fifth-grade math teacher, and I have to think of the most unattractive thing possible to make this raging hard-on go away. It's worked in the past," he confesses but quickly closes his eyes when realizing what he's just said.

"You've done this before?" I gasp incredulously.

"Red, just—" But as he opens his eyes, he sees I won't stop until I know the full story.

"Yes." He sighs, playfully narrowing his eyes at me. "There were times when all I would do is fucking count."

I can't help the laugh that rips from my throat because although I shouldn't be laughing, this is kinda funny. And if I don't laugh, I'll cry, and I've done enough of that.

"Why didn't you just…" I gesture a backward forward motion with my hand as I cluck my tongue twice.

Quinn groans, reading my hand charades perfectly. "Can

we please stop talking about this? This conversation is really not helping the situation at hand."

"I could always lend a hand."

"It's not your hand I want," he boldly confesses, staring at my mouth.

My skin instantly prickles with his lewd suggestion because goddamn, I want that, too.

"I would be more than willing to do whatever I can to help you out because, I mean, times tables? Quinn, that's kinda lame."

"It's the only thing that kept me from…what are you doing?" he quickly says, not finishing his initial sentence as he watches me sit up and reach for the hem of my tank.

"It's the only thing that kept you from what?" I ask, slowly drawing the tank up my body and eventually slipping it off, so I'm sitting in nothing but my black underwear.

Quinn's eyes focus in on my nipples, and his heated stare has my entire body humming in need.

"I'm sorry, were we talking?" he huskily replies, attempting to sit up, but I place my palm on his chest and push him back down.

His eyes widen in shock, and quite frankly, so do mine as a surge of confidence overtakes me, and I slowly straddle his body.

He stares up at me, a cocky smile tugging at his full, sinful lips, and I barely suppress a groan as I feel his arousal press against my core.

"We can't. I still don't have any protection," he says with a hiss as I reach my hand between us and begin palming his erection through his boxers.

"This is me not caring," I defiantly reply, speeding up my movement.

"Two times two is four," he moans as I slip my hand underneath the waistband of his boxers and grip his shaft. "Two times, oh shit, fuck…"

I watch in hunger as his mouth parts in desire.

I quite enjoy being in control, so without breaking contact, I carefully lift my hips and wiggle out of my underwear so I'm naked.

Before Quinn can question what I'm doing, I yank down his boxers and rub myself against his hard cock.

We both moan because it feels so fucking good, and after tonight, we both need to feel good.

"Red, stop, I'll hurt you," Quinn barely chokes out as I begin lowering myself onto him.

The painful intrusion burns, but the burn feels so damn good; there's no way I'm about to stop.

Quinn's fingers claw into my hip, steadying me as I take him into me. My slow movements only heighten the already mind-blowing sensation.

When he's about halfway in, I hold my breath and look into his eyes. "Isn't this much better than times tables?"

Quinn chews on his hoop, his eyes dropping to half mast as he replies, "This is better than anything in the entire world."

"Entire world?"

"Yes…this is perfect." And with that heartfelt declaration, he swiftly raises his hips, impaling me so deeply, tears spring to my eyes.

But perfection has never tasted so good.

We both remain perfectly still, both breathless from our union.

I peer down at Quinn, placing my hands against his chest. I love that his heart beats as quickly as mine.

He doesn't move. This is entirely my show. Having him

surrender is a beautiful thing, so I rock my hips and begin to move.

He feels incredible, more so than the first time. My body isn't screaming at the intrusion; it welcomes it.

I use his chest as an anchor when I quicken my movements and begin to ride him faster and harder. Being on top is intense, and every movement hits me in just the right way. I lift my hips and slam back down, crying out when he sinks into me so fucking deep.

I circle my hips. I lift them. I'm not shy when I lose rhythm because Quinn doesn't judge. He allows me to use him how I want, and that is the hottest thing in the world. He lets me do what I want, and for someone who rarely gives up control, this within itself has me fucking him wildly.

I toss my head back, arching my neck and moaning as Quinn grips my waist to help me rock against him with ease. He encourages me to squat over him, and when I do, I almost collapse forward because this angle robs me of breath.

I bounce on his cock as he lifts his hips, and my legs don't tire because he holds my weight with his hands wrapped around my hips.

"Baby, you're beautiful," he says, his eyes filled with love and desire. "Fuck me and take what you want. It's yours. All of it."

Hearing him speak during sex is almost too much, and I moan, increasing the speed of my movements.

The room is our own personal haven, and when Quinn's eyes drop to our connection, I don't stand a chance. I come so loudly, but to stop my cries, Quinn gives me his fist to bite down on.

Again, so hot.

The moment I'm done, Quinn lifts me off and is about to

come on my stomach. But as I look at his mouth, I get an idea.

I quickly take his cock into my mouth, and he doesn't have a choice when he comes down my throat. I swallow it all because this is so hot, I can't stop.

Once the final tremor racks his frame, he drags me up his body and slams his mouth over mine. We kiss like starved lovers, and nothing has felt more perfect than it does right now.

Fourteen

Today is a brand-new day. That's my motto, and I'm sticking to it.

I'm sick of hardships, and I'm sick of pain. Looking down at Quinn, who sleeps soundly beside me, I'm determined for our future to be happy and normal. Well, as normal as we can be.

I will not allow my past to dictate how I live because I'm sick of living in the shadows.

Today is a brand-new day.

Slipping out of bed, I step into the bathroom and take a hot shower. This is the first step to sticking to my motto. Surely, starting the day with a hot shower is the correct antidote for embracing my new positive approach to life.

I always feel better after a shower, so I have a little skip to my step when I walk back into the bedroom and see that

Quinn is awake.

"Good morning."

I blush when I see Quinn's tousled hair—the hair I was yanking on a few hours ago.

"Did you leave me any hot water?"

"Maybe some."

He gets out of bed, planting a chaste kiss to my lips.

"Well, I better be quick then." He smirks, and as he turns in the direction of the bathroom, I can't help myself and slap him on the ass.

I decide to take a seat on the chaise under the windowsill and wait for Quinn, and as I look out at my surroundings, a sense of peace overwhelms me.

I don't know where this newfound tranquility has come from, but I welcome it with open arms.

Deep down, I'm hoping that today just may be the day when Tabitha tells us the news I so long to hear.

Fixated with the greenness in the distance, I fail to see a glimpse of black until it emerges into my full line of sight. It takes a second for me to realize that the black belongs to a van, which has come to a stop on the front lawn, just near the gravel driveway.

I wonder if maybe they've made a wrong turn, but I doubt that's the case since this house is hidden away from the desolate road.

My skin instantly prickles in fear, and suddenly, my fight-or-flight instinct takes over.

I charge over to the bedside dresser, frantically searching for my gun.

Ensuring it's fully loaded, I reach for my knife and shove it securely into my boot, not wanting to be caught unarmed.

I don't know why I need my weapons; I just know that I

do.

Brushing my hair off my face, I see the comb I wore to the ball sitting on the dresser, so I reach for it and quickly twist my hair into a bun, as I need my vision totally unimpaired for what I'm about to face.

Just as I'm about to charge back over to the window to see if the van is still there, Quinn comes out of the bathroom, wearing nothing but a towel. The moment he sees me, he freezes.

"What's wrong?" he asks, rushing to my side.

Taking a deep breath, I gesture with my head toward the window, wanting Quinn to witness what I did for himself. I need to know if it's real.

He wastes no time charging over to the glass and curses the moment he stands in front of it.

"Shit. How long have they been there?" he asks, dropping his towel and reaching for whatever clothes he can find.

"Not long."

"Stay here," Quinn says, rushing over to his bedside table and pulling out his gun.

"There is no way in hell I'm staying here," I argue, and just as he's about to rebuke, our bedroom door crashes open, and Tristan runs in.

"Someone's here," he pants, eyeing Quinn and me as we look like we're about to square off.

"I know," I reply, panic soon replacing my calm.

"Here," Quinn says, handing Tristan his gun as he storms toward him. "You know how to use it?"

Tristan looks down at the piece, and then back up at Quinn with a firm nod.

When Quinn darts over to his backpack, producing a revolver, I hate that it's come to this.

"Stay with Polly and Cynthia," I order Tristan, and he only laughs, proving to be just as stubborn as Quinn.

"I need you to protect them, Tristan. We need the upper hand just in case this goes south really, really quickly," I plead, hoping to influence his reasonable side.

Thankfully, it works, but he's not happy.

Quinn sprints back to the window, watching and waiting to see what happens next.

I creep up behind him, hoping the lace curtain provides us with some covering against whoever stands on the other side. The car is still idling, and I cross my fingers that it's just a lost traveler.

But I think our day has finally arrived.

When the engine switches off, I know that whoever is in that car is here to stay.

"Shit," I curse as I reach for the gun in the waistband of my jeans and pull back the hammer.

"You're not going out there," Quinn reiterates, his eyes never leaving the scene before him.

"Don't you get it? I have to go out there. There is no other choice. When I woke up this morning, I told myself that it was a brand-new day, and this is fate's way of telling me that this, right here, this is my day. This is my day of reckoning and redemption. Don't take it away from me.

"You have no right to."

"It's too dangerous," he simply replies, but thankfully, he turns, meeting my pleading eyes. "If anything happens to you, Mia, I would never forgive myself."

I know how dire our circumstances must be because he used my name, something which he only does when things are fucking serious. Like right now.

"It's Abi!" Tristan suddenly says, breaking Quinn's and my

stare-off.

"What?" I gasp. Quinn and I spin toward the window and see what Tristan said is true.

Standing before us on the green, lush grass is my best friend, and she's never looked so beautiful. Her long red hair is braided to one side, and she looks exactly how I remember her looking—like a fucking angel.

"What's she doing here?" I ask breathlessly, my eyes never wavering from her form.

"I don't know."

"What's the matter with her?" Tristan suddenly asks, and I turn toward him, confused.

"Why is she just standing there?" he explains, nodding his head toward the window.

"She's scared," I say, dread forming in the pit of my stomach.

"Yeah, but why?" Tristan questions, concern apparent in his soft tone.

Tabitha looks absolutely terrified, and although she's yards away, I can still see the apprehensive look marring her usual happy, bright face.

"I don't know, but I'm going to find out." I place my gun on the dresser, about to go meet my friend.

"Stop, Red," Quinn stresses, latching onto my bicep.

"What? Why? What's the matter with you?" I beseech, pulling out of his grip. "It's Abi down there!"

As I watch Quinn's face fall and turn an ashen white, I know something is wrong. Something is horribly wrong.

"She's not alone," Quinn chokes out, and I don't understand what he means until I spin around and see Lucifer himself step out of the van, the early morning light gleaming off his bald head.

The air gets sucked from my lungs, and I almost collapse because this is surely a dream. But the moment Phil smugly waves to us, I know this is all too fucking real.

I knew this day would come, but I never anticipated Abi would be here when it did.

"I've gotta go down there!" I scream, lunging for my gun, tears blurring my vision. "She's scared, and she's alone with them."

"No, Red, wait," Quinn says, quickly standing in the way.

"Move out of my way."

"Wait, we can't just go down there. We need to come up with a plan," he says, arms raised in surrender as he remembers the last time he stood in the way of my vengeance.

"The plan is I shoot, they die."

"You shoot, Abi dies," Quinn corrects, his eyes begging me to stop being unreasonable and listen to him.

He's right.

Look what happened the last time I was irrational. Hank paid with his life. And so will Abi if I don't stop and pull it together.

Taking a calming breath, I nod, although I wish I wasn't.

"So what's the plan?" I ask, my eyes zeroing in on Phil as he picks some invisible fluff off his shirt, not at all bothered that Tabitha stands beside him, crying.

"You and Tristan stay up here," he of course says, and I turn around, glaring at him. "Let me finish…"

He huffs, and I nod. "I go out there, try and buy us some time while you sneak round the back, and catch them unawares."

"That isn't going to work for so many reasons. Anyone other than me going out there means Abi is as good as dead. They won't shoot me, but you, they will," I say, my heart about to launch from my chest.

"How do you know that?"

"I just do," I reply, avoiding Tristan's stare because he knows what I'm about to do.

He's the only person who knows what Phil and Thomas have planned for me. And in the end, I always knew it would come to this.

"I'm going out there, Quinn, and you can either come with me, or you can stay in here," I state with finality. This is no longer up for discussion.

Slamming my gun onto the dresser, I look at Quinn with nothing but regret in my eyes.

I'm so sorry I have put him through this, but I know he wouldn't have it any other way.

"Lose the piece if you're coming with me. We go out there armed, they kill Abi."

Quinn hates this as much as I do, but he knows I'm right. "Give this to Polly or Cynthia. Protect them, Tristan," he says, grabbing Tristan by the shoulders and giving him a stiff nod.

Tristan hates that he's been left behind, but he knows neither Quinn nor I would have it any other way. And this is Tabitha's life we're dealing with.

So he doesn't argue as he accepts Quinn's gun and nods. "Be careful. I'll be watching from the front window, and if that fucker steps out of line, I won't miss."

Giving Tristan a weak smile, admiring his courage, I look at Quinn, who nods, because it's showtime.

Latching onto the lacy edge, I rip the curtain aside so nothing shields me from the evil, predatory stare of Phil.

The moment he sees me, he has the audacity to laugh, happy to have finally caught his prey.

My knees shake, and my legs threaten to give out at any

time, but I must appear strong. I refuse to show this bastard any weakness. Tabitha takes a step toward me when she sees me standing at the window, but Phil grips her arm, violently shoving her backward.

I bite my tongue to keep from crying out. My poker face must not slip because Abi's life depends on it.

Crossing my arms defiantly over my chest, I glare at Phil, waiting for him to make his move. Remember, this is Phil's game, and I have to play by his rules.

"Come out, come out, wherever you are," he pathetically calls out, and I roll my eyes because this guy is an absolute loser. "I've always wanted to say that."

I motion with my finger for this to get moving along, and Phil's smirk suddenly dies down to a scowl.

"Two minutes," I shout, holding up two fingers, looking at Phil and only Phil, because the moment I meet Abi's tearstained eyes, my entire hard exterior will crumble down into the bullshit facade that it is.

Phil looks bored as he nods, but just for good measure, he wraps his arm around Abi's trembling shoulders and leans toward her, smelling her hair.

Abi cries out, but I refuse to take the bait and keep my eyes focused on him. He's doing this to scare her, and I know how much Phil loves the smell of fear.

Turning around, I see Tristan and Quinn standing a few feet away, nervously eyeing the window.

"Protect them," I say to Tristan, placing my hand over his frantic heart.

He nods and places his palm over mine.

"And you," he says as he leans forward, softly kissing my cheek.

Giving him a small smile, I memorize every piece that

makes up Tristan Berkeley because I don't know when I'll ever see him again.

"That wasn't goodbye," he says with a sad smile, but I don't reply and only nod.

"Let's do this," Quinn barks, and I pull my hand away from Tristan's chest, my body sagging with the sadness of what we're about to do.

"Let me do the talking," I instruct Quinn, who nods, but I'm not convinced.

"Catch ya soon," Quinn says, turning to Tristan as he affectionately cradles the back of his neck.

"Be careful, man," Tristan replies, bringing him in for a quick hug.

Their earnest goodbye has tears stinging my eyes because it's my fault they are once again bidding each other farewell.

But I wipe away my unshed tears and suck it up because my tears can wait.

Once they've said their goodbyes, Quinn looks at me with a confident smile. "Let's do this."

Taking a deep breath, I reach for his hand, and we take our first step toward freedom because I know what I have to do.

Polly and Cynthia wait for us at the top of the stairs, both frightened and in tears.

"This is my fault," Polly cries, her hands covering her face. "If I never went out, they would have never found us."

Cynthia soothes her, running a hand down her back, which only induces a loud sobbing fit.

"This is my fault as much as it is yours," I gently say, and as Polly lifts her tearstained face, I can see the confusion in her eyes.

"It'll be over soon, and then, then you can go back to the

way things were." I smile because that future sounds like a good future to me.

But Polly surprises me when she unexpectedly throws herself into my arms, sobbing.

I don't know what to do, but my arms rise of their own accord, and I wrap her into a tight embrace. She weeps into my shoulder, and I rub her back, just like Cynthia did.

"It'll be okay. Tristan is here to protect you."

However, she pulls out of our hug, wiping away her tears with the back of her hand. "I'm not worried about us. I'm worried about you. Who's going to protect you?" she says, and I stare, stunned. Why would she care?

"I will," Quinn states, snapping me out of my thoughts.

I look up at him with a weak smile because no one can protect me—I'm beyond being saved.

But I nod, knowing the lie will end soon.

"Protect my sister," Polly bawls, nodding at Quinn, silently begging him to shelter me from what I have to do.

"With my life," he replies, and I sadly smile at Polly's term of endearment because their efforts are all in vain.

Cynthia is an inconsolable mess, and I doubt she'll have anything coherent to say. So I decide to speak for both of us because I only wish to say one simple thing.

"I forgive you."

A gut-wrenching howl tears from Cynthia's throat, and she holds the banister for support, her tears clouding her vision. But I don't make a move to comfort her since my words have provided her with the reprieve she needs.

I need her to know I get it, and I don't want her to live with this regret a second longer. I wish her all the happiness in life. She no longer has to grieve for her daughter because her daughter is finally free.

I leave my family sobbing on the stairs and look at my man with a firm nod. "I'm ready."

Interlacing my fingers through his, we descend the stairs slowly, and as each step brings me closer to my freedom, my steady heartbeat begins to slow.

Everything up until this moment flashes before my eyes, and although it's now the end, I'm not nervous or scared. I'm calm, just like the eye of the storm.

We arrive at the front door, and as I reach for the handle, Quinn pulls me back. "You're not about to be a martyr, are you?"

Sighing, I stand on tippy-toes and kiss the lips I've grown to love. "I'll do whatever it takes to protect my family," I reply, and Quinn cocks an eyebrow.

But I don't give him time to respond as I yank open the door, facing my worst nightmare.

A few feet away stands Phil, who holds a sobbing Abi by the back of the neck.

I finally allow my eyes to meet hers, and when they do, my entire world comes crashing down around me.

I see Hank's pain reflected in her eyes, and that's all the motivation I need to surrender.

"Let her go," I snarl, looking down at him from the porch.

"Hello to you too, dear niece." Phil smirks.

"Cut the crap. Let's do this, you asshole," I snap, and I can sense Quinn tense up near me, not understanding what's going on.

"Straight to the point these days, aren't you? My, my, you have changed. Maybe it's got to do with this young man over here," he says, his eyes landing on Quinn.

"Nope, it's all me," I reply instead, nodding at Abi, indicating that it'll be over soon.

MONICA JAMES

"I don't think I like this little attitude of yours, Mia Lee," he scolds like I'm a naughty child.

"Well, lucky for me, I don't give a shit what you think. Hand her over," I snap, faking confidence while I'm slowly dying inside.

Phil contemplates my demand as he tries to stare me down, but I'm done being the underdog.

"Maybe I've gotta hurt this little strawberry shortcake for you to submit," Phil suddenly says, squeezing the back of Abi's neck until she cries out in pain.

Gnawing my teeth together, I try to remain calm and collected.

"You're wasting my time." I fake yawn, examining my fingernails.

I can see the confusion hidden among Phil's cocky demeanor, and this is exactly what I want.

How do you outsmart a con? By playing him at his own game, of course.

"So you wouldn't mind if I had my fun with this little lamb while you watched?" Phil snickers, tonguing the side of Abi's face in one wet lick.

She whimpers, her eyes widening, begging me to save her.

"Oh, on the contrary. You hurting her will destroy me, just like you killing Hank did," I snarl, my body shuddering at the memory of Hank dying before my eyes. "So quit it with the melodramatics because you know I'm the one you really want."

"Red!" This is the first thing that has come out of Quinn's mouth, but I know that's not because he doesn't have anything to say.

He's silently watching and observing, trying to figure out what the hell I'm playing at.

And this is the reason why I never told him what Phil wanted me to do. Because if push comes to shove, Quinn would sacrifice anybody to save me, and I can't allow that.

Not ever again.

Ignoring Quinn, I focus on the asshole in front of me.

"You're right, I do want you, but this attitude of yours, I don't like it. I think I may need to break you…or maybe break a few fingers to rein you back in."

Before I have time to protest, he reaches for Abi's pointer finger and bends it backward, snapping it with a sickening sound. She howls in pain, her hand cradling her broken finger while Phil laughs, clapping his hands in delight.

"Ah, music to my ears." He smirks, cupping a hand over his ear, hoping to amplify Abi's sobs.

"Red, what are you doing?" Quinn whispers, but I barely hear it above Abi's wailing.

"Forgive me," I whisper back, now understanding the words he whispered to me when the tables were turned.

Before he has time to question me, I step forward, hands raised in surrender. "Let her go, and I'll come willingly."

"Red, no!" Quinn screams, gripping my arm and stopping me from taking another step.

He now gets it. He, better than anybody, understands what an ultimatum looks like.

Although our situations are miles apart, when given a choice, you have to choose the right one. And this, this is the right choice. This is right for everybody.

"Let her go, or I break another finger," Phil threatens, snatching up Abi's hand.

When Quinn hears Abi whimper, he reluctantly releases me.

"You see, we all want the same thing." He drops Abi's hand

like he has her best interests at heart.

Walking down the first step, I look toward the van and know Thomas is hiding inside with an assortment of weaponry on hand. I can only hope Tristan doesn't come to my rescue because he'll be dead before he can fire a single round.

As I descend the last step, I try not to recoil as I come face to face with my enemy. He looks the same.

Same shit-eating grin.

Same cold, dead eyes.

Same overconfident stature.

But most of all, same greedy, motherfucking smell of victory.

We're all pawns to Phil, some more valuable than others. But we're all movable game pieces in Phil's mind, and he'll do anything to call checkmate.

"I'm sorry, Abi," I say, my wavering voice betraying my emotions.

"No, I'm the one who's sorry," she cries, her big eyes filling with more tears. "I couldn't wait to tell you…we did it."

And I know by "did it," she means we're finally free.

I close my eyes in relief. The joy I feel knowing Quinn is free and no longer a fugitive has a single tear slipping down my cheek.

Her words give me the strength I need, and I open my eyes with fierce determination.

"Thank you. He's free because of you," I whisper, and Abi bites her lip, understanding what I'm about to do.

"I'll do it," I state, looking at Phil, who watches our exchange with interest.

"What couldn't she wait to tell you?" he asks instead. He's not as dumb as he looks.

A part of me hoped that if I went willingly with him, that

maybe the police would eventually catch up to him, and he would finally pay for his crimes.

But sadly, I always knew it would come to this.

"Abi, call your dad, tell him to destroy everything he has on Phil. And Thomas," I say, glaring at the van. I want Thomas to know I know he's hiding.

"What? I don't…why?" she questions, her eyes darting behind me, no doubt looking at Quinn for answers.

"Because it's the only way for you to stay safe. Can your dad guarantee Quinn's freedom if he does that?"

"But…" she refutes. Phil suddenly twists her arm behind her, threatening to snap it if she doesn't obey.

"Ouch!" she cries but nods quickly, silently apologizing to me with her tears.

But I shake my head because no one is to blame but me.

"Mia, I never took you for a Good Samaritan. I mean, you were a drug dealer. You do remember that, right? I know you remember selling to whoring kids, accepting their dirty money with cum still on their chin.

"And I know you remember selling to Lacey," he sneers, and I rub at my tattoo, remembering the memory all too well.

"I know what I did," I counter with venom. "You'll never let me forget it."

Phil snickers, loving this back-and-forth banter.

"I'll go with you," I say, holding up my finger, "on one condition."

Phil laughs, rubbing his jaw. "And what's that?"

"You let everyone go, and you give me your word that no harm will ever come to them. Once this is done, you forget they exist. All of them," I reiterate, as Cynthia is part of my bargaining.

Phil taps his chin, deep in thought. "And what if I agree to this little bargain and this little cherry pie's daddy is still out for my blood?"

Swallowing down my terror, I reply, "If that happens, then I turn myself over and say I did it. I'll confess to…Hank's murder. I'll confess to the drug dealing, to everything. I'll take the fall for it all."

I don't hear or see Quinn, but I know he's come to my rescue as Phil pulls a 9mm from the waistband of his pants and aims it at my temple.

"Take one more step, and she's dead." He presses the muzzle of the gun to my brow.

You'd think having a gun pressed to my temple would freak me out, but I'm so fucking tired, and if he blew my brains out right now, it would result in an endless slumber.

But I can't rest until I've saved my family.

This won't be over until I'm guaranteed their clemency.

"Quinn, it's fine," I say, extending my hand out behind me, asking him to retreat.

"Like hell it is!" he defies, and I know there's no way he'll back down without a fight.

However, he must submit because Phil lowers the gun, satisfied he no longer needs it for the time being.

"Do we have a deal?"

Phil taps his chin with the barrel of the 9mm, looking to be deep in thought. If he doesn't say yes, then I don't know what I'll do. Because if he doesn't say yes, then we all die.

"Well?"

"You've got my word," he finally replies with a victorious sneer. "Welcome back."

"NO!" Quinn roars, and I can hear his feet pounding on the gravel behind me as he desperately charges toward me.

Spinning around, I turn to face him and quickly shake my

head, begging him to stop. But of course, he doesn't.

"What are you doing?" he yells, latching onto my upper arms and shaking me with brute force.

"I'm saving you," I reply, allowing a tear to betray my pain. "I do this, and you're all free. I was an idiot to think we could have it any other way. Please, forgive me."

My heart is breaking because I know this is torture for him.

But what other choice do I have? If I don't do this, then Phil will kill us all.

And I will not allow another death to be in vain.

"You're the one who said self-sacrifice is not honorable but a coward's way out. What you're proposing, Red, it's suicide." Quinn begs me to rethink my decision.

But I don't have time for second thoughts because this was always going to be my future.

"You would do the same for me," I whisper, and Quinn opens his mouth, but he knows I'm right. "You have."

"Take me instead," Quinn quickly says, looking over my shoulder to Phil. "I'll do whatever you want."

"Quinn, no!" I yell, latching onto his arm as he steps toward Phil.

But he shrugs me off, sadly whispering, "You go with him, I'm as good as dead. You're my girl, Red, and I protect what's mine."

Squeezing my eyes shut, I will my tears away, as I must be strong.

"You have my attention," Phil says, addressing Quinn with interest.

I have to stop this now because there's no way Quinn is doing this.

"No," I spit out, spinning around to face Phil. "We don't

have a deal if you take him instead of me."

Phil holds up his palm, indicating I'm to stop talking.

Quinn advances confidently and begins bargaining with the devil. "Do you manufacture your own stuff?" he asks Phil, who raises an eyebrow as Quinn has piqued his interest.

Quinn can see it, too, so he continues. "Well, I can do it for you. We cut out the middleman and manufacture most of the stuff ourselves. I cook it, I sell it, and you reap all the benefits. Where I stand, that's a good fucking deal."

Quinn is reasoning with Phil's gluttony, a sure bet that he'll get what he wants.

"No!" I yell but shut my mouth immediately as Phil raises his gun and presses it to Abi's temple.

"One more word out of you, and I'll shoot her where she stands," he warns, and I know he's not bluffing.

"You know how to cook?" Phil asks, looking at Quinn with intrigue.

Quinn responds with a dark chuckle. "You have no idea what I'm capable of."

"Oh, that's my boy. The rotting corpse of that traitor is proof of that."

I gasp, as I know Phil is referring to Justin.

So I was right.

The wound Quinn inflicted on him was life-threatening, resulting in Justin's death. And although that bastard deserved it, Quinn has blood on his hands because of me.

"I did what I had to. Given the choice again, I would do the same," Quinn says with no emotion, and I know he means every word.

The moment Phil's thin, sly lips tip up into a sinister smile, I know Quinn has won him over. But it'll be a cold day in hell before I subject Quinn to my future.

Holding up my hand, I gesture that it's now my turn to talk.

Phil sighs, nodding as he lowers the gun from Abi's temple.

Taking a deep breath, I feel like I'm going to hurl with what I'm about to say. "I'll be your...whore," I spit out, feeling dirty and unclean that those words ever left my lips.

But I have no other choice than to offer Phil a deal he can't say no to, because this is what started my demise, and now it's time to end it.

As I watch Phil's eyes darken in hunger, I know I've won. And so does Quinn.

"I'll be your drug bitch, and I'll be your whore. You own me, Phil. You've won. I won't try to run or fight you. I'll do whatever you want me to do. I'm yours."

Quinn's pained gasp has the final piece of my broken heart collapsing within me because I once promised him the same thing not too long ago. But no matter what I do, who I screw over, and who I fuck, my heart will always belong to him.

"Deal," Phil quickly says, his smile disgustingly big.

"And I have your word that Quinn will be free? I'm sure you know how to make the charges against him go away," I say, ensuring this sacrifice will exempt my family from further pain.

"You have my word." Phil nods, and I know it may seem stupid to believe a liar and a cheat like Phil, but he has more to lose by going back on his word than sticking to it.

"Fine, let's do this. Let her go."

Phil steeples his fingers in front of his lips, looking deep in concentration. "I still don't trust she'll tell her father," he says, flicking her braid with the muzzle of his gun.

"You can trust her." I nod, encouraging her to say yes as I

walk toward her. "Because if she doesn't, we're all dead."

Abi snivels, and I hate that I've put her into this awful position.

"It'll be okay," I whisper, placing my hands on her tearstained cheeks.

I barely contain the sob caught in my throat as it's been so long since I've been this close to her. "Thank you for everything. I'll never forget you."

I lean forward, giving her a tight hug.

She weeps into my shoulder, and this time around, I allow a tear to fall because it'll be the last I ever shed.

Reluctantly, I let her go and turn my eyes to Quinn.

I will not cry because I can't show him how weak and scared I feel. I want our last memory together to consist of love and adoration, not fear and pain.

"I love you."

"This isn't goodbye," he stubbornly says as he turns over his shoulder, looking directly at the front window where Tristan stands.

Just as I'm about to call out to him to stop, the front door opens, and out comes Cynthia, hands raised in surrender. Polly and Tristan follow closely, mimicking her stance.

"They've got nothing to do with this!" I cry, turning to Phil as I see him leering at them, pleased he has more people to control.

"Oh, I beg to differ." He steps forward, opening his arms to Cynthia. "Sister, it's so good to see you."

When she hesitates, he demands, "Come down here and give your brother a hug. Now."

I flinch at the hardness behind his request. This is not an act of love—it's an act of power. And Cynthia knows it, too.

She slowly descends the stairs, taking measured steps as

she walks toward the man she once called brother.

It takes all my willpower not to reach out and stop her from making this mistake because once she's in his clutches, he'll never let her go.

Quinn places his hand on my forearm, holding me back because seeing Cynthia in the hands of this monster burns my throat raw.

"Phillip," she says, addressing him curtly as she steps into his embrace.

"I've missed you, little sister," he replies while inhaling her fragrance, lost in the past.

"Let Mia go," she pleads against his shoulder. "I beg of you, Phillip, let her go."

The moment she pleads to his humanity, Phil snarls, pushing her away. "I haven't seen you for so long, and you want to ruin it by begging for her life. You haven't changed," he spits, looking at her with disgust.

"She's my daughter!" she cries. "And she's your niece. You promised me you would look after her!"

I stand spellbound by the scene before me because I know the last piece of the puzzle is about to be revealed.

"You are pathetic, sister. And you're still so fucking weak. No one forced you to leave; you made that choice all on your own."

"I was going to come back!" she shouts, wiping away her tears.

"What?"

She was going to come back?

She never told me this. But I guess I never gave her the chance.

"Yes, your runaway mother was going to come back after she decided to grow a conscience," Phil snaps, curling his lip in disgust as he looks at a sniveling Cynthia.

"But she didn't?" I say, phrasing it as a question because I don't remember her ever coming back.

"Of course she didn't," Phil replies with a wave of his hand. "She was too busy being a whore!"

Cynthia flinches but stands her ground. "You told me that she was happy, and that she didn't remember me! You told me I would ruin her if I came back into her life, taking her away from the only family she ever knew. You lied to me."

"I never prohibited you from seeing her. It was your choice to leave her in the first place." Phil shrugs, refusing to take the blame.

"I know," Cynthia sobs. "And it's a decision I will have to live with for the rest of my life. But I thought she was happy. You told me you loved her and that you were looking after her. I trusted you!"

"You believed what you wanted to believe because facing the truth was too hard. You left her because you are a coward, and you're weak. I did her a favor by raising her because if she stayed in your care, she would have grown into a weak victim...just like you. I'm ashamed to call you family," he concludes, looking at her like she's a piece of shit under his shoe.

"That's not true," Cynthia says, shaking her head. "You ruined her life!"

"She's strong because of me!" he yells, jabbing his finger into his chest. "You would have only turned her into a sentimental fool, and I needed a winner. Someone who could help build my empire, and she did."

"You're sick," I whisper, my hands shaking in rage. "You manipulated me, just like you did my mother."

Cynthia gasps since this is the first time I have referred to her in such a way.

"I did what I had to," he simply replies with a nonchalant shrug. "You are a somebody, Mia, not a nobody. You're special. I could see it the minute you were born."

"You used me!" I scream, storming over to him, not caring if he shoots me down. "I was just a child!"

"I looked after you," he replies with a scowl.

Scoffing, I can't stop the sarcastic laugh that bubbles from my throat. "Looked after me? You used me. And I did it because of him," I snarl, pointing toward the van.

There is one thing, however, I can't figure out.

If Phil was around, why don't I have clearer memories of him? Surely, I would unquestionably remember calling him Uncle?

Wouldn't I?

Then I realize that my self-preservation undoubtedly kicked in, blocking out the horrendous memories of my childhood. This explains the blackout period of my infancy because my mind was obviously learning to protect me from an ugly reality.

Some deep, suppressed memories rattle around in my mind, and when they're finally unleashed, I know I'll never be the same.

"I turned you into an unstoppable force, and this is how you repay me?"

"I never asked you to. I just wanted to be normal," I sadly reply, shaking my head. "But I will never be normal, thanks to you."

I see a flicker of...something flash behind Phil's eyes, but before I can question it, his detached mask slips back into place.

"Call it what you will, but I never abandoned you. Unlike

her," Phil says, pointing his finger toward Cynthia, who hangs her head in shame.

"I did it because I was young and stupid. I loved Chandler, and being with him made me happy."

"You were married," Phil says, reminding her of her sins.

"I know," she replies with regret. "But Thomas, he changed. He turned into you."

Suddenly, everything slows down to single moments in time.

I watch in horror as the van's side door slides open, and Thomas emerges with a rifle in hand. He aims and shoots, and the noise is so loud that I cover my ears. But as my rattled brain processes what just happened, I frantically turn and drop to my knees in disbelief.

Cynthia lies in a bloody pool, feet away from where she once stood, as the force of the high-powered rifle literally knocked the shoes she wore right off her feet. Her blood gushes from a wound in her abdomen, and the lush grass, which was once green, is now stained a bright red.

Polly's scream echoes in my ringing ears when she runs down the stairs, charging over to her mother's side as she lies dying, gagging on her own blood.

I will my body to move, but I can't, all I can do is watch.

Abi's high-pitched screams pierce my eardrums, and I resist the urge to cover them because I can vaguely hear a soft voice coaxing me back to reality. That voice is my only tether to this universe because I feel like I'm slowly dying inside.

Each breath I take, I swear it'll be my last because I feel my organs shutting down, unable to accept what I'm currently witnessing.

I don't know how, but I clearly see Phil charge over to Thomas, seizing the rifle from his hands and slapping him across the face.

Thomas covers his mouth, looking at the bedlam his jealousy has just caused.

"Red...oh, fuck. Mia...breathe!" That warm voice resonates once again, begging for my awareness.

My sluggish mind recognizes that voice as my lifeline, and I hold on tight, as I need it to pull me out before I'm lost for good.

I take a deep, ragged breath, and my starved lungs sing in relief as I allow my depleted organs to fill up with air.

"Oh, thank God," Quinn cries, his hands on my cheeks as he kisses my face over and over.

Everything is still so fuzzy—I realize that my body went into shock.

But now that I'm semi-alert, my reality comes crashing down with a loud bang.

"Cynthia!" I cry, scrambling toward her bleeding form on my knees.

The minute I reach her, my body threatens to give out once again, but Polly's pleas for help give me the strength I need.

Ripping off my sweater, I place the material on her gaping wound, trying to apply as much pressure as I can without hurting her. The fact she isn't dead is a fucking miracle, but I know she doesn't have long.

"She needs to go to a hospital!" I scream over my shoulder, my eyes landing on Phil.

Tristan, Abi, Quinn, and Polly surround me, watching and waiting for my command.

But I don't have the answers, and I didn't have them for Hank, either. But unlike Hank, I won't allow her to die.

I'll do whatever I have to, to save her life.

"Tristan, hold this to her wound, but not too tight, okay?" I say, giving him a firm nod, encouraging him that he can do this.

"Polly, go inside and get me Cynthia's doctor friend's number."

When she hesitates, not wanting to leave her mother, I urge, "Go…her life depends on it."

Polly wipes away her tears, leaving behind a streak of her mother's blood on her pale, terrified face, but she does as I ask and bolts inside.

"Cynthia, can you hear me?" I breathlessly ask, hoping to keep the terror from my tone.

After a long moment, her eyes flicker open as she attempts to focus on my voice.

"Mia?" she wheezes, her lungs protesting with every breath she takes.

"Yes, it's me," I reply, clutching her deathly cold hand in mine. "You got shot. But you're going to be okay. I'm going to get you to a hospital, I promise."

"I'm…dying," she gasps, bloodied spittle covering her chin.

"No, no, you're not. You're going to be fine."

I can feel Quinn stiffen near me, not as certain as I am of Cynthia's outcome.

But I need her to stay positive because she will survive. She has to.

"I've gotta go now, okay? But I'll be back real soon."

"Where…are you going?" she breathlessly asks, her mouth opening and closing like a fish out of water.

"I'm going to make you better." I lean forward, pressing a kiss to her clammy forehead.

Her limp hand rises to caress my head, and in the process,

her fingers pass over the comb in my hair. She floppily fingers the jewels, a small smile touching her lips.

"Cara Mia, mine. I'll be your love till the end of time," she sings softly, her voice breaking with exhaustion.

"What?" I gasp, pulling out of her grip.

But she doesn't need to answer because memories so sharp ricochet in my mind, and I almost fall backward with the clarity of them. The universe spirals into a whirlwind of color, and I am no longer in Canada.

Nor am I nineteen years old.

I am being cradled against the breast of a woman who smells of wildflowers and peppermint. Her voice is like an angel's as she softly sings to me, over and over, "Cara Mia, mine."

My childlike eyes gaze at the pink unicorns glowing in the dark on the ceiling as my mother sings to me.

My eyes then focus on a comb sitting snugly in her hair. The beautiful black stone glitters in the light, and I reach out with chubby fingers, wanting to touch it.

"One day, it'll be yours, my darling. I love you, Mia." She continues humming the song on the radio.

Reality kicks back in, and as I look down at Cynthia, a small smile spreads on her trembling lips.

"You remember."

With trembling fingers, she reaches for the locket around her neck, attempting to open it. But her bloodied fingers are too slippery, so I reach down and open it for her.

The moment I see what's inside, my heart is smashed to smithereens, and my eyes fill with heavy, ugly tears.

It's a picture of me as a baby, sitting in a nursery with soft purple walls. A soft purple I have seen before because I only saw it days ago.

305

"It now makes sense." Polly sniffles, standing a few feet away. "She would always go into that room and cry. Sometimes I would hear her sing that song, but most times, she would just cry. I never knew what was inside, but now I know what it was.

"She replicated your nursery because if she pretended you were still with her, she could pretend that she never left you behind," Polly explains, confirming what I know to be true.

The locked room that I stumbled upon, the one with the purple door—that was my room. Cynthia never let me go.

"My middle name is Cara," Polly says with a sob. "I never knew why, but now, now I know why."

She loved me.

This entire time, she loved me.

She wore my picture around her neck and devoted a room to me, never letting me go.

Touching the comb in my hair, I realize it looked so familiar because it was Cynthia's.

And eventually, it would have been mine.

Weakly reaching for the locket around her neck, Cynthia attempts to take it off, but she's too frail to raise her arms. So Polly bends down beside her and softly unclasps it from around her neck.

"Here, this belongs to you," she cries, tears falling down her face.

I look down at Cynthia, and as she gives me a weak smile, I see her life expiring before me.

We're running out of time.

Accepting the locket, I slip it around my neck and bend forward, kissing Cynthia lightly on the forehead once again.

"You're going to live, I promise you."

As her eyes drift shut and her breathing becomes shallow,

I whisper with a sob, "I love you…Mom."

A smile touches Cynthia's lips, and she looks peaceful, almost relieved, and I know if she were to die, she'd be happy.

But that's not fucking happening.

Not on my watch.

Kissing her forehead one final time, I stand, more determined than ever to take back my life.

"Is that the number?" I ask Polly, nodding to the bloody piece of paper in her hand.

She nods and hands it to me. "Please save our mom."

I throw my arms around her and hug her harder than I've ever hugged her before because she isn't the bratty little half sister I once knew. No, she is my sister, through and through.

"I will," I reply with complete determination, as I mean every word.

"Abi, I love you. Thank you for everything you've done for me. Thank you for giving me my normal." I wrap her into a tight embrace, holding on for as long as I can before we break apart because it's time.

"Let's go," I breathlessly demand, calling out to Phil who stands feet away, watching his sister die before his eyes.

My curt command snaps him back to reality, and he shakes his head, transporting him back to the here and now.

He nods because although he looks overcome that his sister has been shot, it's still business as usual, and our agreement still stands.

I wasn't expecting a happy ending because no matter what, Phil is, and will always be, number one.

I still owe him money, and after this little "mishap," he needs to flee the crime scene more than ever before.

"Call an ambulance the minute we leave," I order. "And call her doctor friend as well. He can look after her until the ambulance arrives."

Phil surprisingly nods, agreeing to my terms.

Turning around, I know there will never be an adequate amount of time to say goodbye to Quinn and Tristan. So I have to make do with the minimal minutes I have.

Throwing my arms around Tristan's neck, I inhale his fragrance one final time. "I love you, Tristan," I cry, holding back my tears.

It's the only thing I can say that'll express how much he means to me.

Pulling away, I lightly kiss his stunned lips and stroke his cheek with a smile.

The kiss is chaste.

Tristan nods, understanding it'll never be any different between us.

"I love you, too. I'll come find you, I promise," he swears, but it's all in vain.

Where I'm going—no one will ever find me.

But I nod, and then, then I look toward Quinn—my prince in blood-splattered war paint.

"I wish it could have been different for us. But for what it's worth, each moment spent with you have been the best moments of my life."

The sob I have been trying to hold back breaks free, and a river of broken tears spills down my cheeks, and I cry ugly, thunderous tears.

"Shh, Red. I'll never let you go," Quinn promises, wrapping his arms around me and giving me his strength before I evaporate into the blood-soaked earth beneath me.

"Oh, Mia, no need to get all sentimental," Phil suddenly says, and his smug tone has my body shivering in fear.

"What?" I ask, turning around to face him, not caring

that he can see my tears.

"Choose," he simply says.

"Choose what?"

"Choose brother one. Or choose brother two," he arrogantly replies, pointing his gun toward Quinn and then toward Tristan.

"No! That was never part of the deal!" I cry, shaking my head in fury.

"Well, things have changed. Now that your mother's life hangs in the balance, I need to know that you won't rebel if she...doesn't make it," he concludes, his eyes glancing at her quickly.

"No!" I snarl, my fists bunching by my sides, as I would never jeopardize either of their lives this way.

"If you don't choose one, then I shoot them both!" he screams, spittle covering his chin, and I know he's sick of this game.

"Why?" I scream back, as I need to know what he's got planned.

"I use one for collateral, of course. You don't do as I say, I shoot him. You go to the police, I shoot him. You try and run, I shoot him. You—"

"Okay, enough! I get it!"

But how can I choose?

I can't.

How can I condemn one when I want to save them both?

"Red, I'm coming with you," Quinn angrily states, no doubt hurt as he sees me mulling over my decision.

"No!" I shout, turning around to face him.

He steps backward, his mouth parted in shock, clearly hurt that he isn't my first pick. But as I hear Polly howling in the distance, I know who I have to choose.

"Tristan, I choose Tristan!" I roar, my eyes never leaving Quinn's as he shakes his head, his pained eyes begging me to take him instead.

"Forgive me," I sob, but the hurt on Quinn's face will forever scar my very existence for as long as I live.

"Happy, you sadistic asshole?" I scream at Phil.

"Very," he replies and takes a step toward the van with a smile.

Tristan is wordlessly at my side in an instant, and I can't face him because I'm so ashamed of myself.

But this decision was made with our survival in mind, and I just hope Quinn will one day understand that.

As Tristan and I take our first step toward imprisonment, Phil suddenly spins around, his eyes twinkling in pleasure.

"Why did you choose him?" he questions, looking at Tristan.

No, I internally gasp because I know what he wants me to say.

"I did what you wanted! Let's just leave."

But Phil shakes his head, pulling the gun from the small of his back and pressing the muzzle to Tristan's cheek.

Quinn rushes to our side, but Thomas appears from the van, pointing the gun directly at my head.

"Tell me, Mia. Tell me why you chose him, and this will all be over with. Just tell me," he chides, and as Polly's screams echo in my ears, I know what I have to do.

"I chose him because he's weak!"

Both Quinn and Tristan gasp. My entire body shuts down around me, and I don't think I'll ever pull away from this alive.

"There's the girl I raised." Phil snickers. "No matter what you say, Mia, we're more alike than you think."

"I'm nothing like you," I growl, barely containing my

nausea.

"We'll see." He chuckles, removing the gun from Tristan's face.

"Weak?" Tristan gasps, his mouth agape as he slowly turns toward me. "You think I'm weak?"

"No," I cry, shaking my head, my body vibrating in pain. "I need Quinn to protect Polly, Abi, and Cynthia."

"And what? You don't think I can do that?"

"No," I softly reply, as we don't have the time to discuss this now.

The final piece of the puzzle falls into place.

"So you chose me because you think I need *your* protection?" he presses, and Quinn quickly reaches for him.

"Fuck off, man!" Tristan yells, pulling from his grasp.

Quinn raises his hands in surrender, and I hate that we've come to this.

"I'll explain everything later," I plead. "We gotta go. Cynthia's life depends on it."

Tristan reluctantly nods, and I turn to look at Quinn, begging him to forgive me.

But he only shakes his head, the wound still too raw.

"I'm sorry, Quinn," I cry, but he clenches his jaw, not meeting my eyes.

His cold dismissal hurts, but we need to move.

"I love you," I say, wiping away my tears. "I always will." I turn my back to him, walking toward a smirking Phil.

I can hear Tristan drag his feet behind me, and I close my eyes as this reality cannot be mine. But it's no one's other than mine, and now Tristan's, thanks to my selfish choice.

As we both reach the door, Phil suddenly steps in front of Tristan, and his Cheshire grin has warning bells sounding loudly in my head.

"How does it feel to be second best?" Phil chuckles, and Tristan growls, his fists clenching by his sides. "But I guess you're accustomed to being second best."

Tristan cocks an eyebrow while I feel like I've just swallowed a vial of acid.

"What are you talking about?" Tristan snarls, but I know. I know that somehow, Phil knows.

And so does Quinn.

"Tristan, don't listen to him!" I implore, standing between him and Phil as Quinn storms over, his face blemished in rage.

"Mia, your bastard friend here has every right to know that you chose his brother, his half brother over him. I mean, tough break that is."

"What?" Tristan wheezes, taking a step back, his face paling to an ashen white.

"Half brother? What the fuck is he talking about?" he yells, looking at Quinn who stands by his side, his head lowered in humiliation.

"Holy shit. It's...true?" he asks, his eyes widening in shock.

This day is on a repeat shit loop, and I close my eyes, wishing it would end.

"Quinn?" Tristan presses, his voice rising in panic. "Is it true?"

"Yes," Quinn finally replies, meeting Tristan's horror-struck face.

Before Quinn has time to explain himself, Phil slams his fist into Tristan's chin, knocking him out cold as he drops to the ground with a nauseating thud.

"NO!" I sob, my eyes not believing yet another tragedy before them.

"Motherfucker!" Quinn roars, charging toward Phil, but

the distinctive feel of a gun barrel being shoved into my back stops Quinn in his tracks.

"Get in the van," Thomas snarls into my ear, and I recoil, sickened by his touch.

When I resist, Phil scolds, "You're wasting time, Mia. Get. In."

I hate that he's right because as I look at Abi, who stands behind Quinn, I know Cynthia doesn't have much time left.

"Fine," I spit, turning around and pushing past Thomas as I get into the back of the van.

"Get in," Phil commands, waving his gun toward Quinn.

"What? No!" I scream, trying to push past Thomas to claw out Phil's eyes.

But Quinn nods, his jaw clenching as he steps over Tristan to get into the van.

Thomas pushes me back into the seat, and I fall as I'm caught off balance. But Quinn is beside me in an instant, steadying me with a firm hand.

We both watch as Phil slides the door shut with a big smirk, and Thomas climbs into the front, turning around and pointing the gun our way.

I look out the window and see Abi weakly dragging Tristan's unconscious body away from harm's way.

How can this be happening? Who's going to protect them now that we're gone?

Phil starts the engine, and as it roars to life, I weep into my hands because I thought I knew what I was doing, but everything is now so fucked up.

"It's okay, Red," Quinn softly coos, wrapping his arm around me, and I sob into his embrace because I don't know what else to do.

The moment the van commences moving, I sob harder,

but I allow myself one final look at the bedlam I've left behind. All I see are victims, victims because of me.

Abi begins screaming as she runs after the van, begging for me to help her, but I can't. I'm just as trapped as she is. Lucky also runs beside her, not understanding why I'm leaving him behind.

I lean over Quinn and place my splayed hand out against the glass, silently promising them that I'm coming back. I'm coming back for them all. I don't know how or when, but I'll find a way.

Abi and Lucky are a distant blur when I finally remove my hand from the window.

Settling low into my seat, I wish I could disappear without a trace.

"Why did you bring him?" I whisper to Phil, who looks at me through the rearview mirror.

Quinn stiffens near me, but I ignore him as I need to know why.

"Because he's valuable to me. And because he's valuable to you, too," he simply replies, dismissing me as he returns his attention to the desolate road ahead.

Phil saw no value in Tristan because he saw the inner strength in Quinn. And being the true predator that he is, Quinn is now Phil's new plaything.

With that disconcerting thought in mind, I lean my head on Quinn's shoulder and try not to cry.

The van is still for minutes, but I break the cruel silence as I sadly whisper, "You were right."

Quinn stills under my comment but doesn't speak. He only glances out the window.

But I know he's heard me, so I desolately declare, "Love really can't save you from your own fate."

Because it sure as shit didn't save me from mine.

Subscribe to my Newsletter:

landing.mailerlite.com/webforms/landing/b4j1v6

Something Like Normal Playlist:

tinyurl.com/bddea5bp

About the Author

Monica James spent her youth devouring the works of Anne Rice, William Shakespeare, and Emily Dickinson.

When she is not writing, Monica is busy running her own business, but she always finds a balance between the two. She enjoys writing honest, heartfelt, and turbulent stories, hoping to leave an imprint on her readers. She draws her inspiration from life.

She is a bestselling author in the U.S.A., Australia, Canada, France, Germany, Israel, and The U.K.

Monica James resides in Melbourne, Australia, with her wonderful family, and menagerie of animals. She is slightly obsessed with cats, chucks, and lip gloss, and secretly wishes she was a ninja on the weekends.

Connect with Monica James

Facebook: facebook.com/authormonicajames
Twitter: twitter.com/monicajames81
Goodreads: goodreads.com/MonicaJames
Instagram: instagram.com/authormonicajames
Website: authormonicajames.com
TikTok: @authormonicajames
BookBub: bookbub.com/authors/monica-james
Amazon: https://amzn.to/2EWZSyS
Join my Reader Group: http://bit.ly/2nUaRyi